"Aurora, do you have any idea what it took to get over what you did to me?"

Aurora gaped at Sean, taken aback both by his words and by this rush of emotion where there had been none until now. Had it been there all along, bottled up inside him? Had he truly become so thoroughly able to hide what she had once been able to read so easily?

She shook her head, like an animal in mortal pain. "Oh, Sean, how you must hate me...."

"I did," he said flatly. "Then."

The emotion had vanished. He was as cool as he'd been before. She made herself look at him, ordering herself not to read anything into his terse answer. But she couldn't stop herself from asking. "And now?"

"Now?" All the mockery was back in his tone. "Now I don't give a damn."

Dear Reader,

What better way to start off this month—or any month—
than with a new book by *New York Times* bestselling author
Nora Roberts? And when that book is the latest installment
in her popular Night Tales series, the good news gets even
better. I think you'll love every word of *Night Smoke* (which
is also this month's American Hero title), so all that remains
is for you to sit back and enjoy.

With *Left at the Altar,* award-winning author Justine Davis
continues our highly popular Romantic Traditions program—
and also brings back Sean Holt, a character many of you have
suggested should have his own book. *Annie and the Outlaw,*
by Sharon Sala, is another special book. This one boasts
the Spellbound flash to tell you it's a little bit unusual—
and as soon as you meet hero Gabriel Donner and discover
his predicament, you'll know exactly what I mean. Our
successful Premiere program continues this month, too,
introducing one new author in each line. Try Kia Cochrane's
Married by a Thread for a deeply emotional reading
experience. And don't forget Maggie Shayne—back with
Forgotten Vows...?— and Cathryn Clare, who checks in
with *The Angel and the Renegade.* All in all, it's another
wonderful month here at Intimate Moments.

I hope you enjoy all our books—this and every month—and
that you'll always feel free to write to me with your thoughts.

Enjoy!

Leslie J. Wainger
Senior Editor and Editorial Coordinator

Please address questions and book requests to:
Silhouette Reader Service
U.S.: 3010 Walden Ave., P.O. Box 1325, Buffalo, NY 14269
Canadian: P.O. Box 609, Fort Erie, Ont. L2A 5X3

LEFT AT
THE ALTAR

Justine
Davis

Published by Silhouette Books
America's Publisher of Contemporary Romance

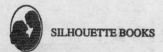 SILHOUETTE BOOKS

ISBN 0-373-07596-0

LEFT AT THE ALTAR

JUSTINE DAVIS

lives in San Clemente, California. Her interests outside of writing are sailing, doing needlework, horseback riding and driving her restored 1967 Corvette roadster—top down, of course.

A policewoman, Justine says that years ago, a young man she worked with encouraged her to try for a promotion to a position that was, at that time, occupied only by men. "I succeeded, became wrapped up in my new job, and that man moved away, never, I thought, to be heard from again. Ten years later he appeared out of the woods of Washington state, saying he'd never forgotten me and would I please marry him? With that history, how could I write anything but romance?"

For Patti,
of Patti's Book Store in Akron, Ohio,
who so wanted Sean to have his own story

Chapter 1

Hospitals. He'd sworn once that he would never set foot in one again. But here he was, Sean Holt thought as he reached the closed double doors, turned and began crossing the small waiting room. If he didn't love his sister so much...

"Sean, why don't you sit—"

"I'm going outside," he said abruptly, and headed for the doors that led out to the parking lot of the small, private hospital. If his mother told him one more time to sit down and stop pacing, he was going to lose it. He didn't want to stop pacing. He didn't care that he would probably pay for it later. He needed the distraction.

The moment a rush of cooling afternoon sea breeze hit his face, he knew he should have done this long ago. Not that it eased his worry about Stevie, but it seemed like he'd been in that tiny room forever. And he absolutely, positively detested hospitals. He'd spent more time than he'd ever wanted to in them, all those years ago.

For some reason he kept thinking about Aurora Sheridan's father. The old man had died in this very hospital three weeks ago, of an unexpected heart attack. When he'd read the headline story in the local paper, he had wondered if Rory would come back, then decided it didn't matter at all if she did or didn't. It didn't even matter that the old man was dead. He even believed it. Almost.

He supposed he could walk over and see if Pete was still at the clinic next-door—no, Sean thought, he couldn't. He'd worked himself into a limp now, and he could feel the strain in his lower back and the tightness that told him his leg was swelling in the socket of the prosthesis. Pete would notice instantly, and Sean would get another of his lectures.

He turned and headed toward the driveway instead, idly noticing the bright red Emergency sign. No ambulances, thankfully, Sean thought as he kept going. Just a golf cart used by the hospital staff, and a sleek, expensive European sedan parked sideways near the entrance.

Maybe he would go see Pete, after all. Maybe a good lecture about changing stump socks when he should would take his mind off Stevie and what she was going through. He knew she truly wanted this baby, but . . .

As he neared the crookedly parked car, Sean heard the emergency room doors open. He had barely noticed it was a woman exiting when he nearly let out a low whistle at the sight of her face. She had a shiner around her right eye the likes of which he'd never seen before. He'd had a few of his own during his football days, but never one that looked like that. This woman looked like . . .

Rory.

It *was* Rory. It didn't matter that he hadn't seen her for five years. He knew. And all the effort he'd put into banishing her from his memory proved wasted in that first split second of recognition.

And all he could do was stand there, awash in the memories he'd tried so hard to bury, memories of an afternoon five years ago that had begun so hopefully and ended so grimly. Oddly, it was Katie, his little niece, he thought of first; her crying had signaled the beginning of the disaster.

"But I wanna be a flower girl!" Katie wailed from the foyer of the packed church, all the wedding guests turning to look.

Sean knew instantly that something was wrong, but not until he was standing on Rory's front porch, her cool, formal note saying she couldn't go through with the wedding clutched in his hand, did he realize just how wrong. The moment the carved oak door swung open and he saw her father there, he knew. . . .

His heart sank; the man was gruff, overbearing and a bit pompous, and he hadn't liked Sean from the moment he'd met him. He hadn't come out and said why, but Sean had a very good—and very bitter—idea.

"I see you couldn't leave well enough alone," Jacob Sheridan said, his voice revealing the disdain his controlled expression hid.

Sean ignored both the disdain and the words. "Where's Rory?"

"Aurora is no longer your concern."

Aurora. That was how she'd signed the note, too. It was crazy, he thought, that the worst part of it was that name. In the beginning he'd teased her about it, about how her nose went up automatically when she corrected anyone who shortened it. It was pretentious, he told her, purposely annoying her by using the "Rory" he preferred. And then, one day, she had stopped being annoyed and begun looking at him in a way that told him his ploy to get her attention had worked.

Now she was back to Aurora. And that, more than anything else, told him how serious she was. The case of prewedding nerves he'd noticed in the past two weeks had clearly been much more serious than he'd realized. His jaw clenched as he faced her father.

"The hell she isn't. Today is our wedding day."

"Not anymore. The wedding is off. It should never even have been planned, let alone allowed to go this far. I should have put a stop to it long ago."

"Damn it," Sean snapped, "where is she?"

"I suggest you leave, Mr. Holt." The man had never once called him Sean, not even after the engagement was announced. "The wedding is off, and if you love my daughter as you say you do, then surely you understand why."

A chill swept over Sean, cooling his anger. He had the sudden feeling that he was about to be hit by a train but was powerless to get out of the way.

"Why?" he asked softly.

"My daughter deserves the best," Sheridan said, his lip curling. "She deserves a man who will make something of himself in the world. A man who can keep her—" he gestured toward the lavish interior of the house behind him "—in the life-style she's grown up with."

Again Jacob Sheridan's gaze lowered, his gaze flickering downward over Sean's body to his legs, as if for emphasis. "Most importantly, she realizes now that she deserves a man who's whole. Not," he added bluntly, "a cripple she'd have to close her eyes to stomach going to bed with."

The memory of those cold words, so long buried, hit Sean now like a blow to the gut as he looked at the woman who had delivered that blow. He had gone on a year-long binge of self-pity after his humiliation at her front door, leaving town, later even the state, trying to pretend she'd never existed. He'd once thought that losing his leg would be the worst pain he'd ever face in his life; he had been a fool to think that fate was through with him.

When he had at last come back, Stevie had quietly told him that Rory was gone, nothing more. It had been Stevie's husband, Chase, with more experience at facing all the ugliness at once, who'd told him that she'd left town within a week of running out on him, and with another man—a rich, whole man. Sean had known Chase wasn't being cruel. He was furious, and his anger had, in an odd sort of way, made Sean feel better.

In his shock now, it took Sean a moment to realize she was still heading straight toward him. She was dressed in a slim, pink silk suit—odd, she'd never cared for pink— matching pumps and small pearl earrings. He could see the golden glint of the chain that held a heart-shaped locket beneath her throat. A set of keys dangled from her fingers, on a ring that also held the symbol of the white car he was standing beside. Hers? He glanced again at the luxury vehicle. Of course, he thought, bitterness welling up inside him.

She didn't even look at him, just reached out to put the key in the door. Sean's mind was screaming a warning, ordering him to turn and walk away before she looked at him, but he couldn't seem to do it. She turned the key, then reached for the door handle.

"Nice shiner."

Rory jerked, and her face went white, stark beside the ugly bruise. She looked up and gasped, one slender hand going to her mouth.

God, what the hell had possessed him to say that? Sean wondered as he stared at her. And why was she looking at him that way? Shocked, yet as if she'd expected this meeting. Or dreaded it. The silence spun out, building its own kind of pressure, until at last she spoke.

"I ... I bumped into something."

Her voice was tiny, wavering under Sean's stare. He felt a ridiculous urge to comfort her. He was saved from his own foolishness by the approach of a young man in hospital whites. Sean hadn't even heard the doors open.

"Are you all right, Miss Sheridan?"

Miss Sheridan. So she hadn't married the guy. Or it hadn't lasted. Not, Sean told himself, that it mattered one whit to him.

"Is this man bothering you?" The young man gave Sean a sideways look that was rank with suspicion.

Jeez, he thought, you'd think I gave her the black eye.

"N-no," Rory said, in a stumbling little voice Sean couldn't believe was hers. "He's not. I'm fine. Thank you."

The man lingered, eyeing Sean warily, as if assessing his six-foot height, the breadth of his chest and shoulders, lingering on the strongly muscled arms that stretched the sleeves of his polo shirt. Try pushing a wheelchair around for a couple of years, Sean silently told the man.

"We're... old friends," Sean managed to tone down the irony in his voice.

When Rory didn't protest, the young man nodded and left. Silence spun out between them as they studied each other. Her hair was as honey blond as always, although now it was clawed back in a tight little bun. She seemed thinner, Sean thought, minus weight she couldn't really afford to lose.

She looked older, of course, Sean thought, but it wasn't just that. There was a difference about her, an edginess, like some frightened creature that wants nothing more than to find a safe lair. There was a fragility about her, a brittleness that had nothing to do with the ugly bruise that marred her face.

And when his gaze went back to that face, there was a look in her hazel-green eyes that even the bruise couldn't hide. She was watching Sean with a hunger that was so palpable it staggered him. And then, in the instant he'd noticed it, it was gone. Or hidden, behind an emotionless mask he'd never seen her wear before.

That, he told himself, didn't matter, either. None of it did. Not anymore. It was ancient history. He hadn't wasted time or energy on regrets for years, just as he'd given up railing at fate for the loss of his leg. It had taken him a long time, but he had finally realized that both activities were useless.

"I didn't know you were back," he said, striving for a casual tone. Simply two old friends, meeting unexpectedly, he told himself.

"I . . . just moved back. A couple of weeks ago."

"To your father's house?"

"Yes."

Sean lifted a brow, wondering why he hadn't seen her before now. Everyone ran into everyone in La Pacifica in the space of two weeks. It was a tiny coastal town in northern San Diego County, with this the sole hospital and medical building, and with the single sizable shopping center across the street. The only residential areas were on the bluffs overlooking the ocean, where Chase had built Stevie the house that was so special to them, the apartment complex where Sean himself lived, and the older, wealthy area in the foothills, which he hadn't gone near for five years.

"I . . . don't get out much," she said, as if she'd read his thoughts.

Don't get out much? Rory? Rory, who used to be on the go eighteen hours out of every twenty-four, who begrudged the necessity of sleep, who had once joked that she would simply have to live to be one hundred years old, because it would take that long to see all she wanted to see and do all she wanted to do? She had infected him with her enthusiasm, made him see a whole new world opening up before him to replace the one that had been taken away.

He didn't like remembering the way she'd made him feel back then. It made him realize painfully what a young fool he'd been, believing life had handed him something in place of his loss, believing that there truly was some fairness in life after all, that Rory would balance the scales that had been so viciously tilted the day a drunk driver had forced a college football team's bus off the road....

"With those kind of wheels," he said hastily, gesturing at the sleek sedan, "I'm surprised you're not driving around all the time."

"I... don't get out much," she repeated.

Her voice, small, hesitant, almost timid, bothered him more than he cared to admit. It was so unlike her. Or, at least, unlike the Rory he remembered. The Rory who had been the bright sun come to warm his dreary days. The Rory who had made him hope for things he'd given up on. The Rory who had stirred his blood like no other.

And still did. It hit him like a blow to the belly. God, after all this time, after what she'd done, how the hell could he react like this? How could he be standing here, his pulse suddenly racing? If anything, he should be feeling distaste, or at the least indifference. Certainly not this sudden male-female awareness.

He automatically took a step back, as if distance were a defense against her potent lure. He knew better, he thought ruefully. Distance had never saved him before; she'd always been able to turn him to mush from across a room with one look from those wide eyes.

She seemed to find the distance enough, though, because after a moment she spoke. Her words came softly, with an undertone that told him she'd tried to hold them back.

"You look... good, Sean."

"For a cripple, you mean?"

He hadn't meant to say it, and he certainly hadn't meant to sound so acid. The old, forgotten bitterness had risen up out of nowhere, and the words were out before he could stop them.

Rory paled. Her lips parted, but she didn't speak. Then she whirled and yanked the car door open. Just as quickly, she was inside and slamming the door. She had the engine started and was pulling away in seconds. Sean had to back up to get out of the way of the black sedan that pulled out just behind her. But he couldn't seem to turn away; he watched the white car until it was out of sight.

Even after it had vanished, he just stood there, looking after the woman who was supposed to have been his wife.

It was well past ten when he got home. He tugged off his jacket and sat down wearily. Thoughts tumbled through his mind in a sort of ricocheting chaos. It had been a tough day for everyone. Stevie's lengthy labor had been hard on her and on Chase, but the squalling, healthy boy who had resulted had brought tears to everyone's eyes. Sean had assigned himself his own task, that of keeping his fussy mother under control—and of shooing both her and his father down to the nursery to look at their new grandson when he caught the plea in Chase's eyes. Stevie, he thought, was going to have her work cut out for her if she wanted another child; Sean doubted Chase would ever willingly let her go through this again.

Chase, wreck that he was, had thankfully accepted Sean's offer to pick up his parents at the airport and bring them back to the hospital to greet their new grandchild. His sister, Cassie—better known to the world as Cassandra, the newest supermodel—was off on a photo shoot in the Caribbean somewhere and wouldn't arrive for a while yet. Sean was looking forward to that. Cassie was the one sure way to tease Chase; the resemblance between them was startling.

Stevie had been wearily grateful when Sean had also promised to go right to little Katie and tell her that her mom was all right, and that she was still the much loved first-born. Sean didn't mind all the tasks. They had kept his mind occupied. Occupied almost enough to make him stop thinking about the fact that his sister and her husband were sharing a joy he doubted he would ever know. Occupied almost enough to ignore his mother's semiaccusing sidelong glances, as if she were thinking the same thing. And occupied almost enough to keep it off a certain green-eyed honey-blonde.

But now there was little left to distract him except his own exhaustion, and even that wasn't enough to keep him from thinking about her.

So think about her, he told himself. You haven't, not for a good long time. Drag it all out and look at it. Get it over with. Maybe then, when you think about what she did, you'll get over thinking about how she looked today, not just older but . . . worn down somehow. As if life had gone sour on the golden girl.

The golden girl with the extremely black eye.

The image of Rory's battered face lingered vividly in his mind, and Sean remembered the way the hospital staffer had looked at him. Suspiciously, assessingly. And the way Rory had claimed—rather weakly—that she had done the damage herself. Rory, whose innate grace had always made him think of a dancer, limber, lithe and perfectly balanced. He'd been very aware of that quality in her, he supposed because he'd lost so much of the athletic grace he'd once had.

The Rory he remembered might have had an accident, but she would never have just "bumped into" anything hard enough to cause that kind of damage. Nor would she have sounded so panicked at admitting it if she had. Which left a possibility he didn't much care for.

Wrong, he corrected himself. *You don't care at all, remember?* She'd gotten herself into this. She'd made her choice. She'd chosen the whole man, and he was probably beating her. A bleak sense of irony filled him. She hadn't been able to face life with an amputee and had apparently wound up living with an abuser instead. If it was even the same guy she'd left him for in the first place.

And it was those memories, the memories of the pain-filled days after her choice had ripped him apart, that enabled him at last to convince himself that he didn't care one bit what Ms. Aurora Sheridan had gotten herself into.

He let his head loll back wearily on the sofa. His missing ankle itched; he was halfway to scratching it when he remembered and stopped. He stood up long enough to shuck his jeans, catching the hem of the left leg with his toes and tugging it off with the ease of long practice. Sitting back down, he methodically removed the lightweight graphite carbon prosthesis and peeled back the stump sock that had kept him from developing abrasions or blisters during the long hours he'd been on his feet today. He should have changed to a thinner sock much earlier, when he'd first realized edema was tightening the fit of the socket, but by then there had been too much to do.

He massaged the swollen flesh, wishing not for the first time that there was a way to let his brain know the leg was gone. He could live with the fact that the fluids that would normally pass through collected here, unable to make the return trip. It was a nuisance, but a controllable one. It was the phantom pains and itches and twitches that made him crazy. They had lessened over the years, but every once in a while, especially when he was tired, like now, the missing leg would ache and itch like mad.

He told himself it was this that had clouded his joy in the arrival of his new nephew, not thoughts of a spoiled rich girl who clearly had some big problems of her own now.

He looked down at himself, at the long, muscled length of his right leg, then the left, ending neatly but abruptly just above where his knee had been.

He no longer felt much of anything, looking at his asymmetrical body. Not the nausea he'd felt at first, or the anger that had come later. But he'd had almost nine years to get used to it, he thought. Rory had never even seen him, never seen what was left of him, never seen the tidy but still shocking stump. Maybe she had been right; maybe she couldn't have dealt with this.

In a rush of memory, he was back to that night on the beach so long ago. She'd been wearing his ring, looking at it every few moments as if she couldn't quite believe it was there. He'd hidden it in a graceful little seashell he'd bought at one of the innumerable tourist-trap shops, then, when she wasn't looking, dropped it onto the moonlit sand for her to find, knowing she wouldn't be able to resist picking up the unexpectedly perfect shell amid the usual broken ones strewn on the beach by the powerful Pacific.

When he wasn't worrying about walking—uneven sand was not the best surface for the kind of prosthesis he'd had then, which was why he usually avoided it—he'd wondered if she would find his method too corny. But the look that had glowed in her eyes when she'd picked up the shell and the ring fell out into her hands, when she'd looked up at him and realized what it was, had erased any worries.

They had wound up in a secluded corner of the beach, hugging each other as they watched the sun go down. And as the huge orange ball sank below the horizon, their passion rose to a pitch neither had experienced before. They'd done their share of heavy necking, but that night, in the hidden shelter of the rocks, kisses and caresses grew more heated as the air around them grew cooler.

Rory had shuddered as he had at last unbuttoned her silk blouse and unfastened her bra to lave her nipples with his tongue, and he had shuddered in turn as her slender hand had stroked him through the fine wool of his dress slacks. She'd even begun to tug down his zipper, and the thought of her touch on his naked, swollen flesh had nearly made him lose control right then.

They came perilously close to making love right there on the beach that night. But he knew it wasn't right, not for their first time, not on a public beach with the possibility of being discovered at any moment. Besides, he didn't have the nerve, not yet. He believed she loved him, but he wasn't ready to see her face when she saw him for the first time. And he knew that there were things they had to talk about first.

"You mean it, Rory?" he'd asked urgently, knowing that with a few more caresses like that he wouldn't have the breath left to speak. "You'll really marry me?"

"Oh, Sean, I thought you'd never ask."

He reached down and stilled her hand. He had to; she had aroused him to the point of pain.

"Rory, listen…I…we have to talk. There's more to this than just—"

"It doesn't matter," she said quickly. "I love you."

In the face of that simple declaration, he hadn't been able to find words. Words to tell her to think, to be sure. Words to say she didn't yet know what she was saying yes to. Knowing intellectually that he was an amputee and facing the reality were two different things, and no one knew that better than he did. But every time he brought it up, she changed the subject. His heart told him confidently it was because it truly didn't matter to her; his common sense was waving a red flag, telling him it was because she was avoiding the truth.

And somewhere deep inside him, a little voice was whispering that he'd been helping her avoid it by making sure he never got tired enough to limp around her, by making sure the hard plastic of his prosthesis never touched her, by making sure she never saw him without at least jeans and shoes. And by acceding willingly, even gratefully, to her seeming reluctance to make love, telling himself it was only virginal qualms, not fear that once she saw him, saw what was left of him, she wouldn't want him.

He would have saved himself a lot of pain if he'd forced the issue back then, he thought now. Instead he'd waited and had it forced on him on the day she left him to face a church full of people alone.

"God, you're in a fine, self-pitying mood tonight," he muttered to himself.

At one time, in such a mood, he would have called his sister's house. Oddly enough, not to talk to Stevie, although his beloved sister was always more than willing to listen, but to talk to Chase, who would listen, then verbally kick his butt again. Sometimes he needed his brother-in-law's acerbic mockery much more than sympathy. Chase had a very unsentimental view of most of the world; being hunted down and nearly killed by first the racketeer he'd testified against in a murder trial, and then the convicted man's son, who had nearly killed Stevie as well, had given him a sometimes sardonic outlook. Especially when it came to those who threatened those he cared about.

While both Stevie and Chase had been through hell before they'd found their way back to each other, Chase's torment had been physical, as well, and it gave him an understanding of Sean's down times that Stevie, for all her loving compassion, didn't have.

Thinking of his by now no-doubt-exhausted brother-in-law, he reached for the phone. He would call Chase to make sure he didn't need anything—like to be rescued from his mother-in-law—but for nothing else. Not for anything would he intrude his own melancholy on his family's joy.

In spite of his obvious fatigue, Chase laughed at Sean's query. "No, I'm fine. Your mother's sleeping."

"And therefore quiet," Sean retorted.

"Yeah. Thanks for being there today. And not just for Stevie. For me, too."

"It's the least I can do."

He meant it, he thought as he hung up a few minutes later. Chase had done more to pull him out of the nose dive he'd gone into after the fiasco of his aborted wedding than anyone, even Stevie. Chase had hired him to work on the Laurel Tree project. While it might have started as an idea to drag Sean out of the gutter, Sean knew it had become more than that to Chase, who stayed much more involved than he normally would. Just as it had become a cause of sorts for Sean. He'd never built anything before, and to stand in front of the site and watch the specialized apartment complex, carefully designed by Chase for people with various handicaps, rise before him, made Sean understand why Chase loved being an architect.

He sat for a while, pondering what to do. Despite the long, emotionally tough day, he knew he was wound too tightly to sleep. And that if he tried, he would no doubt wind up back on the same subject he was trying so hard to avoid. He had to do something. He reached for the phone again.

It was answered on the second ring. At least, the ringing stopped; all Sean heard was, "Nice shot, Stan! Nick, you let him wheel right around you. Don't forget, these chairs are a lot quicker than you're used to. Let's try it again." Then at last the voice spoke distractedly into the receiver. "Yeah?"

In spite of his mood, Sean grinned. It wasn't at all unusual that they would still be practicing at this hour. The squeak of rubber wheels on the polished gym floor was a familiar sound to Sean after the hours he'd spent watching his best friend push his basketball team for perfection. And what Dar Cordell pushed for, he usually got. He demanded as much effort from others as he gave himself—which usually meant about a hundred and fifty percent. And it worked. They had won the state wheelchair basketball championship last year, less than a year after Dar had reluctantly taken over the job.

"How's practice going?" Sean could almost see the man whose dark hair and broad, strong shoulders often made people mistake them for brothers. Dar would be waving his players into place with one hand while he held the phone with the other; only Dar would consider a mobile phone standard equipment for a wheelchair.

"Never mind that, how's Stevie? Okay?"

"Yes. Tired, but okay. I gave her a hug for you."

"Good. Tell her I'll be waiting to see my new godchild."

Sean smiled. Dar had never had much of a family of his own, and he had practically adopted the whole lot of them, and they him. And everybody felt they'd gotten the best of the arrangement.

"And what have you got for Katie, hmm?" Sean knew that Dar, who had very few soft spots, had a special one for the quicksilver little girl.

"A kiss, of course." Sean could almost see Dar grinning. "Any female who's astute enough at seven to realize that I'm the handsomest man in the world—"

"*After* her father and her uncle," Sean inserted.

"Yeah, well, I love her anyway. And I already talked to her earlier. I thought she might need a little reassurance."

"That she's still your best girl?" Sean teased, but when Dar answered, he sounded solemnly serious.

"The very best."

"On that we agree," Sean said.

There was a pause, oddly silent despite the background noise of the practice drill. "You're a lucky guy, Sean," Dar said at last, his voice uncharacteristically quiet.

Sean knew Dar didn't mean physically; he never dwelt on the differences between them. Sean couldn't imagine what it had been like for Dar, who had lost both legs, one above and one below the knee, to face the maiming of his body alone. At least Sean had his family. And still he'd barely pulled through—and might not have, if Chase hadn't come along.

"Yeah, I know," Sean agreed. "That's why I feel like such a jerk."

"A jerk?"

"I can't explain it, I just..."

As was uncannily frequent with Dar, he didn't have to explain. "Feeling guilty?"

"I...yeah. How'd you know?"

"Nothing like an overdose of other people's happiness to send malcontents like us into the dumps. Want to come over and whine later?"

Sean laughed, already feeling better. "I'll bring the pizza if you've got the beer."

"To cry in? Always. See you in an hour or so."

That would be nearly eleven, but Dar never seemed to sleep much. The night demons, he'd told Sean once, were easier to fight if you were awake. And Sean knew he had some powerful night demons of his own to fight tonight.

Chapter 2

Aurora Sheridan sat staring out the window into the night, thinking that the stark, colorless world, bathed in the chill silver moonlight, was a fitting match for her mood. A match, she thought bitterly, for the ugly mark on her face, around the eye that was still so swollen that it was difficult to see. In fact, she thought grimly, it was a fitting match for her whole life.

She managed, most of the time, not to think about the disaster her life had become. She'd made her choice long ago, and she was honest enough—at least, some part of her was—to know that gave her no right to complain now about how things had turned out. But that had been when she'd been far away from here, when there hadn't been familiar surroundings to remind her every day what her choice had cost her.

And when she had known she wouldn't see Sean.

She had forced him out of her mind every single day of the past five years, knowing she would succumb to despair if she thought about him. She'd been able to do it in the bustle and chaos of Los Angeles, but back here it was impossible. Back here, there were reminders everywhere. The hole-in-the-wall Mexican restaurant they'd loved, the campus of San Diego State University where they'd met, the theater where they'd gone to watch *Casablanca* on the big screen three times in a row, the beach where Sean had given her his ring...

She wrapped her arms around herself tightly, trying to suppress the shiver that rippled through her. She'd carried that picture of him inside her for so long, Sean awash in moonlight, that tentative smile on his face, as if half-afraid she would refuse him.

There had been nothing tentative about him today. Nor did he match the image she'd cherished for so long. The Sean Holt she'd known had been attractive, with his dark hair and thickly lashed dark eyes. But the Sean Holt she'd seen today had shown her how young he had been at twenty-three. His hair was still dark, his dark eyes still as thickly, softly lashed, but there was a difference about him now that was undeniable. The Sean Holt she had met today was a man, a solid, strong-jawed, broad-shouldered man. He had fulfilled every bit of promise she'd ever seen in him.

And she had thrown that promise away.

All the pain, all the guilt, all the need she had been denying for five years, flooded her then in a rush of heavy, swamping feeling that threatened to crush her. She fought the tears that loomed, telling herself that she had no right to them. She had hurt Sean badly, and the fact that she had been coerced by circumstance—or that she had paid for it every day of her life since—didn't change that. Nothing could change what she had done to him.

Although he hadn't looked particularly hurt today.

What did you expect? she asked herself scathingly. *That he would be pining away for you?* He'd come back from harder blows than the one you dealt him, Aurora Sheridan. He obviously picked up the pieces and went on. Again.

Which makes him one hell of a lot stronger than you are.

She allowed no mitigation of that assessment; it was true, and she knew it. It had always been true. If she'd been stronger, she would have found another way. Or made her father find another way. But she hadn't been able to, and so she had ravaged two lives; Sean's and her own.

Or had she? Had Sean really been hurt? He hadn't seemed too upset at seeing her today, merely surprised. Of course he wasn't upset, she told herself. It's been five years, after all. More than enough time for anyone except a neurotic like yourself to get on with life. And Sean's had more practice at that than most.

A memory leapt into her mind, fully formed and vivid, and so strong it made the stark black, white and gray of the world outside fade. She even thought she could smell the ocean breeze, rich with its salty tang. They'd spent the morning in the seaside town of La Jolla, "the jewel," which was just that, a little gem of a place, with a tiny cove and a beautiful park and beach that drew visitors from miles around.

It had been quiet that day in early spring, the summer crowds yet to arrive. She'd been flushed with the glow of falling for this handsome young man she'd only known for three weeks. He was such a gentleman, and seemed quite content to let things go at her pace. He seemed, unlike so many others, in no hurry to get her into bed with him; he was only five years older than she was, but the difference between him and men her own age was remarkable.

Not that he didn't want her. She could tell that, even though her experience was limited. He had, after all, kissed her, and rather thoroughly on occasion, although he'd been careful not to let it go beyond that, another instance of the thoughtfulness she'd been so grateful for. She'd had enough of being pawed and more than enough of male expectations that seemed to revolve around the theory that if you spent enough money on a woman, she had to come across. Well, she'd learned early and painfully that money couldn't buy everything, and she'd put herself into that category long ago.

She was glad they had the park, a wide swath of luxuriously green grass on the bluff overlooking the Pacific, almost to themselves that day. Sean had seemed nervous, waiting until she had taken a seat on a bench facing the ocean, then, oddly, walking past her to sit on her right. He looked around, waiting until there was no one close by before he spoke.

"Rory, I...need to tell you something. I think it's time."

She had felt the little skip her heart took every time he called her that; it was hard to remember that the nickname had once irritated her so much. But his expression worried her.

"What is it, Sean? You look so serious."

She saw him take a quick breath. "I am."

"If you're going to tell me you're married and have a houseful of kids," she teased, "just forget it."

For an instant he looked startled, then one corner of his mouth curved upward in that lopsided grin she so loved.

"No. Not that."

"What, then? What could be so gloomy?"

Sean shifted on the bench as if it were too uncomfortable to sit still on. "I...like you, Rory."

It wasn't the word she'd been hoping to hear, but she was too concerned about his solemnity to worry about it. It was too soon for more, anyway, although she knew she was already well past the liking stage herself.

Trying to lighten his mood, she wrinkled her nose at him. "I like you, too. I must, I let you use that silly nickname."

He smiled then, a full, wide smile that made the dimple in his right cheek flash. "I know. You detested it, though, at first. And me, I think."

"That name always irritated me. Probably because my father always says it sounds like a boy."

"I know. That's why I used it. I knew that way you'd at least notice me."

"I noticed you long before that day in the library. But then you started teasing me with that name, and it took me a while to look past the name to who was saying it." She smiled at him. "I'm glad I finally did."

"So am I," Sean said, and she couldn't doubt that he meant it, not the way he was looking at her.

"So what is it you need to tell me that has you looking so serious?"

He shifted again on the wooden bench. "You've never asked me why I'm only now finishing school."

Rory blinked. She didn't know what she'd been expecting, but that wasn't it. "I haven't really thought about it. I know you've been working in your folks' print shop. I guess I just assumed you weren't able to take the full load of classes to finish before."

"That's part of it." He leaned forward, resting his elbows on his knees and lacing his fingers together. "But I also . . . lost a couple of years."

"Lost?"

"I was in an accident. A drunk driver hit a bus I was on."

Rory straightened up, her eyes widening. "You were hurt? Badly?"

"Bad enough."

"My God, Sean, badly enough to lose two years?" Pain filled her at what he must have gone through. "What happened? You seem fine now—"

"I am. It wasn't just healing that took so long. It was . . . adapting."

"Adapting?" She looked him up and down, wondering what she could have missed. There wasn't a scar to be seen on him, and she knew he could see, hear and talk just fine. "To what?" she asked at last.

"This," he said softly. He reached down with his left hand and rapped his knuckles on his left knee. It took a moment for Rory to register that the hard, odd-sounding knock was actually the result of his action. Her gaze shifted to his face, and she stared at him.

"I don't understand," she said. "Is it a brace or something?"

"No, Rory," he said quietly. Then, as if he couldn't face her when he said the rest, he looked away, out at the rolling ocean. "It's my leg. A prosthesis. I'm an amputee."

Staring at him wide-eyed and stunned, she hadn't been able to speak for a long moment. Too long. Sean took her silence as an answer and let out a long breath. He lowered his eyes to stare at the ground between his feet. When he spoke, it was as if he'd had an expectation fulfilled.

"I'll take you home."

"Sean, no, it's just—"

"It's all right. I understand."

"How can you, when I don't?"

And she hadn't, not then. It had been the next day before she even remembered she'd heard the story, still spoken of in hushed tones on campus, about the accident that had ended the career of one of the best wide receivers the Aztecs had ever had. She had just never realized it was Sean.

She'd been shocked—there had never been a sign in the three weeks she'd known him. He moved like anyone else; she had never even noticed a limp. But she'd been swamped with realization, as well, remembering that she had never seen him in shorts, here in this place where they were standard attire, that he had never wanted to go to the beach when she suggested it but always had a different idea.

And he had never let her close enough to really touch him. Even when he'd kissed her, he had kept their bodies scrupulously apart. His lack of aggressiveness had been for his own sake as much as hers, she realized. It hadn't been solely gentlemanly behavior, he'd been afraid she would find out.

It was his fear that confused her the most. What did he expect her to do? She didn't even know, herself.

God, she'd been so young, she thought now as the vivid image faded. It had taken her days to reach the conclusion she should have reached instantly: he was still Sean, and that was all that mattered. But she'd been afraid, knowing she was already half in love with him, and wondering if she could deal with this. Wondering what limitations it involved, and not knowing who to ask.

And wondering, in her more gruesome dreams, what his body must look like. Was it so grotesque that he always kept it hidden? How could it be, with his broad shoulders, well-muscled chest, trim waist and hips, and his sexy backside? And did it even matter? He was still Sean.

It had been a week before she'd gone to him. By then she'd missed him so much she swore it wouldn't have mattered if he'd lost every limb. She had apologized for her reaction and asked if they could begin again. But she had never forgotten that moment when he'd thought she was rejecting him, that moment when she knew he'd been expecting just that.

She couldn't imagine living like that, always expecting rejection, never sure of your welcome. She decided then that they would go at his pace, and if he didn't feel comfortable revealing the extent of his disability to her, then she wouldn't push. She would leave it to him.

Six months later they had taken that walk on the beach, and she had accepted his ring with joy. Yet still he held back. There were times when she wanted him so fiercely that she barely managed to hang on to her conviction that it wasn't right yet, at least not for him, that he needed to be certain of her love before he took that final risk. And she had been willing to wait until they were married, if that was what it took to prove her love to him.

And now he hated her. He must. He had every right to.

One hand crept up to grasp the locket she wore. It had been her mother's and held a wedding picture of her parents. She had worn it ever since the nurse at the hospital had told her how her father had, at the end, given it to her and continuously asked her to be sure Rory got the locket.

Rory hadn't been able to bring herself to look at the picture, but she'd worn it every day since the nurse had given it to her. But it gave her no strength now, no power to fight the too-vivid memories of the boy she'd loved and the man he'd become.

Perhaps he didn't hate her. Perhaps she didn't matter at all to him anymore. He'd changed so much; there was nothing of the sometimes hesitant, tentative boy she'd known in the man she'd seen today. Had she done that to him? Or was it just a result of maturing in a world that generally looked upon him as handicapped, as someone to be pitied, someone who made people thankful it was him and not themselves?

Perhaps he was immune to her now; perhaps he'd truly gotten over loving her long ago. If so, she envied him; for all her efforts, she'd never quite managed to get over him.

Perhaps, Rory thought suddenly, he'd found someone else. Perhaps some other woman had given him that cool confidence, that inner strength Rory had sensed even in their brief encounter. Was he married? Was he happy? Did they have children, perhaps the dark-haired little boy she'd always dreamed of, or the towheaded baby girl Sean had wanted someday?

Something deep inside her screamed out a protest. She quashed it; if Sean had recovered quickly and easily from her desertion, it was only what she deserved. You have no right to be hurt at the idea, she told herself. Or to envy the woman he might have found.

"If you had any class at all," Rory muttered under her breath, "you'd be glad for him."

Then she laughed lowly, ruefully. She had no idea who Sean even was anymore, and here she was fighting off jealousy of a wife and children who might not even exist. It was ridiculous, considering all the time she'd spent feeling so horribly guilty, fearing she had ruined his life forever. If he'd gone on, if he'd found happiness, she should be rejoicing; it would be a great load lifted off her shoulders. She would hate it if the evil had destroyed both their lives.

She wished she could find out. She wished she could—

"What the hell are you doing?"

Rory tensed, instinctively bracing herself. She didn't think he would hit her again, but then, she hadn't thought he would hit in the first place, either. Torture with words was more Frank Talbot's style

"I couldn't sleep," she said carefully.

"I'd think you'd be sleeping like a baby here in your old home. Aren't you glad to be back?"

She said nothing. If she told him the truth, that seeing him here, in her father's house, touching his things, gloating over the richness of the furnishings, made her sick to her stomach, she was sure she would earn another blow like yesterday's. She didn't dare look at him for fear he would see what she was thinking. She didn't need to look at him. She knew he would be wearing her father's silk robe, belted around his paunchy belly, his thinning hair rumpled from his snoring sleep, his narrow, pale blue eyes cold and hard.

"No comment? Too busy crying over Daddy again?"

Oddly, his biting tone eased her wariness. She'd grown used to dealing with his vicious words, and nothing he said could make her feel any worse than she did right now. At least, that was what she thought. Then he went on.

"I knew you'd be like this, a whining little weakling. That's why I never told you your old man was sick. You would have been useless to me for weeks. You're damn near useless anyway, icy little—"

"You knew?"

Rory was on her feet, staring at him. When the hospital had told her that they had tried to reach her but failed, she had assumed they just hadn't had the right number. Her living with Frank Talbot was not something she or her father cared to advertise. Her father had the number, but he'd been so ill she'd assumed he hadn't been able to remember it.

"Of course I knew," Talbot said.

"You knew he was dying, and you didn't tell me?"

"I wasn't about to put up with any dramatic deathbed reversals, my dear. I've worked damned hard to get here." He gestured at the luxurious room. "To prove I'm as good as all those arrogant 'old boys,' and I'm not going to lose it now."

It was his favorite refrain, and Rory knew he believed it, that having the outward trappings proved he was as good as those who had come by such things legitimately. She had, once, a lifetime ago, felt some sympathy for him and for the feeling of inferiority that drove him. But now she didn't even react. Only one thing he'd said mattered to her.

"You bastard," she hissed. "My father died all alone, because of you!"

"Now, now, Aurora. It seems only fair, doesn't it? After all, he abandoned you to me to save his own skin, didn't he?"

"Only because you forced him to it!"

"I did nothing except . . . take advantage of the opportunity he provided." Talbot smiled, a cold, hard curving of his thin lips that underlined the cold hardness of his eyes. "And the charming daughter he offered. Come back to bed, Aurora. Now."

She knew what he wanted. He liked her this way, angry, fighting. It was why she'd trained herself to become docile over these past five years. He had no interest, sexual or otherwise, in an already meek, compliant woman. His pleasure came from her fear, her anger, or any other sign of defiance.

She thought quickly. "Now?" she asked, pleased that she managed to sound so innocently surprised. "I thought you found this time of the month . . . repulsive."

Talbot's heavy, bushy brows lowered. "Again? You used that excuse three weeks ago."

"Sorry. I told you the doctor said the pill makes things erratic." The doctor had said exactly the opposite, but Talbot had such an abhorrence of even the mention of such intimately female things she had found she could tell him just about anything.

He stared at her now, unwilling to either believe or disbelieve her. "Then have her do something else."

"You know she said I can't tolerate an IUD. There is nothing else. Unless, of course, you'd like to get a vasectomy."

A visible shudder went through him, and Rory got the impression that only her presence kept him from moving his hands to protect his genitals from the very thought. She nearly laughed.

"Or I could just get pregnant," she said, his distaste for babies, which nearly matched his distaste for the facts of female life, allowing her to needle him about something she would die before she let happen.

He called her a name, short and crude, before he turned on his heel and strode away. Back to the master bedroom, the room he'd insisted they inhabit when they'd come back to this house after her father's death. The room was so filled with her father's presence that she couldn't believe Talbot could sleep there.

But then, he had a point. Why should he fear taking her father's place, when her father had so easily stepped aside for him five years ago? For a long time she had seen her decision as the only solution to the dilemma her father's recklessness had brought upon them. But now, after five long, hard years of living with a man who had no more conscience than a cockroach, she knew that she'd been a young, malleable fool. But what excuse, then, had her father had? What excuse for letting his daughter sacrifice herself for his own pride? She would never know now; it was too late for her to ask him why.

But not too late to stop Frank Talbot.

The thought came to her suddenly, but so definitely that she knew some part of her mind must have been playing with it for a long time. Probably since the moment Frank had told her, an elated gleam in his eyes, that her father was dead, and she realized that he'd been waiting for this moment for five years. The moment when he thought he would step into Jacob Sheridan's shoes, his house . . . and his life. The moment when he would put into action the last of his manipulations, the will he had forced her father to change, naming Frank Talbot as heir to his majority interest in Sheridan Manufacturing.

But he had left one small thing out of his clever calculations. Rory had been too dazed with grief to see it until now, when anger had cleared away the fog: she didn't have to protect her father anymore. He was dead, and nothing Talbot could do or say could hurt him anymore.

But then caution welled in her. One hand crept up to gingerly touch the bruised flesh of her face. She'd been shocked when he'd struck her, but later, as she sat in the emergency room, she realized she should have seen it coming. While her father had been alive, Talbot would never have dared to hurt her, at least not visibly. Her father would never have stood for that. But now that he was dead, that last restraint had been lost, and Talbot now felt free to do as he wished. To do whatever it took to return her to the frightened girl she'd once been.

But she would never be that girl again. And it was ironic that Talbot himself had forced her to change, to become tougher. Tough enough, she thought determinedly, to stop him. To foil his plans. Tough enough to start to rebuild what she could of her life. But she had to clear away some wreckage first. Had to undo some of the damage he'd already done.

And she would start, she thought, as she resumed staring out into the bleak night, with Sean. It would no doubt make little difference to him, but she would try to explain. She owed him that much. And it would be the first step on her long road to redemption.

Chapter 3

It was nearly midnight when, pizza box sitting beside him on the seat of his little coupe, Sean pulled up in front of the warehouse. Originally a storehouse for a marine hardware company, the building stood in isolation at the end of a narrow, unpaved road that ran along one of the many saltwater lagoons that dotted the coast. It had in fact been too isolated for the company that had owned it, and after trying to sell it for years, they had gratefully accepted Dar's offer.

Sean had just finished fastening down the T-tops he'd removed to take advantage of the balmy night air when he saw Dar come out the front door. As Sean got out of the racy blue coupe, Dar came speeding down the long ramp, throwing his low-slung chair sideways into a skidding, flamboyant stop that kicked up a cloud of dust at the bottom. Sean coughed.

"Nice, huh?" Dar grinned at him. "I'm thinking of starting a slalom race series to go along with the marathons."

"You would," Sean said dryly.

"Actually, what I really want to do is start a downhill. Can't you just see it, down Mount Palomar Road or someplace? Man, we could get up to the speed limit on that old road and then some."

Dar would do it, too, Sean thought. "I'll look for you in the first Olympic Wheeled Downhill," he said, and Dar grinned.

Then Dar's dark eyes narrowed as he looked Sean up and down, taking in the unusual presence of the crutches he was leaning on, and the fact that he'd come on one foot instead of two; forcing swollen flesh back into the socket of the prosthesis was more than he'd been able to face.

"Tough day?"

Sean shrugged. "Long."

Dar studied him for a moment, and Sean knew he hadn't fooled him for an instant. But his friend seemed content to let it slide for now.

"Better give me the pizza then, gimp," Dar said. "You'll drop it for sure, as klutzy as you are with those."

He gestured at the crutches. Sean chuckled, for he might amaze the techs with how well he'd adapted to the prosthesis—they were always calling him when they had some modification they wanted to try out—but he was worse than clumsy with crutches, and he knew it.

He handed over the pizza box and watched Dar wheel back up the ramp. He did it with no sign of strain, muscles built and honed by hours of workouts and miles of road racing handling the incline as if it were level ground. Sean followed at a quarter the speed, crutches thumping unevenly. He should just have put his leg back on, he muttered to himself. He thought suddenly that this was another thing he'd carefully kept away from Rory—she'd never even seen the crutches, had never seen him without at least the illusion of a whole body.

He forced his mind off that track as he stepped inside the building Dar both lived and worked in. In one end was his workshop, cluttered with designs tacked up on the walls, prototypes of two racing wheelchairs and parts for several others strewn about in an order only Dar could sort out. What had begun as a search for a chair to meet his own demanding requirements had turned into a profitable, if small, business. A Cordell chair was the Indy car of the wheelchair racing world, and the demand far outstripped his ability to supply.

The other end of the warehouse was set up with a sofa, chairs and a table grouped around a big-screen television and a powerful stereo—no sense in living out in the boonies unless you took advantage of it, Dar said. Off to one side sat Dar's weight set and bench, along with a cross-country ski machine, adapted for his use. A true athlete, Dar knew the value of balance and worked to keep what was left of his legs in shape, knowing the weight of muscle would help keep his center of gravity lower for racing and improve his conditioning overall.

There was a tall folding wall that blocked off one corner of the room, behind which, Sean knew, lay a custom-built bathroom and Dar's bedroom. That wall was the only barrier in the open space of the warehouse, and Sean knew that when he was alone, Dar left the wall folded back out of the way.

"Room's a mess again, huh?" Sean joked.

Dar set the pizza box down on a low table by the sofa and flipped it open.

"What makes you think," Dar said as he freed a couple of the cheese-attached pieces, "that I don't have...company?"

"Because," Sean said dryly as he made his way to the huge refrigerator in the kitchen area in one corner, and took out a couple of cans of beer, "you're about as likely to have that kind of company these days as I am."

"Uh-oh," Dar said. "The thunder of hormones is heard in the land." He wheeled over and took his beer from Sean before he'd gone three feet from the refrigerator. "I prefer mine unshaken, thanks," he said. "I keep telling you, wheels are better than those cattle pokers."

"Yes, you do." Sean made his way back to the sofa and sat down. "I don't know, it's just..." He shrugged, unable to explain.

"I know, it's a symbolic thing for you. If you use the chair, you're back where you were when you first got hurt."

Sean blinked. "How did you know that?"

Dar shrugged. "Chase and I had a long talk one night."

"Oh." Sean took a deep swallow of cold beer.

"He's a good man, my friend."

"Yes," Sean said, feeling a surge of satisfaction. He'd finally told Chase how much he appreciated what he'd done for him, the effort he had made—for the second time in their relatively short relationship—to kick him in the butt and get his life started again by giving him Laurel Tree.

"You know," Sean had said, holding his brother-in-law's gaze. "I'm really lucky Stevie's as stubborn as she is."

It had taken a moment, but Sean had known the moment Chase realized he meant the stubbornness that had refused to allow Stevie to let Chase walk out of her life, and thereby Sean's life, too. He knew by the unexpected flush that tinged Chase's face.

"I... Thanks," Chase had said after a moment.

Sean shook his head. "I think that's my line. Thanks, brother."

Chase swallowed, visibly embarrassed. "Wow. What brought this on?"

"I should have said thanks long ago. Both for me—twice—and for making my sister as happy as she deserves to be."

"You go much further with this," Chase said dryly, "and I'll be a candidate for sainthood."

Sean had grinned suddenly. "If you were a saint," he'd teased, "we wouldn't be here in a maternity ward."

Chase grinned back, but then the nurse was there, telling him that they were ready for him. He promptly forgot everything except what his beloved wife was going through.

"You play, you pay," Sean said, grinning.

"Thanks, smart a—" Chase glanced at the nurse and cut off the rest of the word. He grimaced and followed the nurse to change into the sterile gear that would allow him to be with his wife in the delivery room.

Sean had watched him go, wondering if he would have the nerve to watch a woman he loved go through such agony to bring their child into the world. An old, long-buried image flashed through his mind; he'd always pictured Rory when he'd thought of such things. He reburied the scene with the ease of long practice and nearly laughed at himself for thinking he might ever face *that* particular decision.

And only moments later he had walked out of the hospital just in time for her to walk back into his life.

But she hadn't, not really. It had been a chance encounter, inevitable in this small town. But that didn't mean it would ever be repeated.

"I think," Dar said, dragging Sean back to the present, "that he's even good enough for Stevie."

"Yes," Sean said again, taking a drink from his beer. "He is."

Dar grinned. "Wish I'd found that sister of yours first, though." He took a long draw from his own can. "Guess I'll just have to wait for Katie to grow up."

Sean grinned back, as much as he could through a mouthful of pizza. The mutual admiration society his niece and his best friend had going never ceased to amaze him. He knew Katie thought Dar was the most wonderful man in the world who wasn't related to her, and the tough, hard-shelled Dar quite simply let the feisty little girl wrap him around her tiny finger.

"So, what's my new godson's name?"

"Jason," Sean said. "After Chase's brother."

Dar lifted a brow. "The one who was killed in 'Nam?"

Sean nodded. After a moment, so did Dar. "That feels right."

"Yes," Sean agreed. "They thought about naming him after Chase but decided it wasn't fair to Katie."

Dar grinned. "Especially since Stevie wouldn't let Chase name her Stevie, Jr."

"Too bad," Sean said with a laugh. "I think Katie would have liked that."

They ate, finished the beers, then started on seconds. After the pizza was gone, Dar lifted a brow when Sean went back for a third beer, but merely nodded when Sean looked at him questioningly.

"So," Dar said casually as he popped open the can Sean handed him and took a healthy swig, "what brought on this sudden attack of libido?"

Sean nearly choked on his own fresh beer at the out-of-the-blue question. Sometimes Dar saw too damned much.

"Hey," Dar said with a shrug, "you love Stevie and Chase too much to really begrudge them this happiness. So something else must have set you off. And you're way past due, my friend."

Sean shrugged, wishing now that he'd denied it all. Not that it would have done much good. Dar Cordell saw through denial about as quickly as he saw through any other form of deceit. Sean sometimes wondered if, when he'd lost his legs, Dar hadn't gained some sixth sense the rest of the world lacked.

"Who is it, some sexy blond doctor at the hospital?"

Sean downed another long swallow of beer. "You're two-thirds right," he muttered.

Dar's dark brows lifted. "Well, the sexy's a given, or you wouldn't be here to whine. So which other part is it, the blond or the doctor?"

Sean went very still. He studied the beer can he held, then traced a meaningless design in the condensation on the side.

"Come on, buddy," Dar said. "You haven't looked like this since the night you told me about—"

Dar broke off suddenly, and Sean knew he'd stiffened. He heard Dar swear, low, harsh and forcefully.

"Blond," Dar muttered. "She's back, isn't she? That rich bitch who ran you through the wringer? I should have guessed she'd show up after her father died."

"Forget it."

"It *is* her, isn't it? Damn it, Sean—"

"I said forget it, Dar."

"Is she going to stay?"

"It doesn't matter. She's ancient history."

"Right," Dar said acidly. But he didn't ask again. He downed the rest of his beer in three huge gulps, then went for another.

Sean watched him curiously. Two beers was their usual with pizza, three their limit, but Dar was dragging out a full six-pack. As rarely as they did this, that was enough to get them thoroughly intoxicated.

"Are we going to get drunk?" he asked.

"I sincerely hope so," Dar said, his voice flat.

He pulled the cans free of the plastic rings and handed three to Sean. Then he pulled out the folding pocketknife he was rarely without and flicked open the blade. Sean thought suddenly of the beautiful turquoise-inlaid knife Rory had given him, the one he still carried, telling himself it was only because it was so handy and he sometimes needed it to make an adjustment on his leg. He pushed the memory away.

"Still protecting the birds?" Sean asked as Dar folded the plastic rings over, then sliced through them. Dar had been doing this ever since they'd found a beautiful shorebird drowned in the lagoon out front, unable to swim because its feet were caught by one of the six-pack holders.

Dar shrugged, ignoring the question, as Sean had learned he usually did when confronted with any evidence of his own generosity. "Drink up," he said, popping open a new beer. "If we're going to whine, we're going to do it right."

"Are we? Going to whine?"

"That's why you came, isn't it?"

Sean flushed. "It was that obvious?"

"You sounded like you'd been hit by a train," Dar said dryly.

Sean blinked. He'd never quite gotten used to Dar's ability to joke like that; a speeding train was what had cost him his legs. Sean had heard about it when it had happened, although he hadn't known Dar then. It had been big local news for several days, because Dar had been a golden boy, just signed by a major league baseball team to play Triple A ball right out of college.

Sean had gone back to look up the story again after he'd first met Dar at the prosthetist's. Dar had a set of prostheses, and could walk with them and a cane, but to Pete's frustration—despite his lectures, he delighted in having fit, strong clients who pushed his appliances to their limits and beyond—Dar preferred the swift maneuverability of his lightweight, agile chairs.

Sean had easily found the heroically grim story. Dar had been stopped at the lowered gates of a railroad crossing, watching two boys proudly showing off their obviously new mountain bikes. The boys decided they had plenty of time and headed across the tracks. Then one of the boys had gone down right in the path of the oncoming train. Dar had gotten the boy clear. But he hadn't made it himself.

And if you called him a hero, Sean thought, Dar would ignore you. As usual.

"Hit by a *female* train," Dar amended now. "Metaphorically speaking."

Sean's mouth quirked wryly. "Is there any other kind? Metaphorically speaking?"

"All kinds. I've been hit by a few. The diesel was simpler."

Sean blinked again. "Simpler?"

Dar nodded. "It was just a chunk of metal. It didn't pity me or want to nurse me, didn't feel sorry for me or treat me like some kind of noble cripple. Or tell me how sad it is, that I'd be so gorgeous if I was whole."

Sean eyed his friend critically. He himself had been told on occasion that he was good-looking, but even he, with a masculine eye that rarely considered such things, could see that Dar had the kind of looks that graced magazine covers or—he glanced at the can he held—beer commercials. He popped open another can, handed it to Dar, then took one for himself.

"Not all women," Sean said. "How about that little brunette in Encinitas last year? She only had one thing in mind. She practically drooled all over you."

"That's because I was sitting in the 'Vette." Dar had won the racy sports car, adapted with hand controls, in a marathon two years ago. He'd sold it shortly thereafter, putting the money down on the warehouse.

"Maybe, but it was you she asked out, not the car."

Dar studied his can of beer, lifted it to his lips for a long pull, then lowered it. He glanced at Sean, then went back to staring at the can.

"She walked into the restaurant that night," he said quietly, "took one look at me and my chair, and suddenly had something else to do."

Sean gaped at him. "What?"

"She thought because I was driving, the wheelchair in the back must have been yours. It was dark, and she'd never seen my legs."

Sean's stomach knotted. "You never told me that."

Dar shrugged. "At least she was honest about it. That's the good thing about a wheelchair. People know right upfront what they're dealing with. No surprises. No heartache if you wait too long to tell them."

He had a point, Sean thought. A good one. "Maybe I should just wear a button. You know, 'My name's Sean and I'm an amputee.'"

"Sure," Dar said. "Or just start wearing shorts. That's a great conversation starter. And ender."

Something jabbed at Sean through his beer-fogged brain. Dar never did this. He never whined, never indulged in self-pity, despite the fact that he had much more reason to than Sean did. Dar had put all that behind him; he looked upon the maiming of his body as something he had no control over. He just concentrated on making what body he had left the best it could be. And that did not include crying into his beer, especially more than a six-pack of it.

He's doing it for you, dummy.

The answer drifted in out of the fog. He had, on another rare night when he'd overindulged in alcohol, told Dar about Rory. Including what her father had told him about why the wedding was off. The wound had been fresher then, that night four years ago, and Dar had recognized the signs. He had uttered a pungent and incestuous profanity that inexplicably made Sean feel better.

Then he had told Sean how his own father, the only family he had, had been unable to even look at what was left of the son he'd had such hopes for. William Cordell had died three years after Dar's accident, never having once come to his injured son's side.

The shock of that had distracted Sean from his own pain and enabled him to see the parallels between them. Football scouts had been hot on Sean's trail from his first year on the San Diego State Aztecs. Dar had become a friend, gradually his closest friend, close enough to somehow realize he needed that sense of understanding again tonight.

Now Dar lifted the beer again. "So here's to honest women, buddy. I'd rather meet a hundred of 'em than one who wants to rescue me or treat me like a helpless child."

"Here, here," Sean said, taking a chug of his own brew. "Do you know, when I was in the hospital, there was a volunteer there who continually talked baby talk to me? Like I'd lost my mind instead of a leg."

"Must be the same one I had. I think she assumed I'd lost something higher up than my legs, but still below the waist." Dar's mouth quirked upward. "But then there was Gina. She made up for a lot. I swear, if that woman hadn't been married, I would have proposed on the spot."

Sean grinned. "Good-looking?"

"In a Sophia Loren kind of way. Earthy. First time I met her, I'd been feeling pretty down. Half-a-man syndrome. You remember."

"Do I ever," Sean agreed with a wry smile.

"Well, she came in and started talking to me about sex. About then I was figuring my sex life was pretty much over, so I told her to get the hell out."

"Did she?" Sean asked, smothering a hiccup before downing another swallow. He was feeling no pain by now, and that mildly pleasant buzz was making everything seem a bit distant. He lifted the can again.

"Nope. She waltzed over and sat on my lap."

Sean forgot to swallow for a moment. "She what?"

"Yep." Dar hiccuped. "Wiggled that cute little bottom all over me. Started whispering dirty nothings in my ear. By the time she got through with me, I was hot enough to light a firecracker with no match."

Fascinated, Sean stared at his friend. "What happened?"

Dar shrugged. "Nothing. She'd proved her point, so she left. But before she did, she gave me some advice I've never forgotten."

"Wha-hic-at?"

Dar grinned. "She said, 'If you're going to try sex in a wheelchair, Cordell, remember to lock the wheels.'"

Sean burst out laughing, quickly deciding that he'd sadly missed out by not meeting the earthy Gina. He reached for the last two beers.

They were well into them when, watching Dar try to spin the chair he'd designed specifically not to spin, Sean grinned goofily. "Wonder'f you could get arrested for drunk driving in a wheelchair?"

Dar stopped his efforts to give that due consideration. "Sure," he said at last. "Can on a bike, why not a chair? Equal rights, y'know. Must be in the Disability Act somewhere."

"If I went out in one, I'd prob'ly get hit by a drunk in a car again," Sean said morosely. "Gotta be an easier way to get yourself killed."

"Easier," Dar agreed. "But less certain. I tried most of 'em."

Sean blinked. "You?"

"Mmm-hmm. Soon's I realized I was one of those people I didn't even like being around."

Sean knew exactly what he meant. It had been the greatest of shocks to him, in rehab and even later, to look at someone else and feel uncomfortable with their handicap—and then realize others were looking at him in the same way. Still, he had a hard time believing the irrepressible Dar had ever been so far down.

As if he'd read Sean's thoughts, Dar went on. "Tried drivin' off a bridge, but the guardrail held. Was gonna jump off the roof of a building, but back then I was such a wimp I couldn't get up and over the side. Got a gun, but by the time I drank enough to work up my nerve, I was too drunk to load the damned thing."

Sean couldn't help chuckling. "Jeez, all I ever did was try slicing my wrists with a piece of broken mirror."

"Betcha did it wrong."

"Huh?"

"Betcha did it crossways. Never works."

Sean stared at his friend. He saw the corners of Dar's mouth start to twitch. The moment he realized Dar was trying desperately not to laugh, Sean was lost. As he realized, even through the alcoholic haze, what they must have sounded like, humor welled up inside him and escaped as a huge, deep, belly laugh. Dar lost his own battle then and joined him.

"Damn," Sean swore when he was finally able to control himself. He wiped at his eyes. "We are a pitiful pair, aren't we?"

Dar hiccuped, laughed again, then nodded. "Damn pitiful. I think we've whined enough to last us through the next decade, buddy."

Sean's last thought, as he collapsed on the sofa, well aware that he had no business driving, was that he'd made it through nearly an entire hour without thinking about Rory.

Chapter 4

He wasn't listed in the phone book. Rory went to the house where Sean had lived with his parents in La Mesa. Mrs. Holmes, a neighbor, told her that they had moved into a new condo in a building their son-in-law had designed. Sean had an apartment somewhere farther north, the woman said, but she didn't know exactly where.

"I do have his phone number, though," Mrs. Holmes told Rory with a speculative look. "I've been trying to set him up with my niece for a year now."

So he wasn't married, Rory thought, denying that the little rush of feeling that went through her was relief. She had no reason to feel relieved, she told herself. Hadn't she been hoping he'd gotten on with his life, that he'd married and was happy? Besides, unmarried didn't necessarily mean unattached. Her mouth twisted grimly. Who knew that better than she?

"I...could you give it to me? I haven't seen him in years, and I've lost Stevie and Chase's number."

She hoped her familiarity with the family would convince the woman. Mrs. Holmes hesitated for a moment, studying her. Rory wondered if the woman recognized her as the girl Sean had brought home on occasion. Probably not, Rory thought. It had been too long ago, and Rory knew she had changed a great deal. And the woman was clearly distracted by the blatant bruise around Rory's eye. For the first time Rory was grateful for it. Mrs. Holmes might not have given her the number if she'd realized she was giving it to the woman who had abandoned Sean on what was to have been their wedding day.

But at last she did, writing the number down for Rory. Not that it mattered; when she stopped at a phone booth and called—she didn't dare go home to call, not the way Frank checked the phone bills—he didn't answer anyway. But just hearing his voice on the answering machine made something tighten in her chest; she'd been half expecting a woman's voice.

Rory sat in her car, thinking. There was an easy way to find him, but she didn't think she had the nerve to take it. She didn't have the nerve to face Sean's sister, the woman who had become her friend, the woman she had come to know well enough to know that a betrayal of her beloved brother was a betrayal of her, as well.

She knew it would take only minutes for her to drive to Stevie's house. She remembered perfectly well where it was; it was hard to forget once she'd heard the story behind its design, and how the drawing itself—and Stevie's undaunted courage—had been instrumental in saving Chase from a life on the run.

Chase.

Maybe she should go to him. Compared to facing Sean's sister, even facing his darkly handsome, somewhat intimidating brother-in-law seemed easy. Chase knew what it was like to be forced to do something you hated for the sake of someone else. Maybe he would understand.

"He's at home," the helpful young redheaded man at the Cameron and Associates office told her with a wide grin. "Never seen a man go into such a panic over a simple thing like a new baby."

"A new baby? Stevie had a baby?"

"Yep. A boy, late yesterday." The redhead laughed, his affection for his employer clear in his voice. "And the last little Cameron, if Chase has anything to say about it. He was a wreck."

So that was what Sean had been doing at the hospital, she thought. She'd assumed he was there to visit the prosthetist who worked out of the clinic next-door; she'd even driven by on occasion, wondering if he might be there, if she could just get a glimpse of him....

"So Katie has a baby brother," she said softly, feeling a heart-wrenching tug as she remembered the little girl who had made her long for one of her own.

"All eight pounds of him," the young man said, still grinning. "You want to leave a message for Chase?"

Rory shook her head, lost in visions of children who would never be, of dreams thrown away. "No," she murmured, turning to go. "I was really looking for his brother-in-law, anyway."

"Sean? He's out at the Laurel Tree site, south of town."

Rory blinked at the unexpected gift. "What?"

"He should be there for another couple of hours, at least." A phone rang, and the young man turned toward it. But before he picked it up, he looked back over his shoulder at Rory. "Just take Coast Boulevard south to Laurel Road. It's right there."

She left him talking on the phone, and was back in her car and on her way before she realized she had never asked the man what Sean was doing at one of Chase's design sites.

* * *

She saw the job site first, a typical-looking two-story apartment complex that appeared nearly finished. She waited for a large black sedan to pass, then parked her car. It took her only a moment to find the Cameron and Associates sign on the fence around the site, next to a sign labeled Starr Construction. Below that was another sign, describing Laurel Tree as "fully accessible" housing, designed in cooperation with the North San Diego Center for Independent Living.

She puzzled over that as she made her way across a parking lot that looked freshly paved and painted. Painted, she realized, with an inordinate number of blue striped and logoed handicapped parking spaces. She walked toward the building, puzzled.

"Lady? This is a hard-hat zone, please stay back."

She turned at the sound of the voice behind her, saw the bearded man's eyes widen—at her still bruised face, no doubt—then saw him recover quickly. She smiled at him tentatively.

"I'm sorry...I was looking for someone. I was told he was here."

The man's graying brows drew together. "Not many guys working today. We're waiting on some deliveries and the county inspector. Who were you looking for?"

It took her a moment to get it out. "Sean Holt."

The bearded face split into a grin. "Oh, *he's* here. Last I saw, he was arguing with some doofus who got an order wrong. Again. Come on, I'll show you."

He started walking toward a delivery van parked on the far side of the building, assuming she would follow. After a moment of wondering if she shouldn't take to her heels and get out of there, she did follow.

"You a friend of Sean's?" he asked, looking back over his shoulder.

Actually, he hates my guts. "We...went to college together."

"Oh. Never went to college myself, but I don't hold that against him." He grinned through the beard. "Charlie—that's my boss, Charlie Starr—has already signed up to work on the next project like this with him. Sean's a good guy."

"Project like...what?"

"Like this one. You know, places designed for folks with handicaps. Sean works for Cameron and Associates, but he's been involved from the get go, pulling the whole thing together. Took almost three years to get this place off the ground, what with all the agencies involved and the funding. But now they're coming from up and down the state to look at Laurel Tree and to talk to Sean. He's become an authority on handicapped housing."

Pride rang in the man's voice. It made Rory painfully aware of how long it had been since she'd been proud of anything she'd done.

"Best thing Chase Cameron ever did was hire him as a consultant, even if he is his brother-in-law. He's already got a reputation for getting things done."

"He...does?"

"Yep. You should see him, explaining to the bozos who don't understand why the fluorescent lights have to be the special natural, nonflickering kind, for people with limited vision. Or why the faucets and doors have to have lever controls, not knobs, for people who don't have full use of their hands."

"You sound pretty adamant yourself," Rory said quizzically.

"I am. My sister's first on the list to get in here. She's a paraplegic. She's in a nursing home now, has been for over a year, and she hates it. This'll be like getting out of jail for her."

"I didn't realize," Rory said.

"Most people don't. If there were more like Sean around, everybody would, though." He pointed toward the parked van. "There he is. I've got to get back to work."

She hadn't noticed the two men standing at the open back of the van, but now she could hear them talking. And could see, despite the hard hats, that one of them was Sean. She nodded her thanks to the worker, who smiled back and hurried off. She took a few more steps before she realized that the voices she was hearing were raised in a loud discussion, both sounding irritated.

"I just deliver them."

"Fine," Sean said. "You can just deliver them back."

The deliveryman swore, but Sean never blinked when the man shouted, "Doors are doors, for cryin' out loud. They're the right size, and there's fifty of 'em. What's the big deal?"

"The big deal," Sean said, "is that these doors aren't what we ordered."

"It says right here, fifty doors with lever handles, automatic door closers and peepholes. That's what I got here."

"Two peepholes."

The man looked at Sean as if he'd lost his mind. "Two? What the hell would anybody want with two peepholes?"

Rory was close enough now to see Sean's jaw clench. He looked tired, and his eyes were bloodshot. He looked, she thought, like a man you shouldn't tangle with. He leaned over and reached into the van, tugging out a full-sized door with no more apparent effort than if it had been made of cardboard.

"Sit down," he told the deliveryman, gesturing toward the bumper of the truck.

"Huh?"

"Sit down," he said again. Reluctantly, and clearly puzzled, the man did. Sean swung the door around and set it

upright in front of him. "Now look through your damned
peephole."

Still confused, the man started to rise.

"I didn't say anything about getting up."

"So how am I supposed to look through it if I don't stand
up?"

"Exactly," Sean said coldly.

Even then it took the man a moment to get it. "Oh," he
said at last. "I forgot this was one of those places."

Sean's jaw tightened again at the man's slight emphasis on
the word "those," but he said only, "Your boss has two
choices. He can send us the right doors—today—or we can
deduct the cost in time and materials to make these right
from his bill."

"All right, all right, I'll take 'em back. Jeez," the man
muttered as he headed for the driver's side of the van.
"You'd think you were going to live here yourself."

Rory half expected Sean to deliver the verbal blow the
man so richly deserved. Part of her wanted to do it herself.
But just then he spotted her and froze. She saw his gaze linger for a moment on her discolored eye and thought she saw
a flicker of emotion cross his face, but it was gone so quickly
that she couldn't be sure. As the van pulled away, she made
herself take the last few steps between them.

"You sure you want to be here?" he asked. She wasn't at
all sure, but the tone of his voice told her that he meant for
some reason other than her own doubts. "I mean, this place
is designed for people who are even more handicapped than
I am."

Rory drew back, stung. This Sean, mocking, cool, self-
possessed, so different from the earnest, open, sensitive boy
she'd known, had her off balance. Any touch of softness
was gone; the hint of vulnerability that had so moved her at
nineteen had been replaced by a cool, easy confidence. And
both times that she'd seen him, he'd made some comment

like this, and she didn't understand why. Unless it was the only way he could think of to strike back at her for what she'd done.

"So what are you doing here, Ms. Sheridan? And," he added, looking suddenly thoughtful, "how did you find me, anyway?"

She took the coward's way out, answering the easier question. "I . . . went by Chase's office. They told me."

His expression went cold, as if he didn't like the idea of her being anywhere near his family. "Lucky for you Chase wasn't there."

She'd guessed she wouldn't have been welcomed, but it stung to hear it so baldly. "They told me. About the baby, I mean. I'm . . . happy for them."

"You'll pardon me if I don't pass that along. Stevie and Chase are too happy right now to spoil it."

There was no point to this, Rory thought. He would never forgive her, no matter what explanation she gave. All her fine courage, which had seemed so unassailable in the middle of the night, seemed a frail thing in the light of day. And before the unrelenting coldness of this man.

She almost turned to go. But something stopped her, some deep core of honesty, too long unused, that reminded her that she wasn't doing this for forgiveness, which was an impossibility, anyway. She was doing this as payment of a debt. And, she admitted with that same honesty, to ease her guilt. She squared her shoulders and turned back to face him.

"I never wanted to hurt you, Sean."

His eyes widened as he stared at her. "I can't believe you said that. Or that you expect me to believe it."

At least it was a reaction, Rory thought. And it wasn't cold. "It's true. I know you won't believe it, but I didn't want to call off the wedding."

"Funny," Sean said, sounding anything but amused. "I could have sworn it was you who sent that charming little note."

"I did. But I had no choice. At least, that's what I thought."

"No choice?" The mocking tone was back. "You made your choice pretty obvious. Even though you used your father to hide behind."

"My father is...was the reason." The correction still hurt, viciously, especially now that she knew Frank had kept his condition secret from her. "He...was in trouble. Financially. Major trouble. His only way out was help from one of his partners, a man he'd borrowed some money from."

"Fascinating. Or I'm sure it would be, if I felt the least bit sorry about whatever mess your father got himself into. You'll have to excuse me if he wasn't one of my favorite people. Now, if you don't mind, I've got a headache, and a lot of work to do."

Beneath the mocking tones there was a vehemence in his voice that Rory didn't understand. Jacob Sheridan had never really liked the idea of his daughter marrying Sean, as much because Sean had been at loose ends about his future as because of his disability. But she'd convinced her father, who hadn't forbidden the marriage, and they'd never openly clashed that she knew of. At least, not enough to cause this fierce emotion. Stubbornly she kept going.

"That partner, Frank Talbot, offered him a deal. To save himself, and the company. My father had to take it or lose everything."

"Is there a point to this?"

It took every bit of her fledgling nerve to go on in the face of his obvious disinterest.

"The point is," she said, her voice shaky, "that part of that deal . . . was me."

She had his attention now, although it was clearly disbelieving. "What?"

"Frank offered to bail my father out." She tried to steady her voice, to make this a dispassionate explanation. "With a great deal of money. In return, he wanted certain... concessions. And me."

"You?"

"He said... he had wanted me for a long time."

Sean was gaping at her now. "So you're saying... what? Your father made you part of the deal?"

She winced. "No. Not really. I made the choice. To save him. He couldn't have faced ruin, Sean. Or the humiliation. He would have died."

"He did that anyway." Rory paled, swaying on her feet. "I'm sorry," Sean said unexpectedly, his voice gruff. "That was uncalled-for. But do you really expect me to believe this?"

"It's the truth."

He swore, low and derisive. Rory steadied herself. She hadn't anticipated that this would be easy. "I had to do it, Sean. It was either hurt you, knowing you were tough enough to recover... or watch my father slowly die."

Or quickly die, she thought, remembering her horror when she'd discovered that he had purchased a handgun and kept it in his center desk drawer. He'd never mentioned suicide, but it was in his eyes every time she looked at him.

"Let me make sure I have this clear," Sean said slowly. "In order to save himself from losing his precious position and wealth, your father in essence sold you to one of his partners? When did he take up pandering?"

She said nothing; really, there was nothing more to say. Especially when nothing she said seemed to penetrate the cool, mocking facade this new Sean had developed.

"There's more to this, isn't there?" he asked after a moment. "There has to be. Your father wouldn't just...sell you like that. Whatever else he might have been or done, he loved you."

"I know. I told you, I made the choice."

"Why? What aren't you telling me?"

"Nothing that matters," she said wearily. "I'm sorry I bothered you. I just thought it might...make a difference to you to know...I never wanted to do it."

"A difference?" His laugh was so genuine it hurt. "You leave me facing a church full of people with nothing more than a note to explain it, destroy all the plans we'd made, take off with some other guy the same week we were supposed to be married, and you think it should make a difference if you tell me that you were sleeping with this guy to buy your father out of trouble?"

She couldn't look at him. Nor could she speak, not even in her own defense. She deserved every word, for what she'd done to him. She'd tried. She'd tried, and she'd lost. If the rest of her campaign to regain control of her life went as dismally as this encounter had, she might as well go quietly home and get back to being Frank's puppet.

"Tell me something," he said, his voice as level as if he were merely curious. "Suppose I were to believe all this. Why didn't you tell me the truth then?"

"I couldn't." Her voice was flat, emotionless. "It was part of the deal."

"Part of the deal?" He swore, short and pungent, a crude oath she'd never heard him use before. It startled her, as did his sudden anger. "How about my part of this little deal? God, Rory, do you have any idea what it took to get over what you said?"

She gaped at him, taken aback by both his words and this rush of emotion where there had been none until now. Had it been there all along, but bottled up inside him? Had he truly become so thoroughly able to hide what she had once been able to read so easily?

"If it was a lie, couldn't you have come up with a better one?" He laughed, a harsh, humorless sound. "A kinder one, at least? Did you have to leave me the gift of thinking that because I was repulsive to one woman, I must be repulsive to them all?"

"Sean, what are you talking about?"

"I'm asking," he said fiercely, sounding like a man fighting to hold back every word, "why the hell you said it was because of my leg!"

Rory went paler than she had when he'd made the crack about her father's death. Her knees went weak with shock. For a moment she thought she would faint. "I didn't... Sean, I didn't..."

"Your father made it quite clear," he snapped.

"I couldn't... Oh, God, Sean."

Sean's eyes narrowed as he looked at her. Lord, Rory thought numbly, this explained so much, the cynical gibes, the comment he'd made at the hospital yesterday....

She had to talk, had to tell him; she couldn't let him go on thinking something so awful for another instant. But she couldn't seem to find her voice. At last the words came, tiny and stunned.

"He didn't... God, Sean, tell me he didn't say that."

"Believe me," Sean answered grimly, "that's not something I'm likely to forget. 'She deserves a man who's whole, not a cripple she'd have to close her eyes to stomach going to bed with' were the exact words, as I recall."

Rory moaned. "I didn't know. God, I didn't know. Please, Sean, if you don't believe anything else I say, you have to believe that. I would never have let you be hurt like that, not even for my father."

He hesitated, frowning.

"If that's what you've believed all this time..." She shook her head, like an animal in mortal pain. "Oh, Sean, how you must hate me."

"I did," he said flatly. "Then."

The emotion had vanished. He was as cool as he'd been before. She made herself look at him, ordering herself not to read anything into his terse answer. But she couldn't stop herself from asking. "And now?"

"Now? Now," he said, all the mockery back in full force now, "I don't give a damn."

Rory let out a long breath. With a slight nod—there was, after all, nothing more for her to say—she turned to go. Sean stopped her, with a question she'd never expected from him.

"How long has your boyfriend been beating you?"

Rory froze. "I told you . . . it was an accident."

"Right." He clearly didn't believe her. "Why did you come here, Rory? What did you hope to accomplish?"

"I . . . owed you an explanation. The truth. After what I did. And because I . . ."

She let her voice trail away, facing the futility of what she'd been about to say. He would never believe she had truly loved him, not after all the years of pain she'd put him through. Pain that had been greater than she had ever realized, thanks to her father's cruelty.

She walked away without another word.

Chapter 5

"Hey! You with me here, or what?"

"Sorry," Sean muttered, and resumed his position over the barbell stand, although he wasn't sure how much good he would be if Dar dropped the damned thing. On a good day he could bench-press more than his body weight, but Dar was doing twice his and was barely breathing hard.

"Up another twenty," Dar said as he let the bar come back to rest on the stand. "I've got to shave some time off that home stretch."

Sean nodded. He removed the collar that held the weights in place, added a ten-pounder to each end, then put the collar back and fastened it. Dar set his grip and pressed upward. His muscular arms barely wobbled as he held the weight suspended for a full ten count, lowered it, took a breath, then raised it again.

"So," Dar said, as casually as if he weren't lifting well over three hundred pounds, "when do I get to see my new godson?"

"Sure," Sean said, sounding as vague as his eyes looked.

Dar eyed him suspiciously. "I have a present for him."

"Okay."

"It's a motorcycle. Think he'll be able to ride it by tomorrow?"

"Sure."

The weight clattered back onto the stand. "I quit."

Sean focused suddenly. "What?"

"I'm switching to dumbbells. I could die here while my spotter's out in the ozone somewhere."

Sean winced. "Sorry. I'm just—"

"Distracted. I noticed."

Dar sat up, reached out and pulled his chair closer, then levered himself into it in a smooth, fluid motion. With sharp, short motions, he tugged off the fingerless weight lifting gloves he wore. He looked at Sean for a long time before he spoke.

"Take my advice, friend. Stay clear. Have sex with her if you have to, but keep your damned heart intact."

Sean drew back. "What makes you think—"

"I recognize the signs," Dar interrupted. "I was *distracted* like that once."

"You? Hell, Dar, you're the most focused human being I know."

"I wasn't. Not then, right after my accident. All I could think about was Valerie."

"Valerie?"

"My fiancée."

Sean blinked. "Your what?"

Dar gave him a sideways look. "You heard me."

Sean stared at him. "Jeez, man, I've known you for what, four years now? And this is the first I've heard that you were ever engaged."

Dar shrugged. "It's not something I talk about."

"Why? What happened?"

"Simple. When Val realized I didn't have any feet left, she used hers."

Sean swore, low and empathetic.

"Yeah. The worst part was, she tried. She really tried. It was pretty obvious, though, when she'd never look at me, or what was left of my legs. The first time we tried to have sex and my stump touched her . . . she threw up."

"Damn."

"I couldn't really blame her." Dar shrugged. "I threw up, too, first time I looked at myself. Finally I told her to go. It was too tough on both of us."

Then the insouciant Dar was back. "Thank God for Gina, or I'd be missing my manhood as well as my legs. She had me convinced I was so damned sexy she'd leave her husband for me if she didn't love the stuffing out of him." He eyed Sean speculatively. "But you, my friend, didn't have the pleasure of knowing Gina. So who held you together after the little blonde walked?"

Sean opened his mouth, then closed it. He eyed his friend sourly. "Pretty sneaky, Cordell. Open a vein and bleed a little, so you can get me to do the same. You studying psychology on the side?"

Dar grinned. "Hell, why study? I've been through enough sessions with them, I picked it up by osmosis. He eyed Sean again. "So, you want to talk about her?"

"What makes you think that's what—"

"Pu-lease," Dar groaned. "Of course that's what it is. The rich bitch blows back into town, and you're still spinning."

"She's a lot of things, Dar," Sean said slowly, "but a stereotypical rich bitch was never one of them."

"Okay," Dar said agreeably. "Just a selfish bi—"

"Maybe not even that," Sean said. "Maybe even less than your Valerie."

Dar drew back, staring at Sean. "This *is* the cold-hearted, note-writing, cowardly little no-show we're talking about, isn't it?"

Sean sighed. "Yeah. At least, that's what I always thought." And then, because he'd been carrying it around all day and felt as though he had to tell someone or burst, he told Dar what had happened.

"Do you believe her?" Dar asked when he'd finished, sounding doubtful.

"I don't know. But I don't know why she'd lie about it at this late date."

"Guilt?"

"Maybe. But it's a pretty bizarre story."

"So you figure it must be true?"

"I don't know," Sean said again. "But there's not much way to check it out, is there? Her father's dead, and this Talbot guy isn't likely to admit to anything."

"Probably not," Dar admitted. He was silent for a long time. Then, in a very quiet voice, he said, "She must have really loved her father."

Later that night, Sean was still thinking about Dar's rather wistful words. Sometimes he wished he could magically heal his friend, not his maimed body, but his more badly injured soul. Dar had lost so much, yet he kept on, whining only when his best friend needed company in the cathartic process, and never complaining. Four years, Sean thought in amazement. For four years he'd known Dar, probably better than anyone, and he'd never known about Valerie, or her desertion, until today.

There were a lot of things he hadn't known until today. He just wasn't sure if he believed them all. Rory's version of what had happened five years ago indeed seemed bizarre. But in an equally bizarre sort of way, the pieces fit. Her father had always been very conscious of his position in the community—in fact, Sean had thought him a bit of a pompous fool—with the awareness of one who had made his money recently, not lived with it for generations. But that had not precluded his obvious love for his daughter. Rory's mother had died when Rory was twelve, after a long, painful illness, and the two had become very close afterward.

He tried to picture what she must have felt like five years ago, a sheltered nineteen-year-old, faced with the ruin of her beloved father. If what she'd told him was true, was he expecting too much to think she could have found another way? And how could Jacob Sheridan have let his daughter sacrifice herself just to get him out of financial trouble? No, that part didn't make sense. And what the hell kind of man would want a woman who was forced to come to him like that, anyway?

The kind of man who would beat up that woman, Sean answered himself grimly. The kind of man who could take a girl as animated, as vibrant, as Rory had been and turn her into the spiritless creature who had left the construction site today.

If what she'd told him today wasn't true, why would she bother with a lie after all this time? And if it was . . .

No, it was much more likely that she had come to the same realization Dar's fiancée had: she couldn't deal with a husband whose body wasn't whole. But that still didn't answer the question of why she would lie now, when it was years too late to soften the blow.

His entire perception of what she had done five years ago was shifting, becoming liquid where it had once been set in concrete. Lord, but he was tired of thinking about it. He'd done little else all day. Including, he thought suddenly, checking on his new nephew.

When he called, the answering machine picked up.

"Hi," he said after the beep. "Just checking to see if you're surviving—" A click cut him off.

"Hi." Chase's deep voice sounded weary but tinged with an undertone of relief. "I was afraid it was your mother again."

Sean laughed. "I've been meaning to thank you. Since she's calling you all the time, she's leaving me alone."

"You're welcome," Chase said dryly.

After giving Sean the update on Stevie and baby Jason, along with assurances that Katie was adapting to the new addition as well as could be expected—with a lot of help from Dar, who had called to talk to his favorite girl for nearly an hour, wisely exhibiting only mild interest in the baby that had everyone else so fascinated—Chase turned to business.

"Heard you had a little problem at the site today."

Sean's breath caught. "How the hell did you hear about that?"

"Armstrong called to apologize for the mix-up. Whatever you said worked."

Sean's breath came out in a relieved rush. "Oh. The doors."

"Yes," Chase said, his tone quizzical. "What did you think I was talking about?"

"I . . . nothing."

"Is that a nothing I should know about?"

Chase had a right to ask, Sean knew. After all, it was his name on the sign, even though Sean was basically in charge of the project.

"It's . . . nothing to do with the job," he said at last.

"Okay," Chase said, trusting him, accepting his word so easily that Sean felt a tug of gratitude for this man who had done so much for him for little reason other than that he was the brother of the woman Chase loved more than life itself.

Before Sean realized he was going to say them, the words were tumbling out. "Rory showed up. She's back in town."

There was a moment of silence, then a short, explicit curse. Sean hadn't mentioned the encounter at the hospital, but he knew his family had wondered, as he had when he'd heard of her father's death, whether she would be back.

"Yeah. That's kind of how I felt, too. When I first saw her there, I didn't know whether to throttle her or just throw her out."

"Uh, Sean," Chase said, sounding odd, "you didn't, did you?"

"Which?" Sean asked, joking yet puzzled by his brother-in-law's tone.

"Throw her out. That might prove . . . complicated."

"Complicated? What does that mean?"

Chase sighed. "Damn it. I didn't know if it would bother you, but I didn't figure you'd ever have to know."

Sean felt his stomach knot. "Know what?"

Chase paused, then said flatly, "Jacob Sheridan was one of the major contributors to Laurel Tree."

"What?" Sean asked, astonished.

"There was no way to turn him down, Sean. I wanted to, but even if I'd had the authority, which I didn't, it could have set the whole project back six months. It was his contribution that put us over the top."

Stunned, Sean said nothing.

"I thought about pulling out altogether when I found out, but—"

"No," Sean said, finding his voice at last. "That would have been crazy."

He meant it, although the knowledge that Chase had even thought about abandoning the project he'd poured years of energy into for his sake moved Sean in a way he had no words for.

"I knew I could make sure you'd never have to talk to him, or even see him—"

"Chase, it's all right. I'm just . . . surprised, that's all."

"So was I. It hardly seemed in character for him, donating to a project for people with disabilities. I even went to see him after I saw his name on the list."

Sean was startled again. "You did?"

"Don't worry," Chase said wryly. "I managed not to slug him. Although, believe me, the temptation was there. But I wanted to make damned sure he didn't back out later, when it could really steamroller the project."

Sean's stomach knotted up again. "You thought he might do that?"

"After what he did to you, I wouldn't have put it past him to have made the donation for just that reason," Chase said, the grimness of his tone reminding Sean that his brother-in-law had considerable experience with the ugliness people were capable of.

"What . . . did he say?"

"Not much. Just that he knew what Laurel Tree was. And that my company would be designing it." Chase paused. Sean waited. "Then," he added, as Sean had half expected, "I told him that you would be working on it."

"And he still agreed?" Sean asked, feeling a little bewildered.

"In writing."

"What?"

"I made him sign a statement saying he knew all of this before he signed the check. I promised it would stay between him and me, unless he tried to pull a fast one."

"My God," Sean breathed. He'd always known Chase could be intimidating, but to beard Jacob Sheridan in his den like that . . . "Remind me to put in that nomination for your sainthood," Sean said at last.

"Forget it," Chase said brusquely. "I was just covering all the bases."

And looking out for Stevie's little brother. Again. "I don't get it," he said at last. "Why would he do it?"

"Beats me. I asked him, but he wouldn't give me an answer. So, as they say, we took the money and ran." Chase cleared his throat. "I...er, I'm sorry you had to find out like this."

"Never mind. It doesn't matter now."

"No. Laurel Tree's almost finished. But now we'll never know what made him do it, I suppose," Chase said.

"No."

"Sean?"

"What?"

"Be careful, will you? Don't get yourself tangled up with her again. She wasn't tough enough to deal with reality before, don't convince yourself she is now."

"She's got her own problems now," Sean said. "I'll be fine." He wished he felt as sure as he sounded.

Chase's news lingered in Sean's mind long into the night. He was exhausted; he wasn't used to late nights of drinking—he and Dar had ruefully compared hangovers that morning—and it hadn't been a restful day.

He lay staring at the ceiling, his thoughts whirling. Why would a man who had shown such disdain for "cripples" give that much money to a project to benefit the very people he scorned? Or had he merely been relaying Rory's feelings that day five years ago, not his own, meaning she'd been lying today?

Or was the crazy story Rory had told him true? Was the donation some kind of payoff, given to ease a guilty conscience? Jacob Sheridan would be just the kind of man to think enough money could pay any kind of debt.

Or had it perhaps been Rory's idea, a huge bone thrown to the wounded puppy to keep him occupied and out of her life, and maybe ease her own guilt, if she felt any?

He woke up from a couple of hours of broken, uneasy sleep with the same questions still battering at him in the gray light of morning. And a new determination to get the answers.

It was nearly seven when he turned his car down the street he hadn't been on in five years. The street he hadn't been on since the day he'd arrived in Chase's car, wearing a tuxedo, unwilling to believe what the note crumpled beside him on the front seat had said.

And to find out now that the man who had blasted him to pieces that day had been partly responsible for the work that had helped put him back together... There was only one person who could resolve this for him. Any of this.

He couldn't seem to get out of the car. What if Talbot came to the door?

So what if he does? he rebuked himself silently. It couldn't be any worse than the last time Sean had come to this door. Besides, all he wanted to know was why the hell her father had made that donation. Strictly a business discussion, of sorts.

That got him out of the car and up to the door. But only the sound of a car passing by enabled him to finally ring the bell; he was afraid whoever was in the big black sedan would report him as a suspicious character just standing stupidly on the front porch of this opulent house.

He held his breath as the door started to swing open, then released it when he saw it was Rory who had opened it.

The instant she saw him she went starkly white. "Sean!" she gasped, one hand going to her mouth as if she could stop the sound that had already escaped. Her sudden pallor accentuated the still livid bruise around her eye. She was in baggy sweats that made her look fragile, especially with her hair pulled up into a knot atop her head, baring the slender line of her neck.

Quickly she closed the door to a mere crack.

"I need to talk to you," he said without preamble.

"I can't! You have to get out of here," she said urgently.

"It's about your father."

She looked puzzled for a split second, but after a quick glance over her shoulder back into the house, she shook her head. She looked around again, as if some monstrous horror was nipping at her heels.

"Just go," she said, almost wildly.

Perhaps he wasn't far wrong about that monster, Sean realized suddenly. He hadn't thought about this aspect of his coming here. He had no experience with this kind of thing, hadn't thought that this was a woman living with a man who beat her. His mind didn't work that way, and he hadn't thought that by coming here he could be making things even more difficult—and dangerous—for her.

He supposed he shouldn't care; she'd certainly made life difficult enough for him. But he kept looking at her swollen eye, and thinking that he might have let her in for more of that kind of treatment made him a little queasy.

"I'm sorry," he said, a little lamely. "I didn't think."

"Aurora! What is going on out there? Can't I even trust you to answer the damn door?"

Instinctively Sean drew back at the roar of an angry male voice. In the narrow strip of a mirror visible through the barely open door, he saw the reflection of a man approaching, walking with a rolling gait that was almost a swagger.

"Go!" Rory moved quickly, and for the second time in his life, Sean stood staring at a front door that had just been closed on him.

He could hear voices through the door. Or one voice, at least; only the pause between the man's angry words told him that Rory was answering. Common sense told him to get the hell out before Talbot—he assumed it was Talbot—yanked the door open again and found him standing there like a befuddled idiot.

But some other instinct he didn't quite understand made him linger until the voice faded away. He wasn't sure what he would have done if he'd heard the sound of blows, or Rory had screamed; he was just glad it was a decision he didn't have to make.

It was odd, he thought, when he got back to his car and got in. He'd expected Talbot to be younger, an athletic type. The stocky man he'd seen had looked at least twenty-five years older than Rory's twenty-three. Sean sat there, staring at the big house, realizing that that had been an old image, born of the days five years ago when he had pictured Rory choosing the kind of man he'd once been, an athlete in his prime. Days when he'd been convinced she'd left him because he wasn't that kind of man anymore.

He wasn't at all sure he was convinced otherwise now. Her story had sounded so incredible, so impossible…but again, why would she bother to make up something that absurd, especially after all this time?

Maybe he should just wait until Talbot left. Maybe then he could get some answers. But if the man came out and saw him here, Rory might end up in even more trouble. He didn't know. He'd never understood the kind of mind that let a man abuse a woman, so there was no point in trying to speculate on what the man might do.

When he noticed that the occupant of the black sedan, which had parked in front of the next house, was sitting there staring at him, Sean decided he'd better get out of here before the blond man really did call the police on him. A strange car with a lone man in it watching a house in this wealthy neighborhood was no doubt reason enough for a cop to stop by for a chat. And he wasn't quite up to explaining his presence here to a stranger. He wasn't even sure he could explain it to himself.

He wasn't much calmer by the time he got to the site. He almost hoped today's delivery—a dense-nap, nonskid carpet designed for wheelchair traction—would be messed up like the doors; he could use some reason to vent his turmoil. He'd worked damned hard to put the past behind him, and now it seemed to be crashing in on him from all sides. For a moment he wished he was still young enough to see running away as an answer.

It was late, nearly midnight, when the phone rang. Sean rolled over and fumbled for the phone, more than a little irritated. He'd fallen asleep at last after another restless couple of hours of tussling with questions he had no answers for. He started to answer as grumpily as he felt, then caught himself in case it might be Stevie or Chase, calling about something wrong with the baby.

"Yeah?"

He still sounded half-asleep, he thought, and cleared his throat. No answer came. He tried again, more awake now.

"Hello?"

"Sean?"

The voice was faint, tiny, and something about it sent a shiver up his spine. "Rory? Is that you?"

"I...I'm sorry, I know it's late, but...I didn't know who else to call."

He was sitting up now, his hand tightening instinctively around the receiver. "What's wrong? What happened?"

"I . . . Frank found out."

"Found out? Found out *what?*"

"That it was you. This morning. At the house."

The chill that had rippled up his spine now threatened to envelop him. He closed his eyes, but all he could see was Rory's bruised face. He steadied himself.

"Are you hurt?"

"I . . . I don't think so."

Whatever that meant. "Where are you?"

"I shouldn't have called you, I—"

"Where, Rory?"

"A... phone booth. On Coast Boulevard. By the park."

"Stay there," he said. He wedged the phone to his ear with his shoulder and leaned over to grab his prosthesis from the chair next to his bed.

"I'm sorry, Sean. For everything."

"Stay there," he repeated, but he was talking to dead air. Rory had hung up without another word.

When he got there, the phone booth was empty.

Chapter 6

Sean slammed his fist against the steering wheel in frustration as he stared at the glow of the phone booth's light. It had been over an hour since Rory had called. He'd been back to the booth twice, hoping she'd returned, but it always stood unhelpfully empty. He'd searched the area for her car, but he'd found nothing.

He shifted his gaze out toward the sea. He was usually soothed by the nighttime beauty of it, the moonlight painting a gleaming silver swath over dark, rhythmically rolling water. But tonight he could only think of its chill, the unforgiving depths of it, and he looked at it with a kind of fear.

She wouldn't, would she? He couldn't picture Rory seeking such a permanent end to her problems. But then, he couldn't think of her tolerating such treatment in the first place. At least, not the Rory he'd known. Which meant, he supposed, that the question was whether that Rory even existed anymore?

No more than the kid you were then exists anymore, he told himself. The kid he'd been. The naive boy who thought he'd had the world handed back to him when Rory accepted his ring—and him—had been mortally wounded that day on her front porch. It had just taken him a long time to die.

He went suddenly very still. *When Rory had accepted his ring.*

She had done it on the beach below this very park.

When he reached the narrow stairway that led down from the bluff, he took it five steps at a time, using the railing on both sides as support as he swung and slid, coming down hard with his weight on his natural leg. He staggered a little when he hit the loose sand at the bottom but steadied himself quickly. He turned and started walking swiftly along the base of the bluff.

He hadn't set foot on this beach since he'd spent an entire night here after Rory's desertion, weeping like the kid he'd been, railing at the injustice of the world that had first taken his leg, then the woman he'd thought could make him forget about it. Chase had told him once that sometimes you met people who pretended to forget about your scars. And that, rarely, you met people who really did forget. And if you were truly lucky, you someday found the person who made *you* forget. Chase had found Stevie. And Sean, so he'd thought, had found Rory. Only in the end, Rory hadn't been able to pretend any longer. At least, that was what he'd always told himself.

He found his way as easily as if he'd come here every day, and he knew the instant he saw the figure huddled in the dark shelter of the rocks where they'd lain that night so long ago that he'd found her. Even in the shadows the honey gold of her hair gleamed.

She must have heard him before she saw him, because she stiffened and backed up against the craggy rock. It was a fearful, self-protective movement, and it made Sean almost afraid to go close enough to see her.

"Rory, it's me," he said.

For an instant she didn't move. Then he saw her shoulders slump, and although he couldn't hear it over the roll of the waves, he knew she'd let out a sigh of relief. He came forward into the shadow of the rocks and sat on the knee-high boulder she was crouched against. She was dressed only in jeans and a thin blouse, with a pair of canvas slip-on shoes sitting on the sand beside her.

"Are you all right?" Stupid question, he thought as soon as he'd voiced it. Of course she wasn't. "I mean, are you hurt?"

"No."

"Did he . . . ?"

"He tried. I ran."

Sean swore under his breath. Anger bubbled up inside him, the same rage he felt whenever he heard or read of a man brutalizing a woman, yet stronger, fiercer. He told himself it was simply because he knew this woman, and because he'd seen the damage Talbot could do. No matter that he might hate her for what she'd done, she didn't deserve that. No woman did.

"I shouldn't have called you," she said quietly.

"Then why did you?" His anger put an edge in his tone, but she didn't seem to notice.

"Because . . . I knew you would come."

His anger took a perverse twist. Was he so predictable? Did she really think that with a snap of her fingers, Aurora Sheridan could have Sean Holt dancing to her tune again?

"And what the hell made you think that?" he asked gruffly.

"Because you're who you are," she answered simply. "You couldn't have changed that much. You're still the

Sean I knew, at heart. You'd help anyone in my position, even if you . . . hated them.''

Damn. Maybe he *was* that predictable. He was here, wasn't he?

"What happened?"

"I told you. He found out it was you who came to the door this morning."

"How? I've never even met the man." And hopefully I never will, he added silently. "He wouldn't know me if he saw me."

"He . . . he's been having me followed."

"Followed?"

He saw her push a strand of her hair, lifted by the sea breeze, back out of her face. His fingertips tingled involuntarily; how many times had he done that same thing himself, merely for the pleasure of touching her incredibly smooth skin? He waited, letting the silence build.

"He hired someone," she said at last. "A private detective. He's been following me ever since we moved back into Daddy's—" her voice broke for an instant before she went on "—house. I was just too stupid to realize it."

Sean's brows lowered. "Blond guy? Drives a big black boat of a sedan?"

She gave him a startled look. "I don't know. He wouldn't tell me. He just said he's had me watched every day."

"Must be," Sean said. "He pulled out right behind you at the hospital. Then I saw the car yesterday at the Laurel Tree site, and the car and the same man were there again this morning, sitting outside your house. But I didn't put it together until you said that."

Rory nodded, her expression bleak. "Frank said if I leave, he follows me. If not, he just sits there, watching the house until Frank gets home to . . . take over."

"Well, he was watching me this morning." His mouth twisted ruefully. "I was afraid he was going to call the cops on me or something."

Rory lowered her gaze, and Sean thought he saw her shiver. "That must be how Frank knew, then. If that man saw me talking to you at the hospital, and again yesterday..."

Sean nodded. He'd figured that out already. The man Talbot had hired to follow her must have seen that the man she'd talked to at the hospital was the same man Rory had talked to at the Laurel Tree site, and it wasn't much of a jump from there to finding out who he was. One call to the number on the Cameron and Associates sign out front would do it. His position as head consultant and liaison on the project was hardly a secret.

"And then you show up at the house." She shivered again, undeniably this time. Sean understood, he felt a little chilled himself.

"I'm sorry, Rory." He meant it. "It never occurred to me that—"

"How could it?" she burst out. "You don't...think like that. Twisted. God, I've barely been out of that man's sight for five years, and he accused me of...of seeing you all along." She laughed, a sound as bleak as her moonlit expression had been. "As if you'd have anything to do with me."

Something struck him then. "Are you saying he knows...specifically who I am? I mean, that I'm the one you..."

"Left at the altar?" she said bluntly when his voice trailed off. "Yes. He does. He made a point of knowing, in case you didn't..."

"Exit gracefully?" Sean suggested wryly. Her nod was tiny, barely discernible. "What set him off tonight?" he asked.

"He got home late, after midnight. He'd been at... Daddy's office. I was in the kitchen, fixing some hot chocolate, because I couldn't sleep. The minute he came into the house he confronted me. Said he'd been waiting all day to do it, to get good and mad. Told me he knew it was you who'd been at the door."

"What did he do then?" he prompted when she stopped.

"Accused me of inviting you. When I denied it, he..."

"Hit you?" Sean asked, his voice a strained combination of gentleness and anger.

"He tried. I threw the hot chocolate at him and ran. He doesn't move real fast, so I beat him up the stairs. I locked myself in the bathroom. He started to break down the door, so I piled everything I could behind it. Then I climbed out the window."

Sean's brow lifted. "Upstairs?"

"That bathroom is over the back patio. I just dropped down to the patio roof, then to the ground." She shrugged. "It was the only room he hadn't gotten around to changing the knob on yet."

"The knob?"

"The doorknob. He took out all the inside ones with locks." She grimaced. Sean saw the glint of moonlight on the locket that was still around her neck, the gold looking oddly devoid of its warm glow in this bleak light. "He said it was his house now, and he wouldn't have any door in it locked against him."

Sean swore, beginning to get an inkling of what the past five years had been like for her. And wondering how—and why—she had stood it. The Rory he'd known never would have. Except, perhaps, he amended silently, for the sake of her father.

"It's not, is it? His house?" Sean asked.

Her head came up. "No. No, it's not. Daddy made sure of that, at least."

At least? What did that mean? Sean wondered. But he delayed his questions for the moment; they had other things to worry about.

"Did you take your car?"

"No. I knew he'd hear it and come after me in his. He was so furious, I didn't want him after me in a car. So I went through the backyard and over the fence into the Gerards' backyard. Thank God old Pepper still recognized me. He didn't even bark."

Sean felt himself unexpectedly start to smile at the sudden image of the huge, gamboling sheepdog that had lived behind Rory's house. He must be twelve years old by now, he thought.

"Then what?" he prodded when Rory stopped.

"I came here."

"You walked?" It was every bit of five miles, most of it hills.

"Yes." She gave him a sideways look. "I didn't think it made much sense to escape Frank, then get killed by some maniac who picks up lone female hitchhikers."

Now that, Sean thought, was more like the old Rory. "You should call the police, you know."

The flash of spirit wavered. "No. No, I can't."

"Rory—"

"I can't," she repeated doggedly.

He sighed. "All right. For now." He glanced at his watch. "Let's get out of here. It's two, it's getting chilly, and you don't even have a jacket."

"I didn't have time to pack," she said wryly, that touch of liveliness showing again, stronger this time. "All I have is what was in my pockets. My keys and two sticks of gum."

Odd, he thought, that now, when she should logically be at her lowest ebb, she was starting to sound a bit like the girl he'd once known. He stood up, holding his hand out to help her up. She shook her head.

"No, Sean. I shouldn't have called you. If Frank were to find out you helped me—"

"You going to tell him?"

"Of course not, but—"

"Let's go, then."

"But he must be looking for me. And he's probably got that man he hired looking by now, too."

"Probably. That's why we need to move fast."

Still she held back. "You don't understand. When I said he made a point of knowing about you, I meant it. He made my father tell him everything he knew about you. He knows who you are, even your parents' names. Sean, he knows who Stevie is, and Chase."

The words in themselves weren't inherently threatening, but the context made him very uneasy. A threat to himself he could deal with, but his family...

"And now he knows that you're working for Chase," Rory added, "so he'll be able to find you."

"Not if I warn Chase first," Sean said flatly. "He's had some experience with fending off predators, remember?"

He'd once told Rory a slightly edited version of Chase's time as a protected witness, and how Chase and Stevie had both nearly been killed by the son of the man he'd testified against.

"I know," Rory said, her voice shaky. "But I don't want to bring this down on them. Or you. It's my problem, and I should handle it."

"You're right," Sean agreed. Rory looked up sharply, as if she'd expected him to deny it. "I've learned," he said dryly, "that there are some things no one else can make go away for you." Then he held his hand out to her again. "But you need some breathing room, time to think. You can use my place until you decide what to do. Come on."

"I should go to a motel or something."

"At two in the morning? With no bags and no ID?"

"But what if he finds out where you live—"

"That'll take him a while. Long enough for you to rest a little."

After a silent moment, she took his hand. And as easily as that, the connection between them was reestablished. Sean remembered, with a jolt that left him sweating, all the times he'd pulled back from her, shaking with need, all the nights he'd awakened from erotic dreams and had to beat down the desire this honey-haired, green-eyed woman roused in him, all the times they'd teased each other into a near frenzy.

And he remembered the fear, the apprehension, that when the time finally came she would take one look at him and do... exactly what she'd done. Walk away.

He pushed the thoughts out of his mind. It wasn't Rory he was trying to help here, not really. It was a woman in need, a woman who was trying to deal with something no woman should have to, yet so many did; a man who used his strength and power against her. That it was the woman he'd once loved made it both more poignant and a hell of a lot harder.

When he realized he was still holding her hand, long after she was on her feet, he dropped it hastily. She flexed her fingers, looking at them with an expression of surprise, as if she, too, had felt the unexpected connection, as strong as if the past five years had never been. They walked toward the beach stairs without a word.

They were almost at the foot of the steps when Rory said tentatively, "You... don't have trouble on sand anymore."

Sean shrugged. "It's a new system I'm testing out for Pete. A Japanese design. They call it an 'intelligent prosthesis.'"

"Intelligent?"

He realized suddenly that this was the first time she'd ever asked him anything about it. He hadn't even realized that she'd noticed walking on sand hadn't been easy for him, before.

"Yeah," he said, keeping his tone casual. "It has a pneumatic system with microprocessors that sense my walking rate and adjust the flex of the knee to different speeds. The leg works more naturally than the old one, which was permanently set to an average pace."

"It's computerized?"

He was surprised. She seemed genuinely interested. He answered as they started up the stairs.

"Sort of. The processor controls a valve that sets the pneumatic pressure. When it's high, the knee moves faster, so I can walk faster. Go up stairs easier. And stumble less—like on sand. Only problem is, my batteries go dead every ten months or so."

Rory turned her head to look at him, as if she weren't sure whether he was kidding or not.

"No joke. Lithium batteries. To power the microprocessors."

"Amazing," she said.

And it was, he supposed. But what was more amazing than the leg itself was that, in the casual conversation they had just had, they had talked more about it than they had in all the time they'd been together before. But then, it was easy to be curious when it wasn't...personal. She could ask now, he supposed. Now that she wasn't faced with living with it.

That realization kept him silent all the way to his apartment. That, and constantly watching the rearview mirror for a large, black sedan.

"You want to tell me the rest of it?"

Rory stopped her pacing. She watched him lean back in the big chair that sat at right angles to the comfortable-looking sofa. She wondered if he'd chosen to sit in the single chair to guard against the chance of her sitting next to him. She wouldn't blame him if he had.

In an easy, unbroken motion, Sean locked his right foot under his left ankle, and lifted his left foot to rest on the long, low table in front of the sofa and chair, then crossed his right ankle over the left, assuming the posture of a man settling in for what was likely to be a very long discussion.

He did it so smoothly that it was a moment before she realized the significance of the first part of the action, that he was lifting the artificial leg with the real one. But the significance of his stance needed no interpretation: he was waiting for her to answer him.

For a long moment Rory said nothing. Her hand went to the locket in what had become a habitual gesture as she began to move around the room again, looking at the books on the shelves, the photos on the wall. She liked this room, liked the rich, deep colors of the furniture and framed prints—she recognized some of Stevie's ad work over the sofa—set against the plain white walls, the high, airy ceilings. She imagined that in daylight, when the California sun poured through the skylight above, the place looked like a jewel box lined in white velvet, the white the perfect setting for the deep colors, the colors emphasizing the purity of their setting.

"I like your place."

He shrugged. "Stevie did it."

She wasn't surprised. The Cameron house had the same look of space and airiness, along with the comfort and balance of the deep, jewel colors. She wondered if Chase had designed this building, too.

She looked at the group of framed photographs again, smothering a pang as she saw one of a younger Sean, holding baby Katie like the doting uncle he was. Next to it, was a lovely portrait of Stevie, her red gold hair a lustrous flame. And then one of her and Chase, his vivid green eyes so full of love as he looked at his wife that it made Rory's heart ache. Then another shot of Katie caught her eye.

It had to be a recent photo, she looked about six or seven. So this was how that precious little girl looked now, Rory thought. More than ever the living image of her father, green eyes lit with happiness as she clung to the man who held her. Except that the man in the photo wasn't Chase. His eyes were nearly as dark as his hair, and, she added with a rather detached feminine appreciation, he was damned near perfect. His jaw was strong, his grin as he looked at the little girl a masterpiece of dimpled masculine appeal, his body straight and strong, with a pair of shoulders that surpassed even Sean's.

"Who's this with Katie?" she asked.

Sean laughed. It wasn't a necessarily pleasant sound. "Dar Cordell. My best friend. And Katie's, too, as you can see."

"He's—"

"Yes, he is. Lots of women agree. But don't even think about it, honey. He's not your type."

There was nothing sweet in the endearment. She made herself turn to look at him. "What's that supposed to mean?"

"It means he spends most of his time in a wheelchair. As I said, not your type."

He said it flippantly, not bitterly, but it still stabbed deep. He obviously didn't believe that she'd never sent that message through her father. His words reminded her that this man might help her, but it would be because of who he was at the core, not because he'd forgiven or forgotten.

"Who is this Talbot character?" he asked.

He deserved an answer to *that,* at least, she supposed. She let go of the locket and turned to face him. "I told you. He was one of Daddy's partners. He had been for years. Since I was thirteen."

She didn't think her expression changed, but Sean's eyes narrowed. "You remember that rather specifically. At thirteen, most kids don't pay that much attention to Daddy's business."

"I didn't, at first. Frank came to the house for dinner a couple of times, before Mom got so sick. About a year after she died he started coming more often. And he... changed."

"Changed?"

"He was... creepy. He kept looking at me. Saying crude things when Daddy couldn't hear him. Trying to touch me."

Sean drew back a little. "You never told me that. How old were you then?"

"Fourteen." His mouth curved in an expression of distaste. She nodded in agreement. "I finally threatened to tell my father. He tried to convince me that Daddy wouldn't believe me, but I knew he would. I guess my certainty must have shaken him."

"He backed off?"

Her mouth twisted at the ugly memories. "Yes."

"But?"

She sighed; this new Sean was also tenacious. "He promised that he'd be back when I was eighteen. And he told me in more detail than I understood then what he was going to teach me."

"Bastard," Sean muttered.

"Yes. He is a bastard. Literally. It's one of the things that drives him, I think. And his mother was an alcoholic, and that didn't help."

"But he left you alone, after that?"

"Yes, mostly." Her lips curved in rueful self-reproach. "Naive little fool that I was, I thought it was over for good."

Sean was silent for a long moment. Then, his voice cool, he asked, "And I'm supposed to believe this is the man your father sold you to? To salvage his pride?"

Rory tensed. "I keep telling you, it was—"

"Your choice. I know. Why don't I believe it?"

"Probably," Rory said wearily, "because you don't want to believe anything I say."

It was probably true, she thought, but all she could do was tell the truth; she couldn't control whether or not Sean believed her. And if she let herself think about it, she would never be able to finish the ugly story.

"I did, once," Sean said. "I believed you when you said you loved me. And look where that got me."

If he had sounded bitter, she could have handled it better. That would mean he at least felt something, even if it was anger. But he said it so lightly that it was as if he were talking about someone else, not himself. But then, she thought, maybe he was. The Sean she'd known didn't seem to exist any longer. The Sean who had loved her. The Sean she had no doubt destroyed with her own hands.

She didn't know why she felt driven to explain, except that he deserved to know. And she had no one left to protect anymore. Besides, she was too tired to resist any longer.

"You were right," she said suddenly. "There was more to it."

If he was surprised at her sudden capitulation, he didn't show it. Not a flicker of expression crossed his handsome face. Still more evidence of how far he'd come from the boy whose every emotion had once been reflected in the deep brown of his eyes. He said nothing. He'd gained that, too, a patience that let him wait until the pressure built up inside her and the words came tumbling out.

"My father...got into a tight spot. Really tight."

Again Sean waited silently. She wasn't sure if it bothered her because it made her want to fill the silence, or because it was such an obvious measure of how much he'd changed. She decided to see if she could rattle that cool of his.

"I didn't know much about it, because I wasn't paying much attention to…anything about then. I'd met this man a few months before, you see, and I was already half in love."

She thought his eyes narrowed slightly, but if they had, he controlled it so quickly that she couldn't be sure. She gave up the idea of trying to shake him. He might have let his emotions slip for a few seconds the day she'd gone to see him at Laurel Tree, but they were obviously completely in check now. She sighed and went on.

"My father wanted to back a new computer software company that had developed a program he thought was going to really take off. So he got a group of investors together. Some real high-profile people, a group he'd been trying for years to get in with. He always wanted to—"

"Play with the big boys. I know."

Rory stared at him. "You do?"

Sean shrugged. "Your father was never satisfied with what he'd already accomplished. He didn't just want to have money, he wanted it to be old money. Since he couldn't have that, the best he could hope for was to be accepted by the old money."

"How do you know that?" Rory asked, stunned at his perception.

"Snobs sneering at the nouveau riche have been around for centuries. Too bad your father was one of the worst of them. It must have torn him apart, hating himself for what he was."

How did he know all this? It had taken her years to understand why her father was the way he was. Then it came to her; Sean had more experience than most with the experience of hating yourself for what you were. He'd told her once of the time when he had hated what he saw in the mirror every day.

"So let me guess," Sean said with thinly veiled derision. "The old money decided to let him play, as long as he paid big for the privilege and provided the ball, right?"

The years had made him a cynic, as well, Rory thought. No, a realist, she amended silently. Because he was absolutely right.

"Yes," she admitted. "Daddy had to pledge a lot of his own money to entice them. He was counting on a cash influx from a government contract he was sure was going to Sheridan Manufacturing to provide him with his share of the money."

There was a second of silence before Sean asked, "He didn't get the contract?"

"Oh, he did. Eventually. After nearly two years of delay. The government project got bogged down in a bureaucratic fight. Then there was an election, the wind shifted, and it finally went through."

"But not in time to cover your father's pledge."

"No."

"So the other deal fell through?"

"No. And it was a good deal. The software company really took off."

Sean frowned, then understanding cleared his brow. He'd never been slow, Rory thought, and he wasn't now. He let out a low whistle.

"He robbed Peter to pay Paul."

"Yes," she said flatly, beyond cloaking her father's actions with any kinder words. "He took the money from Sheridan Manufacturing. Money that couldn't be spent without approval from the board of directors. Money that shouldn't have been used to finance what was purely a personal project."

She tried to find the words to explain the rest, but Sean saved her the trouble, his agile mind having already made the next leap.

"That's it, isn't it?" he said, going very still in the chair. "That's what Talbot had on your father. He caught him, didn't he? Embezzling the money? And that's why you won't go to the police now, isn't it?"

Rory nodded. "He started blackmailing Daddy. Threatened to go to the board or the police with the records of the transaction. Daddy would have been ruined."

"How much?"

"What?"

"How much did he milk your father for?"

"I...don't know. I just know he started coming to the house every week. I stayed away those nights. I didn't find out until later that it was to...collect."

He looked at her, letting the silence stretch out again. God, she hated this new ability of his to just...wait. She gave in and kept on, as he must have known she would.

"Daddy paid him for months. Until...May, five years ago."

She saw the significance of the date hit him; it had been on May first that he had proposed to her. He slowly sat up straight in the chair. Her hand went to the locket once more, as if the lovely old piece that had been her mother's could somehow give her strength.

"Daddy mentioned...our engagement at the office. It got back to Frank. He came to Daddy that night and offered him a final deal."

Her throat tightened, and she suddenly didn't know if she could finish this after all. She swallowed tightly. Sean was staring at her, but his eyes, those expressive brown eyes she'd always been able to read so easily, told her nothing now. She shivered.

As if her involuntary movement had prompted him, he asked flatly, "What final deal?"

She tried to pull herself together, but she wasn't sure how successful she was; she didn't seem to be able to stop shivering. At last, by avoiding that penetrating gaze, she got it out.

"A trade. Daddy would get all the evidence Frank had against him. And Frank's silence."

"And Frank got you?"

She nodded mutely. He said nothing, and at last she lifted her gaze to him once more. He just looked at her for so long that it took every shred of her remaining courage not to look away.

"And you, Ms. Sheridan," he said coolly. "What did you get out of this... deal? Besides saving your precious father's pride?"

"Nothing." One corner of her mouth twisted as she realized that wasn't quite true. "I take that back. I did get one thing. My one condition to accepting Frank's terms."

"Which was?"

"You. Out of sight."

He blinked, brows furrowing. "What?"

"That was my condition. That we move away from here, so there wouldn't be any chance I would ever have to see you again."

"No. He refused."

Sean blinked, as if surprised. He clearly hadn't believed her when she'd told him that she had made her own choice. She started pacing again, as if that could steady her enough to go on.

"After Daddy said no, Frank kept after him. When he wouldn't give in, Frank came to me. Two weeks before...our wedding."

Sean's dark brows rose, as if she'd solved a puzzle for him. His words told her that she was right.

"So that's why you were such a wreck. I thought you were just getting cold feet."

Rory winced. No wonder he'd so easily accepted her father's cruelty; he'd half expected her to call it off anyway. She made herself go on.

"He told me what my father had done. Showed me the evidence he had, records of the money transfer, dates, copies of the documents with my father's signature. And he explained exactly how he would ruin my father's reputation. And that Daddy might even go to jail."

Sean waited, making her wonder where the compulsion to fill silence with talk came from. And why she was the only one here who seemed to feel it. She supposed he learned a lot this way, but it was hell on her nerves. She tried to pull together the rapidly unraveling threads of her composure.

"He told me what he wanted," she went on finally. "And what he would do if he didn't get it. That he would make sure my father would go to jail. But that Daddy would be eaten alive by the media first."

She remembered the rest of what Frank Talbot had said that night, she remembered it so vividly that it still had the power to make her shake. But not for anything would she tell Sean the other threat that had been made that night, the threat that had been the true deciding point for her. When Frank had told her if she ever went near Sean again he would kill him, she'd truly known she had no choice. But she couldn't tell Sean that part, not when it might make him feel under an obligation to her. She'd spent five years in hell because of her sense of obligation; she wasn't about to subject Sean to the same thing. He'd been hurt too much already.

"So you agreed," Sean said, his voice flat. "You traded yourself for your father's pride."

"For his life," Rory said. "He never would have survived it. I know that. He would have killed himself first. He'd even bought a gun. I couldn't have borne that."

For a long moment Sean just looked at her, the usually warm brown of his thickly lashed eyes revealing nothing. A lock of dark hair fell forward almost to his brows, and she remembered suddenly how she had always brushed that stubborn piece back, just for the chance to touch the heavy silk of his hair.

"When did the beatings start?"

Rory sighed. It showed, she supposed, how far out of sync they were. She was remembering touching him with love, with longing, while he was thinking of her being struck in violence.

"This—" she gestured toward her blackened eye "—was the second time. The first time wasn't this bad. It was right before we came back here. He found out I'd been looking for a job."

She thought Sean's jaw tightened slightly, but he'd gotten so damned good at hiding his emotions....

"And the eye?"

Rory grimaced. "He found my stash of money. I'd been squirreling it away, just in case I ever got the chance to...disappear." She sighed. "That must be why he started having me watched. He must have sensed somehow that I...couldn't take much more."

"Why start hitting you now? After five years?"

She shrugged. "The same reason, I suppose. He guessed I was looking for a way to get away from him. I wondered if it was because he felt...able to now, after Daddy died. But the first time was while Daddy was still—"

She broke off suddenly as the connection she should have made the moment she'd discovered Frank had known for weeks that her father was ill fell into place.

"He knew," she whispered, her eyes going unfocused as she remembered. "God, he knew Daddy was dying, that he didn't have to worry about him anymore. The first time he hit me was right after Daddy went into the hospital. I just didn't know it then."

"You didn't know your father was dying?"

"I didn't even know he was sick. Frank...kept it from me. He said he didn't want any...dramatic deathbed reversals."

"You think that's why he didn't hit you before? Why would he worry about what your father would do when he was blackmailing him in the first place?"

"He must have known Daddy would never stand for him hitting me."

"Oh?" Sean's voice was deceptively mild. "It was okay for your father to sell you, but the buyer can't abuse you, is that it?"

She winced, but more at the truth of the words than the fact that it was Sean saying them. She had long ago recognized her father's cowardice in letting her pay for his actions. And her own foolishness for thinking she could save him from the consequences of what he'd done.

Then, as casually as if he were inquiring about the weather, Sean asked, "Was it worth it, Rory?"

Her legs felt suddenly weighted, as if all the strain and tension of the past two days had collected in her knees. She sank down onto the sofa, not looking at him.

"I don't know," she said wearily. "I only know that I was eighteen, I loved my father, and I didn't think I had any other choice."

Sean let out a harsh, short sound that could have been incredulity or anger. "Miss Aurora Sheridan, reduced to peddling her lovely body—"

Rory's already worn composure snapped. "Yes! Is that what you want to hear? That I prostituted myself, sold myself like any hooker on the street, only for a different price? Do you think I haven't thought that, too? And that my father, who should have been protecting me, let me do it, for his sake? My God, Sean, I've done nothing else for five years! And the only thing that's kept me sane is the knowledge that I didn't have any other choice!"

"But you did," Sean said, anger creeping into his voice for the first time. "You could have come to me, could have told me the truth."

"And what would you have done? What *could* you have done?"

"It doesn't matter," he snapped out. "You never gave me the chance."

"And you're angry about that?" She stood up again, the vitalizing flood of her own anger giving her strength. She glared at him. "Well, let me tell you how angry I was at you, Sean Holt!"

Sean blinked, looking startled. "At me?"

"Yes, damn you! Do you have any idea how often I prayed that you would come back for me? I couldn't believe that you just let my father send you away. That you didn't believe in my love enough to... to see through the whole charade."

Sean was staring at her now, an expression on his face she couldn't even begin to put a name to.

"God, I was such a fool. Every night I waited, hoping like some naive child, waiting for the hero on the white horse to come riding in and rescue me from an impossible situation. I knew you would, I just knew it. I loved you, and you would never abandon me. But you never came."

"Rory," Sean whispered, sounding shaken for the first time.

"You believed him. He said those awful things, and you believed him."

"I..." Sean stopped, shaking his head.

Rory bit back the tears that were suddenly threatening. If she broke down now, she was afraid she would never stop crying. It took all her slight remaining energy; she was only vaguely aware of Sean's silence.

She didn't know how much time had passed when at last, in a tone of realization she'd never heard from him before, Sean said quietly, "I did believe him. I believed everything he said. Because I'd been expecting it."

Rory lifted her head then to look at him. Oddly, he was rubbing at his left knee as if it were aching. The knee that wasn't there anymore. His gaze was unfocused, distant, his expression tight, as if he were confronting something unpleasant.

"I expected it," he repeated slowly. "I expected you to hate this—" he rapped his knuckles on the prosthesis "—because I did. I expected you to reject it, and me, because I was still rejecting it myself. Rejecting what had happened, rejecting the damage to my body, all of it."

"Sean—"

"I was trying to pretend it hadn't happened. To pretend that all I needed was the outward appearance of a normal, whole life and I would have it again. And you were part of that."

Rory watched him, her own tears ebbing away as she understood that Sean had never confronted this before, that only now was he actually seeing his reasons for so easily accepting her father's words that day. She'd gone through too many similar unhappy realizations herself in the past five years not to recognize the process.

Then his last words came home to her. *And you were part of that.* Was that all she'd been? Part of his attempt to pretend nothing was wrong, his attempt to rebuild his world and his life into what they had been before that drunk driver had forced the team bus off the road? Was that why he was able to be so cool now, because he'd never truly loved her before?

Wouldn't that just be poetic justice? Rory thought, tears threatening again. A new weariness descended upon her, and she shivered under its force.

Slowly, moving as if every muscle hurt, Sean stood up. So did Rory, knowing exactly how he felt; her every muscle *did* hurt. He dragged a hand over his face, rubbing at his eyes. Then he looked at her. They stood there for a long moment, bare inches apart in physical distance, miles apart in memories and choices made. Silence stretched out between them.

He took a deep breath. And then, so quickly she wasn't sure how it had happened, or which one of them had moved, she was in his arms. They held on as if seeking comfort in the contact, like old friends who had once shared a crisis, brought back together years later to find they had little else in common but painful memories.

"God, Rory," he said at last, sounding as if he were as exhausted as she was, "we were so young. So blindly, stupidly young."

"Yes," she whispered. "But we've certainly grown up now, haven't we?"

His mouth twisted. "Yeah. And it ain't what it's cracked up to be, is it?"

"No."

She felt the movement of his chest as if he'd drawn a deep breath. A moment later she felt the soft stirring of her hair

as he sighed. She wondered if he was sighing for what they'd
lost, or for the fools they'd been, her for thinking she could
make up for what her father had done, him for believing in
her.

The warmth of his embrace seemed to sap what little
strength she had left. She didn't mean to sag against him,
but she couldn't seem to help it. His hands slid up to her
shoulders, and he eased her away from him.

"It's late," he said. "You need some rest." His mouth
quirked wryly. "We both do."

She looked up at him. He hadn't released her, and she
could feel the heat of his hands on her shoulders. For a long,
silent moment he just stood there, looking at her. The heat
from his hands seemed to grow, to spread, making her realize how very cold she was.

It had been so long since she had stood like this, looking
up into Sean's face. Once her entire future had been held in
those dark, deep brown eyes. A future she had turned her
back on.

She saw the moment when his eyes changed, when the
weariness and strain and sadness were joined by heat and
awareness. Her breath caught, then eased away when she
realized there was as much wariness as warmth in his look.
Her lips parted for breath, and in that instant the heat
flared.

She felt his reluctance, the battle within him, knew herself that this was quite probably the most foolish thing they
could do, yet she couldn't seem to move, either to stop him
or to avoid what she knew was coming. She wanted this, and
in this moment she was too tired to fight her own desire.

He lowered his head slowly, as if fighting against the motion every inch of the way. His fingers tightened on her
shoulders. His breathing, quicker now, was audible. She felt
everything as if it were magnified somehow, as if every sense

had been amplified, in a way she had only known with this man.

And then his mouth was on hers, at first a feather-light brush of warm lips that sent a burst of sensation through her. She felt him start to pull back, as if he were determined to leave it at that, a brief contact under tight control. Then she heard a low groan that sounded like half pleasure, half pain. After that she knew nothing except that he was kissing her fiercely, hungrily, his mouth taking hers with an insistence she couldn't have denied even had she wanted to.

For the second time she sagged against him, but this time it was his lips that sapped her strength. And his tongue, when he flicked it over her lips, coaxing, asking, then demanding. She gave in, knowing she had no energy—or desire—to resist. The moment her lips parted, he let his tongue dart inside, as if he'd been starved for her taste for all the years they'd been apart.

It was hotter, sweeter, than she remembered, as if the years had refined his taste to something fuller, more masculine. Everything about him was that way, from the strong line of his jaw to the breadth of his chest and shoulders, from the cool glint in his eyes to his no doubt hard-won patience, allowing her no lingering doubts that the boy had become a man.

She raised her hands between them, flattening her palms on his chest, her fingers flexing involuntarily at the heat and solidity of him. His hands moved up to cradle her head, his fingers sliding through her hair as he tilted her head back. His tongue probed forward, searching, tracing the even ridge of her teeth, savoring the softness of the inside of her lips.

At last, unable to stop herself, she tentatively reached out with her own tongue, seeking his. At the first connection she felt him go still, waiting. She stroked him, hesitantly, uncertain until he returned the motion. Then they began the age-old dance, darting, teasing, savoring the bursts of sensation as hot, wet velvet met and slid together.

She moaned, moving her hands from his chest; they were keeping them too far apart. She slid her arms around him, hoping he would answer in kind; he did, and pulled her tight against him. Her breasts flattened against his chest, and she felt as if they were taking on his heat; she felt suddenly swollen and aching.

Her knees felt near to collapse. She tried to steady them, but her effort somehow turned into an arching, sinuous caress of her body against his. She heard a sound rumble up from deep in his chest, half groan, half growl. She felt his body go rigid. He wrenched his mouth away from hers, and she heard him suck in a quick, deep breath. Then, slowly, his hands went back to her shoulders and he eased her away.

Dazedly she looked up at him.

"Sean?" she whispered.

He just looked at her, his breath coming in quick pants through parted lips. The haze of pleasure that had so swiftly enveloped her began to fade. As she watched, the heat ebbed from his eyes, the hunger from the shape of his mouth. He came back to himself so quickly—much faster than she seemed able to—that she half expected him to come right out and say how stupid this had been.

She knew that. She knew it all too well. Her body had responded as if they had never been apart, as only Sean had ever been able to make her respond, but her mind knew they were only complicating an already impossible situation, taunting themselves with what had been lost, never to be regained.

He released her abruptly. His first words proved that he knew it, too.

"I'm . . . sorry," he said, still sounding a little breathless. It was some small comfort to know he'd been as affected as she had been. "I shouldn't have done that."

"Oh, Sean, I wish . . ."

"Don't. Wishing is pointless."

And so was kissing her, Rory guessed he was thinking. But could she blame him, when she'd been thinking the same thing?

"This doesn't need to be any more complicated," Sean said, eerily echoing her earlier thoughts. "It won't happen again."

How could she tell him that that was what she was afraid of? That she would never know that swirling pleasure again, that she would never, ever know the heights they could have taken each other to, had not circumstances—and her own sad judgment—intervened.

He turned and walked away without a word, opening a door behind them and going into what was obviously the bedroom. She saw a light go on, then he came out carrying a pillow and a pale blue blanket. He dropped them onto the couch.

"Go to bed," he said, with a sharp gesture toward the other room. The light he'd left on threw a parallelogram of light onto the carpet. "I'll take the couch."

"I don't want to put you out of—"

"Don't argue, Rory. We're both too tired. Just go. The bathroom's to the left."

"Sean—"

"Please, Rory. Not now."

He was right. Now was not the time. Not for them, anyway. She was carrying far too much baggage for easy solutions. Maybe the time would never come. Maybe what they'd had was all they ever *would* have.

She nodded, not looking at him, not able to look at him. Without a word she turned and walked toward the open door, wondering how on earth he expected her to sleep in his bedroom, in his bed.

She kicked off her shoes and sat on the edge of the bed, looking around her at the bedroom that matched the living room in vivid intensity. Stevie again, she thought. Better than that imagined female she'd gotten so ridiculously angry at before.

This room was marked rather pleasantly with male clutter. A shirt hung on the bedpost, a belt was draped over a doorknob, a robe was tossed over a chair, and, oddly, a can of talcum powder sat on the dresser. It seemed so normal, so unlike Frank's disturbing combination of fastidiousness and perversion.

Slowly she reached out and picked up the shirt that hung over the bedpost. It was a pale blue knit polo shirt that would set off Sean's dark hair beautifully, she thought. It would have to stretch to cover his broad chest, and the short sleeves would be strained by his muscled arms. She caught a faint scent, a combination of spicy after-shave and something that was purely Sean; that, at least, had not changed, that pleasant, masculine scent she remembered.

She fought the urge to hug the shirt to her, to hold it as she couldn't hold its owner. But she found herself clutching it close anyway, her fingers trembling. She lay down, rolling to her side and drawing her knees up in a semifetal curl. She recognized the position for what it was, the posture of an animal hurt beyond bearing, trying to protect its vital parts. She wondered why she was bothering; she felt as if all her vital parts had been ripped out long ago.

She closed her eyes and only then realized that she didn't need the shirt at all; the faint scent of Sean lingered on the pillow that cradled her head. She shuddered, knowing that if that first tear fell, the dam would rupture and she would weep for hours.

And in the end she didn't know whether to weep or laugh at the irony of it; she'd finally made it into Sean Holt's bed, but there wasn't a chance on earth that he would ever join her there.

Chapter 8

Sean hadn't expected to be able to sleep much, but the strain of the past couple of days seemed to have caught up with him, and he rested deeply for a few hours. When he woke up looking at the back of the couch, he thought for a moment that he'd just fallen asleep out there, as he'd done on occasion before. But then the presence of the pillow and the blanket that was tangled around him registered, and the memories came flooding back.

He let out a sigh, thinking of everything that would have to be dealt with today. Idly he kicked at the tangled blanket with his foot, then, yawning, he rolled over onto his back. And froze, nearly choking on the aborted yawn.

Rory was sitting in the chair he'd been in last night, watching him. And from all appearances, she'd been there for some time. She was dressed in the same clothes as last night, her hair brushed and pulled back with a rubber band at the nape of her neck. Her face was damp, as if she'd splashed water on it—or as if she'd been crying. The eye that wasn't blackened was nearly as darkly circled as the one that was, and he wondered if she'd slept at all.

Slowly, rubbing at gritty eyes, he sat up. Only then did he realize he'd kicked the blanket nearly off his hips, and that the fact that he was clad only in briefs was obvious. In another second, he saw, the blanket was going to slide off altogether; instinctively he reached to pull it back, to shield himself and the stump of his leg from Rory's gaze.

As he did, Rory made a tiny sound, and his gaze shot back to her face.

"Are you hiding because you're modest?" she asked softly. "Or because you still believe what my father told you?"

He went very still. "What he said doesn't matter anymore. I accepted myself as I am a long time ago."

She looked at him steadily. "Yes," she said after a moment, "I think you have. You've changed, Sean. Grown up, I suppose."

"Happens to the best of us," he quipped, uneasy with the way she was looking at him. She wasn't staring, her eyes fixed on one point; instead, her gaze moved over him with an odd slowness, lingering on his shoulders, his chest, his belly, then flicking downward over the blanket for a moment, once more making him too aware of his state of undress. It was then that it struck him, then that he realized Rory was looking at him with hunger, a hunger he belatedly recognized as purely sexual.

The realization hit him like a blow to the gut, tightening his belly and stealing his breath. Rory's gaze shot to his face, and he wondered if she'd been able to see his reaction. The parting of her lips and the sudden darkening of her eyes told him that she had, and warnings began to clamor in his head. But the alarms were muted by the memory of that kiss last night, of those moments when he had nearly drowned in the unexpected heat and sweetness of it, when things had nearly spun out of control.

Out of control. The words echoed in his head. Out of control was something he couldn't afford to be around this woman. No matter how she looked at him. She had once taught him a hard and bitter lesson, and he wasn't about to forget it. It was too damned likely that she would teach it to him all over again if he did.

So maybe, he thought, it was time he taught her one.

He shifted his weight on the couch, twisting to put his foot on the floor. Then, in one continuous motion, he threw off the blanket and stood up on his remaining leg, balancing himself with the ease of long experience. After an instant in which surprise flickered across her face, Rory slowly stood up, too, her gaze never leaving him.

"Take a good look," he said, keeping his voice even with an effort as he gestured at his stump, then at the prosthesis on the floor beside him. "This is how it is. This is what you couldn't even bear to talk about, let alone look at."

Surprisingly, she did look. Carefully. He well knew what she was seeing, knew that the tidy, smooth job the surgeon had done, sculpting the stump in such a way that he had enough musculature to manipulate the prosthesis easily, surprised some people who expected something scarred and twisted.

She looked at him for so long that he began to feel foolish, standing there in his briefs, concentrating on his balance so he wouldn't wobble. Then, slowly, her eyes lifted to his face.

"Do you really think," she asked slowly, never shirking his gaze, "that I never thought about this when we were together? That I never imagined it, even though you would never let me see you?"

In truth, he *had* wondered, but he'd never had the nerve to ask her then. "So why didn't you ask?"

"I didn't want to push."

"Push? I asked you to marry me, for God's sake. You said yes, without ever...didn't you think you had a right to know what you were getting?"

"I knew what I was getting," Rory answered quietly, with a sincerity that was undeniable. "Everything that mattered, anyway." She shrugged. "I was waiting until you were ready. I knew you weren't. You couldn't let me look at you when you could barely look at yourself."

Sean stared at her, silenced by her unexpected candidness—and her perceptiveness. He'd never known she had been so aware of his feelings about his injury. He had thought she was ignoring it, had feared it was out of distaste, a fear he'd tried to overlook in his desperation to go on with his life as if nothing had ever happened. And all the while Rory had simply been reacting to his own feelings, playing off his own self-rejection, his own deeply buried refusal to accept the maiming of his body.

If, of course, he believed her. If he believed her unfeasible story of embezzlement and blackmail. If he believed her tale of five years of hell under the thumb of the man who'd held her first with threats and now with blows, the man who'd imprisoned her in a cage fashioned from her love for her father.

But if he believed all that, he might as well believe the rest, too. Believe that her father had been lying that day. Believe that she hadn't wanted to leave him literally standing at the altar. Believe that, at eighteen, she had truly believed she had no choice.

And while you're believing, Sean told himself acidly, *why don't you believe in that kiss, too?*

He wanted to believe in it, he thought as his gaze shifted to her mouth. He wanted to believe in the sweetness of it, in the hot, quick response it had built in her. And that knowledge alone scared him to the core.

Suddenly, unexpectedly, Rory moved. She covered the space between them in two quick steps and enveloped him in an embrace that startled him even as it sent his pulse racing. The feel of her against him, of her hands on the naked skin of his back, made him shiver, but he suppressed it.

"Rory," he began, looking down into her face. But what he saw there made him forget the words of withdrawal that had been going to come next. He felt as if the warning his mind was shouting had been seared away by the heat in her eyes.

And without that warning, there was nothing to stop him from pulling her closer and lowering his mouth to hers, nothing to prevent him from tasting her once more, nothing to forestall him from probing the depths of her honeyeyed sweetness with a tongue that was suddenly hungrier for the taste of her than he could ever remember being for anything in his life. And it was a hunger he couldn't resist.

He felt a little shiver go through her as she welcomed him, meeting his tongue with her own, luring him deeper. He went eagerly, wondering how he had survived the loss of this wondrous pleasure. Sensation rippled through him, nearly swamping him, and in response to some dim echo of his mind's warnings, he pulled back.

Rory moaned a protest, and when his tongue began to withdraw she followed it with her own. Her arms tightened around him, as if she feared he would move his body back from her, as well, and the feel of her drawing him so close shattered the last of his restraints and his precarious balance. He broke the kiss. With a smothered groan he sank down onto the couch. Rory went with him in a willing, clinging heap.

Instinctively Sean shifted, stretching out so that she was sprawled atop him. He savored the amazingly pleasant feel of her weight, the sensation of her being pressed full-length against him. Then she was kissing him, probing the depths of his mouth as he had done hers, and the thrill that raced down his spine nearly made him gasp.

She squirmed, as if she wanted to be even closer. She was, Sean thought vaguely, quite close enough already; every movement aroused him more, and in a moment she was going to realize just what she was doing to him. She couldn't help but realize it. There was no way to hide it, half-naked as he was.

She released his mouth then, and Sean gulped in a breath, trying to rein in his reeling senses. But no sooner did he take in that desperately needed air than it shot out of him again as Rory began to lay a path of hot little kisses along the line of his jaw.

"Rory," he gasped at last. "Stop."

She froze for an instant, then lifted her head to look at him. Color flooded her cheeks, adding a bright red to the black-and-yellow bruise already marking her face.

"Oh, Sean," she moaned. "I didn't . . . I know you don't want— "

He didn't want to hear what he didn't want. "Just get up," he said, her stricken look making him grateful that he had managed not to say "get off me" with the desperate undertone he heard in his own voice.

"I'm sorry," she choked out, narrowly missing unmanning him completely with her knee as she rolled off him onto the floor, turning her back to him as she buried her face in her hands. "I don't know what I was thinking."

"There wasn't a lot of thinking at all going on here." Sean's tone was dry as he sat up rather awkwardly, aware that he was so blatantly aroused that he didn't have a prayer of hiding it if she turned to look at him.

"No," she said, sounding distressed, "there wasn't. I'm sorry, Sean. You were right. This doesn't need to be any more complicated than it already is."

But it *was* more complicated, Sean thought, still able to feel her kiss on his lips, still feeling the tingle where her mouth had traced his jaw. He'd never forgotten the taste of her. His mind had apparently filed it away as accurately as the taste of summer peaches. She tasted as honeyed now as then, yet different, as if she'd mellowed somehow, as if the years had ripened her to the peak of sweetness.

And he wanted that sweetness again. He wanted all of it, her mouth, her body, so badly that he ached with it. And he knew he couldn't have it. He silenced the little voice that tried to say she owed him something for what she'd done five years ago. He'd learned long ago to ignore the little imp of bitterness that urged him to try to balance a scale that could never be balanced. He'd seen too many others go down that useless road, looking for fairness in an unfair world.

Slowly he sat up. He shifted himself away from Rory and moved to the far end of the couch. He had himself under control, but he didn't trust himself to stay that way if she gave him that hungry look again. That, too, scared him. She'd put him through such hell that he should be immune to her lure, yet in three short days she had him tied up in knots once more.

"I have to go to work for a while," he said suddenly, not caring that he sounded gruff. "I'll be back this afternoon."

"I understand," Rory said, still without moving.

"You'll have to move."

Rory lifted her head then, looking at him blankly.

"You're on top of my leg," Sean explained.

Puzzlement crossed her face, then a quick look of understanding as she glanced down and saw the prosthesis beneath her legs. She moved hastily, and Sean picked up the leg. Rory watched with what could have been either morbid or genuine curiosity; he didn't know which and wasn't sure he wanted to know. The only thing he was sure of was that he had to get away from her, that he needed time to figure out why, after all she'd done and after all this time, this woman could still turn him into a quivering mass of desire.

"According to Antonio, the plumbing should be ready for the final inspection by Friday," Sean said, shuffling through a sheaf of papers in his hand.

"I know," Chase said, looking at his brother-in-law rather oddly.

"The electrician's going to finish up next week, then we'll be ready for that inspection, too."

"Are you all right?"

Sean looked up from the papers and focused on Chase, who was looking at him with an almost worried expression.

"What?"

"Sean, we talked about all this two days ago."

"Oh."

"What's with you?" Chase asked, leaning against his desk. "You're even more distracted than I am."

Sean's mouth quirked. "You've probably had more sleep, baby and all."

Chase looked startled, then curious. Sean cringed inwardly, wishing he could call back the remark. Chase was too damned sharp, and now he had to divert him, never an easy task.

"The right doors finally arrived," he said hastily. "And the hand-held showerheads."

"Fine. You want to talk about it?"

Sean knew he didn't mean the shower heads. He wandered over to the window and looked out into the brilliant sunlight. "No," he said.

Chase looked at him for a moment, then said quietly, "Okay. But if you do—"

A commotion from the outer office interrupted Chase's words. A man burst in, followed by the small, older woman who served as their receptionist. She looked frazzled and almost fearful as the intruder swaggered across the room.

"I'm so sorry, Mr. Cameron, I tried to stop him, but he just pushed past me!"

Sean froze, staring, as Chase stood up straight and looked at the woman in concern.

"Are you all right, Mrs. Stewart?"

"Yes, I think so."

"Go ahead back to your desk, then. I'll deal with this."

As she left, closing the office door behind her, Chase turned on the man, glaring down on him from his four-inch advantage in height.

"I don't know who you are," Chase snapped, "but I don't care for men who bully people smaller and older than they are. Get out."

The shorter, stockier man's lips curled into a snarl. He moved his arms in a practiced gesture that let the sunlight catch the big, square gold cuff links that held two gaudily large diamonds. "Who the hell do you think you're talking to?"

"A trespasser, as far as I know," Chase said coolly.

Sean knew that after what Chase had been through in his life, it would take much more than a blustering braggart to intimidate him. But this wasn't Chase's problem, it was his—and all because he'd been unable to resist a phone call in the night.

"I think," he said, walking back toward the desk from the window, "that our trespasser is looking for me."

Frank Talbot whirled, startled by Sean's voice coming from behind him. His eyes flicked up and down doubtfully, but then his gaze came to rest on Sean's face, and his eyes narrowed in recognition. "So," the man hissed, "it *is* you."

Sean started to make a wisecrack about the efficiency of the detective Talbot had hired, then realized it might be wisest—and safest for Rory—if he pretended to know nothing about the man who'd been following her.

"You want something, Talbot?"

"You know damned well what I want. Where is she?"

Sean kept his voice innocently casual. "I presume by 'she' you mean Ms. Sheridan?"

Sean saw Chase stiffen and felt the sudden intensity of his brother-in-law's gaze. He hadn't told Chase or Stevie any more about his encounter with his former fiancée—or anything at all about the man who had just stormed his way into the office.

"I have no idea where she is," Sean lied without a qualm.

Talbot swore, low and crude. "You're lying. I know she came to you."

"Who is this clown, Sean?" Chase asked.

Sean nearly grinned at the fury that flashed across Talbot's face, a fury that he quickly turned on Sean when he answered lightly, "I'm reasonably sure he goes by Frank Talbot, although I've thankfully never had the pleasure of meeting him before."

"Listen, you nobody!" Talbot exclaimed, Sean's ease seeming to infuriate him. "You're going to tell me where she is or I'll—"

"What you'll do is get the hell out of my office," Chase snapped. "I don't care who you think you are."

"He's the man Aurora Sheridan dumped me for," Sean said bluntly, hoping his words and tone would convince the man he knew nothing more. Chase's brows shot upward as he glanced at Sean, then shifted his gaze back to Talbot, looking so disbelieving that his expression was an insult in itself. Again Sean stifled a grin. Then he realized that this was a chance to discover exactly how much Talbot knew. He shifted his own gaze to the man.

"Even if she did come to me, what in hell makes you think I'd even speak to her?"

"I suppose now you're going to lie about being at my house yesterday," Talbot said.

Sean didn't see any point in denying it and couldn't resist pointing out the truth anyway. "I wasn't at *your* house. I was at the Sheridan house."

Rage suffused Talbot's face, and he cocked his arm back. For a moment, Sean thought the man was going to take a swing at him, and he instinctively tensed, ready to move. Chase apparently had the same thought, because Sean saw him go suddenly still, eyes fastened on Talbot as if wishing he would try it.

Talbot seemed to suddenly realize he was dealing with two men who wouldn't hesitate to give him a taste of his own medicine, and he dropped his arm. He dug into a pocket of his suit coat, yanked out a small photograph and held it out to Sean with a look of disdain.

"You think I'm a fool? I know you're seeing her, that you probably have been since we came back here, if not before."

Sean looked at the picture, a sharply focused shot that left no doubt that the man in the black sedan had brought a camera with an excellent telephoto lens the day Rory had come to the construction site.

Sean shrugged, handing the picture back as if it meant nothing. Little did Talbot know that he had spiked his own guns; the photograph showed Rory's blackened eye clearly and reinforced Sean's determination to keep the other man away from her. Not, he told himself, because of any feelings he still had for her, not even because he had once loved her, but because, as she'd said, he would do the same for anyone in her position.

"She was checking on her father's investment," Sean said casually. "That's also why I was at the house. Or didn't you know he was a big contributor to the project?"

Talbot looked nonplussed. "Er, of course I knew. But Aurora knows nothing about the business."

"True. She didn't even know I was there," Sean lied again, that image of Rory's bruised face making it easy. "And I have no idea where she went after that. Nor," he added, allowing a little bitterness to creep into his voice, "do I care. I had enough of Aurora Sheridan five years ago to last me a lifetime."

Talbot stared at Sean for a long moment, and Sean could almost feel the man considering, assessing, trying to decide if he believed him or not. Up until four days ago Sean would have sworn those words were nothing less than the truth, and the fact that even one particle of his certainty was shaken disturbed him immensely.

"She's not worth it, you know," Talbot said, almost conversationally, as if he didn't want to accuse Sean of lying face-to-face, but wanted to warn him off anyway. "She's as frigid as the north pole."

Frigid. Sean felt a burst of heat flash through him at the memory of their kiss that morning, of her slight, soft weight sprawled all over him, of her mouth blazing a path over his jaw, of her breasts, nipples peaked, pressing against his chest. Frigid. He nearly laughed aloud, pleasure of an entirely different sort welling up inside him, a purely male satisfaction as ancient as time, based in the knowledge that his woman responded to him alone. It was new to him, and heady stuff; it made the transition to shocked alarm when he realized he had actually thought of her as *his* woman even more chilling.

"Stay away from her," Talbot said in that same easy tone.

Sean lifted a brow at the obvious contradiction. "If she isn't worth it, why warn me off?"

"She's mine, Holt. I own her. And I never give up what I own."

His pale blue eyes flicked over Sean, down his body, lingering on his legs for a moment, then skittering back up to his face.

"Especially to half a man," he said contemptuously.

Sean tensed, not at the insult—he'd heard similar things too many times before—but at the proof that what Rory had told him was true. It also explained the doubtful look Talbot had given him; he must have been looking for an obvious sign that Sean was an amputee and been surprised, as many were, at how easily he moved. Sean had learned from Chase's nightmare experience that almost any information was available for a price; that this man knew so much about him, and, in turn, probably his family, made him very nervous.

Chase had gone rigid the moment Talbot spoke. "Get out," he spat now. "Before I throw you out."

Talbot glanced at Chase warily, but threw a last threat at Sean. "I'll find her," he promised, "and she'll be sorry she ever thought of leaving. And if you're helping her, you'll be even sorrier."

Sean fought down the fury that rose in him; God, he despised bullies. "I'd have to go some," he said, keeping his tone scornfully cool, "to be sorrier than you."

Even as he spoke, Sean's mind was racing. Talbot might be many things, but he wasn't stupid. He'd said he would find Rory, and he'd meant it. And with the kind of help he was able to pay for—with her own father's money, no doubt—he could probably do it. Fast. Which meant he himself had to move faster.

He could sense that Chase was on the edge of losing his temper, so he decided to give him something to do. He hoped he would also divert Talbot at the same time. Or at least delay him.

"I don't much like being followed around," he observed mildly, grinning at his brother-in-law, knowing his cheerfulness would irritate Talbot even more. "I've got work to do, and I don't want him in my way. Keep him off my back for a while, will you?"

Chase's green eyes narrowed, and Sean knew he would eventually have a lot of explaining to do. But he was counting on the fact that Chase had never let him down, and hoping that he would pick up on the seriousness hidden in the jocular request. Chase's mouth twisted wryly; then one corner lifted in acceptance.

"Sure," he said, looking at Talbot. "We have something to discuss, anyway."

Talbot looked startled and backed up a step. "What are you talking about?"

"I'm talking about whether I call the police and file trespassing charges against you. And assault charges, as well, for Mrs. Stewart."

Sean's grin widened as Talbot sputtered, "You can't—"

"Can't he?" Sean laughed. "He has no more patience for bullies than I do. Good luck talking him out of calling the cops."

Talbot turned, eyeing the closed door as if he were contemplating making a run for it.

"I wouldn't," Chase advised mildly. He nodded at Sean. "He's damned quick."

Talbot seemed startled at that idea, and his brows lowered as he looked at Sean. Sean grinned at him once more, enjoying the way his refusal to take Talbot's bluster seriously infuriated the man. Then he glanced at Chase.

"See ya," Sean said breezily, and walked out the door Talbot hadn't had the nerve to try for.

Chapter 9

Sean checked his rearview mirror constantly, but there was no sign that the big black sedan or any other car was following him.

Talbot might have his flunky out looking for Rory, Sean thought, figuring he could handle ''half a man'' by himself. Still, he made random turns, stopped at a doughnut shop for a cup of coffee he didn't want, and twice made quick turns and pulled to a stop around the corner, watching to see if anyone came after him. No one did.

As he neared home, Sean was thinking swiftly. Talbot might seem a swaggering blowhard, but Sean had to assume that the man he'd hired was a pro. So he would be careful and assume he was being watched even if it wasn't obvious. And instead of continuing on to the residential street that led to his apartment, he turned onto the busy boulevard that came first.

He pulled his car into the rear parking lot of a small convenience store that backed up to his apartment building, then he glanced around, especially at the opening in the wall between the store and the apartments, put there so the residents would have easy access. He saw nothing moving anywhere and got out of the car.

He ran toward the gap, a little awkwardly. He swore softly; to really run with any kind of efficiency he needed his Seattle foot, the one designed to add flex to his step, and provide the stability of a natural foot. But he made it without being seen as far as he could tell.

There was no sign of Rory in the living room or the kitchen when he went in. The steps up to his door weren't particularly quiet, and he realized that if she'd heard him, she might be afraid Talbot had found her. He started to call out to her, then stopped. What if Talbot's muscle man was already here? What if he was holding Rory, waiting for Sean to come bumbling in looking for her?

He felt the sudden hammering of his pulse, the flood of adrenaline to his muscles. God, he wondered briefly, irrelevantly, how had Chase stood it, all that time on the run, knowing they were after you and never knowing where they would turn up next?

He didn't have much in the way of weapons, so he grabbed the only thing that looked likely, one of his aluminum crutches. Holding it at his side the way a police officer held a baton, he slowly made his way toward the bedroom and bathroom. The bedroom door was open, the bathroom door—the only interior door that locked—closed.

He glanced into the bedroom to make sure it was empty. As he expected, it was, the bed tidily made up, no sign that anyone other than himself had ever been there. He hesitated, wondering what to do. If he called out to her and she wasn't alone, she could be forced to answer him as if all was well. He didn't know if the man in the black sedan was armed, but he didn't relish the idea of betting his life that he wasn't and walking in on an ambush. But if he tried the

door without calling out to her and she *was* alone, she would
be terrified.

He had to think of something else, some way to let her
know it was him without making it seem as if he suspected
she wasn't alone. But what the hell could he—

It came to him seemingly out of nowhere. A memory of
a night long ago, as they had walked along a darkened
street, still caught up in the mood of their favorite classic
movie. He thought about it for a second, then decided it was
his best chance. If she recognized it as a signal, she would
come out on her own. If she didn't, he would have to assume she couldn't. He began to whistle, as if idly, from the
hallway outside the bathroom door.

He was into the second bar of "As Time Goes By" when
the door of the bathroom burst open and Rory tumbled into
his arms.

"Oh, God, Sean, I was so scared. I heard someone come
in, and I didn't know...I thought it was Frank, or that man
who's been following me."

Instinctively his arms went around her reassuringly. "It's
all right, Rory. You're safe."

She jerked away from him. "Me? It was you I was afraid
for. If Frank found out you'd helped me, he'd—"

"I know. He told me."

Rory blinked. "What?"

"I already got the threat. In person."

"In person?" Her eyes widened. "You saw him?"

"He came to the office." Her eyes widened, then flicked
over him, as if searching for injuries. Sean's mouth twisted
wryly. "He never laid a hand on me. He might not think I'm
much of an adversary, but Chase is another matter altogether."

Rory paled at his words, as if she knew exactly what Talbot had said. Maybe she did, Sean thought. Maybe he'd

been telling her for years how lucky she was to have escaped being shackled to half a man.

She lowered her gaze. "God, Sean, I'm so sorry. I'm sorry I got you into this, sorry you had to deal with him. I'm sorry... for everything. All I ever seem to do is cause you pain."

He couldn't deny that. She'd whipped up his hard-won calm like a tropical storm that blew in out of nowhere and went on to the same place. The difference was, when the storm was over, the sea turned calm again; he wasn't sure he ever would.

She lifted her head and looked at him for a long moment before saying softly, "You've turned out to be everything I always knew you could be. And more. You deserved better, Sean. I should have found another way."

Surprise kicked through him as she echoed his own earlier thoughts. And, perversely, he found himself defending her. "Maybe you couldn't have," he said, running a hand through his hair.

"I should have," she insisted, her eyes dark with remorse as she shook her head. "But instead I...sold myself." He saw her lips thin with repugnance, but then her expression went oddly blank. "It's just as well, Sean. It only proves I was never good enough for you."

Never in his life would Sean have thought to hear those words from the lips of Aurora Sheridan. "Is that how you think of yourself? Not good enough? Is that what he's got you believing?"

He saw a shiver ripple through her, saw her make an effort to control it, and knew his words had struck close to home.

"Frank knows why I...went to him. And he's a man who takes great joy in knowing—and flaunting—that he has that kind of power. He made certain everyone knew I was...bought and paid for."

Was this what she'd lived with for five years? Sean wondered. Had she been paraded as a possession, on a par with the diamond tiepin and gaudy cuff links Talbot wore? He could only imagine what that would do to a woman as proud as the Aurora Sheridan he'd known.

I prostituted myself, sold myself like any hooker on the street, only for a different price.

Her self-castigating words came back to him, but only now did he realize the true extent of her humiliation. And, he admitted reluctantly, what strength it had taken her to survive.

"No matter what you think of yourself," he said quietly, reaching up to touch her bruised face with care, "you don't deserve this. No one does."

"I know that."

"Then why did you stay? After the first time?"

She sighed. "I suppose I was in shock. It was such a surprise. He'd never done it before. Words were his weapon. Then . . . then Daddy died."

There was such anguish in her eyes that Sean couldn't dredge up the anger he'd always felt at the mention of the man. He was dead now, so what did it matter what he'd once said or done?

"Did he really know your father was sick and not tell you about it?"

She nodded. "I just found that out. The night after I saw you at the hospital. He was . . . gloating about it." Her mouth twisted so painfully that it was all Sean could do to keep from reaching out for her. "Daddy died alone, asking for me. He must have thought I didn't care."

Her voice cracked, and the next thing Sean knew he was reaching out for her. He pulled her into his arms, cradling her head to him as she fought not to weep. He tried to imagine how she felt. His own mother was judgmental, fussy and sometimes, albeit unwittingly, sharp-tongued, but he did love her, and if she were dying...

"Shh," he soothed as Rory trembled. "He wouldn't think that, Rory."

"But I didn't go to him."

"Do you think he didn't guess why? Your father may have been a lot of things, Rory, but he wasn't a fool. He knew Talbot. He would have known why."

And in a way, Sean thought, that made it worse. Her father had to have known who and what Talbot was, and he'd sacrificed Rory to him anyway. That fact must have been driven home to him in the days before his death, as he lay alone, knowing why. Perhaps the realization of what he'd really done to his daughter had even contributed to his illness. Jacob Sheridan had not been an old man, nor had he had any history of heart trouble. For the first time Sean felt a stirring of pity for the man.

It wasn't long before pity gave way to another emotion, a much more disturbing, much more dangerous, one. He became aware of Rory's body pressed against his, of the feel of her breasts against his chest, the soft tickle of her lashes against the skin of his throat. Heat began to build, and he wondered why he had ever thought he could be immune to this woman. Even when he'd thought he hated her, when he was angry, when she turned to him only for comfort, even when comfort was the reason he held her, he couldn't seem to stop himself from responding to her.

Maybe he'd just been celibate too damned long. He hadn't really thought about how long it had been, he'd found that the need eased after a while. Especially when, for him, the prospect of becoming intimate with someone involved considerably more than just the "how soon is too soon" question. Most of the time he decided it wasn't worth the trouble.

Or maybe, he thought grimly, as his arms seemed to tighten around her of their own volition, there just wasn't a damned woman in the world who got to him the way this one did.

Rory tilted her head back to look at him, and Sean was stunned to see her expression. As if her own thoughts had followed his, her pain had faded away, to be replaced by a heat as fierce as what he was feeling himself. So fierce that he was unable to draw back, unable to pull away from the potent lure of need glowing in her eyes.

Before he could even think, or listen to the warnings his mind was trying to send, she had risen up on her toes and pressed her mouth to his. He was surprised that there was no crack of sound from the electricity that leapt between them.

Her mouth was soft, warm and far too tempting to resist. He bent his head and deepened the kiss, accepting the invitation of her parted lips. He felt the sigh of her breath, heard the tiny sound of pleasure she made, and his body surged to readiness with the swiftness he'd known only with her.

Her hands slid up around the back of his neck, and he felt her fingers slide into his hair. Once, long ago, she'd told him that she loved to touch his hair, that it felt like thick, heavy silk against her skin. That had set him to wondering about what the honey gold strands of her hair would feel like stroking across some rather intimate areas of his own.

He nearly groaned. Those long-ago thoughts had lost none of their impact in the intervening years. They still had the power to nearly bring him to his knees. The oddity of that hit him—how could she manage to make him feel weakness in a limb he didn't have anymore? It was the strangest sensation he'd had since the phantom pains had eased up over the past couple of years.

That was the last rational thought he had. Rory was clinging to him, kissing him fiercely, and he was lost in the maelstrom she created. He let his hands slip down her back to her slender waist, pulling her even closer. Her tongue was probing, tasting the depths of his mouth, lingering as if she were finding the sweetest of nectars there. Her urgency fired his already heated blood, and his pulse began to pound in his ears.

She twisted against him, as if she wanted to be closer. Her breasts rubbed against his chest, and he could feel the taut points of her nipples even through the layers of cloth between them. Those hardened crests were an enticement he couldn't resist, and slowly, so very slowly, his hands slid up the sides of her rib cage until he was cradling the soft, feminine curves.

Rory moaned, and his hands froze. But then she twisted against him again, as if she craved the sweet friction. When he pulled back she made a tiny sound of protest that turned to a gasp of pleasure when his thumbs crept up to rub over her nipples.

He toyed with them until she cried out, his name breaking from her on a panting breath as she at last tore her mouth away from his. This time it was he who mourned the loss, and he quickly moved to regain the contact, to nibble gently on her lower lip until she sighed and opened for his tongue.

The intimacy of being allowed into her body in this small way made him even more desperate to complete the full joining, to ease the unbearable ache that was settling low and deep inside him, making him feel more swollen and hard than he'd ever been in his life.

He moved again, his hands returning to her waist, then slipping lower. He grasped her hips and pulled her to him urgently, breaking the kiss himself when the feel of her body against his hardened flesh made him let his breath out in a gasp.

"Oh, Sean," she murmured, sounding as breathless as he felt. "It's never been like this. Only with you, only us."

Only with you. Sweet words, Sean thought. Proof that Talbot was wrong about her. She was no more frigid than—

Talbot.

The name slammed into his consciousness, sending the heat and passion and need skittering before it like leaves on a windy street. He'd completely forgotten.

"Damn," he said, forcing himself to pull back.

Rory looked up at him, still seeming a little dazed. He knew just how she felt, he thought. He'd let the danger of the situation completely slip his mind, been so wrapped up in the haze of pleasure she spun around him that he could think of nothing else.

"We've got to get out of here. Chase is going to hold Talbot for as long as he can, but we won't have much time before he'll be on the prowl again."

Rory took a couple of deep breaths, as if she were finding it hard to retreat to reality. He knew how that felt, too.

"I . . . do you think he'll find us here? You're not listed in the phone book. I only got your number because I went to your old neighbors."

He'd wondered about that. Mrs. Holmes, he supposed. The old woman was a font of information and didn't know what a secret was.

"As Stevie and I found out when we were looking for Chase, there are ways, lots of places your name is public record. He may already know where I live, could have had me followed, if he's as . . . unhinged as he seems. . . ."

"He is," she said grimly. "I have to leave, Sean. I can't endanger you anymore."

"Don't worry about me. I can take care of myself, contrary to what Talbot might think."

An image came to him then, of Dar, that devilish grin curving his mouth as he told Sean not to get upset when people assumed he was helpless in a physically tough situation, because being underestimated was one of the most effective weapons a person could have. He'd had the feeling then Dar was speaking from experience, but when he'd asked, his friend had merely grinned again.

"Worry about yourself," Sean told Rory. "What do you want to do?"

Her brow furrowed. "I wish...I could get back into the house, just for a few minutes. There are some things I'd like to get. This—" she lifted the gold chain that held the locket she still wore "—is all I was able to bring with me, and only because I haven't taken it off since..." Her voice wavered, then she finished quietly, "Daddy wanted me to have it. It was my mother's. He had it with him when they took him to the hospital, and me getting this locket was the only thing he talked about at the end, the nurse said."

Odd, Sean thought. What a thing to worry about when you were dying. And what a thing for him to be thinking about, when they should be on the move.

"All right," he said briskly, "we'll try the house. There'll probably never be a better time. We'll have to look out for your watchdog, though. Why don't you call the house and make sure there's no answer?"

Rory nodded in understanding. She made the call, and after several rings got only the answering machine. She hung up and turned back to Sean, shaking her head. He took the phone from her and dialed quickly.

"Cameron and Associates."

"Are you at your desk, Mrs. Stewart?"

"Why, yes. Sean, is that you?"

"Yes. Look, I just need to know if that visitor we had is still there."

"Well, yes, he is, but he's getting quite upset that Mr. Cameron won't let him leave until I decide whether I want to press charges." Mrs. Stewart sounded quite delighted with the idea. "I'm afraid it's taking me a while."

"Thanks," Sean said, grinning. "You take all the time you want, okay? The longer the better."

"I understand. I'm just so upset," the woman said with a dramatic sigh, and Sean chuckled. She was enjoying this. "He really is quite rude, isn't he?"

"Quite," Sean agreed. "Just tell Chase to hold him as long as he can, but not to worry about it."

After he'd hung up, he turned to look at Rory. "He's still there," he said, "so we'll go. But you'll have to make it fast."

"I only want a few things. Papers, identification and Daddy's will." She grimaced. "I wouldn't put it past Frank to try to alter it, or forge a new one to replace it, giving him everything."

Sean frowned. Despite all the painful revelations she'd made, he couldn't shake the feeling that there was more to this than he knew.

"Why would he expect anyone to believe—" He broke off, realizing that this wasn't the time. "Later. Let's go."

Rory followed him out the door. She gave him a sideways look as he led her to where he'd parked. He shrugged. "I figured I'd be cautious, in case Chase couldn't hold him for long."

Rory smiled slightly. "My money's on Chase."

"Mine too."

Sean couldn't help the grin that curved his mouth. Rory had, as most women did, gone into wide-eyed shock the first time she'd seen Chase. And Sean had felt, for the first time, a twinge of jealousy of his brother-in-law, whose dark good looks and vivid green eyes never failed to stop feminine traffic in its tracks.

But Rory had eased his pang, even made him ashamed of it later. She'd shaken her head in awe, saying, "Whew, it's a good thing Stevie has him wrapped up and off the streets. He's dangerous.'' Then she'd turned to him, eyeing him possessively. "And you'd better be the same, Mr. Holt."

"The same?" he'd asked, puzzled.

She'd nodded. "You'd better make it as clear as he does that you're crazy about your wife, or I'll never let you out of my sight."

At the time, never being out of her sight had seemed like a pleasurable idea. And he had murmured a silent apology to his brother-in-law for his momentary lapse into wounded male pride, never realizing just how bad wounded male pride could be. He'd found out, though. The hard way. Rory had taught him, the day she'd left him standing at the altar.

Sean's grin faded as he started the car and began to drive. He'd never thought there could be a reason to forgive Rory. Although he tried to keep the memories well buried, the pain was vividly etched into his mind, and it was a pain that had changed him forever. He'd lost whatever boyish innocence he'd had left and nearly all of what little faith he had in the fairness of life. Only the happiness of his sister and Chase had enabled him to hang on to any semblance of hope at all. Those were losses he'd never thought he would get over, let alone forgive.

But then, he'd never expected to hear a tale like the one Rory had told him. And, he admitted silently, any doubts he still had about her story had been greatly shaken by this confrontation with Talbot. The man seemed capable of everything she'd said, and more. For the first time he saw Rory as a victim in what had happened five years ago, perhaps as much of a victim as he himself had been. And in the next moment he wondered if that meant he'd begun to forgive her, if perhaps it was more than just a desire to help a woman in trouble that had made him so willing to entangle himself in this mess.

The idea startled him, then unnerved him. He'd hated her for so long that it had become a part of him, a part he wasn't sure he could let go of. He tried to tell himself it was only what Rory had said, that he would help anyone in her situation, but he wasn't certain.

What he *was* certain of was that he wouldn't feel compelled to take just any woman in her situation to bed for a month or so. He couldn't remember ever feeling that compulsion before, not even with Rory. He'd been far too nervous, afraid that his leg was the source of her seeming wariness of sex with him, even as she told him that she loved him. He wasn't sure if the change had occurred naturally in him, or simply happened because she'd seen him now and hadn't recoiled in repugnance. But he knew he'd never felt so much heat so fast as when he touched her.

But when he wasn't touching her, he felt oddly empty, as if the hatred he'd carried around for so long had taken up more room inside him than he'd realized.

So what was left, if he had forgiven her? What caused his sudden, fierce wanting? Pure lust?

Well, there was certainly that, he thought, giving her a sideways look. She was sitting quietly in the passenger seat, fiddling with her keys, her eyes cast downward except for an occasional wary glance in the right-side mirror.

When he'd first met her, he'd wanted her for his own with the single-minded purity of purpose that now seemed possible only in the young. He wondered if it had been a test of sorts, a dare to life to make up for what it had done to him. You took my leg, but give me Rory and I'll call it even. God, he'd been so young and stupid.

So don't be stupid again, he warned himself. Admit to lusting after her, if you have to—and he could hardly deny it, he thought ruefully, considering how his body went into overdrive every time he got close to her—but nothing more.

Anything more would just be setting yourself up for a fall all over again.

"How's the new baby?" Rory asked, sounding as if the silence in the car was getting to her.

"Fine. Sleeping, mostly."

"Have they named him yet?"

"Jason. Jason Steven, after Chase's brother and my dad."

She smiled then. "I'll bet your father liked that."

"Yes."

"How's Katie taking it?"

Sean couldn't help smiling then. "She wasn't real sure about it, but then her boyfriend called and convinced her she was still the most special girl on the planet."

"Her boyfriend?" Rory looked startled.

"My friend Dar. The guy in the picture you saw. Katie adores him, and the feeling is mutual. And Dar doesn't easily adore anyone."

Rory looked at him speculatively for a long moment before she said quietly, "And neither do you."

"Not anymore," he said, glancing away before the regret that flickered in her eyes could stir him.

The remainder of the drive was silent except for the sound of the wind through the open top of the car. Yet there was a building tension that was almost audible as they neared the house. From the side street, they could see that there were only three vehicles parked on the street in Rory's block; most of the expensive cars in this neighborhood were kept securely locked in multicar garages. None of the three was the black sedan.

Of course, Sean thought, their watchdog could have traded cars, now that he knew Rory knew she had been followed. But there was no reason for them to assume she knew what kind of car her tail was driving; indeed, she hadn't, until Sean had pointed it out to her. But none of the three vehicles parked on the street was occupied, and the big house looked quiet, deserted. Still, he backed into the driveway so the car would be pointing outward, ready to roll.

He went in with her to be sure the house was empty—which took a few minutes, with the size of the place—but then told her that he would wait outside, to watch for Talbot and the watchdog. It was true, as far as it went, but the much more powerful reason was that he didn't want to spend any more time than he had to in that place. It reminded him too much of the painful past, and he had enough of that to wrestle with already.

He was still wrestling with it when Rory came out and tossed a designer handbag into the back of the car, assuring him that she had only one more trip to make, to get some clothes. He told her to hurry, then went back to pacing on the front porch, trying to keep from dwelling on the chaos of his emotions by watching. Occasionally a car would drive down the side street, but the street in front of the house remained deserted.

He would help her get out of here, get out of reach of Talbot's fists, he told himself, and then he was through. After that, she was on her own; he wasn't about to get tangled up with Rory Sheridan again. Dar was right. Stay clear, he'd said.

Of course, he'd also said have sex with her if you have to. And God knows there had been times in the past four days when it had been a damned close thing, when he'd felt as if he had to have her more than he had to have his next breath. But he also knew there was no way he could do that and follow the rest of Dar's advice: *"... but keep your damned heart intact."* Dar might be able to do it, but Sean knew his own protective shell wasn't that thick, wasn't as impenetrable as Dar's. Unlike Dar, he'd always had his family, especially Stevie, and that had kept him from closing himself off completely. He—

He abruptly stopped his pacing and turned sharply, peering down toward the side street. It was empty. Had he really seen it, or was it a figment of an overactive imagination? Had he seen the tail end of a big black sedan when the sound of a motor made him automatically look up?

He couldn't be sure, but it was enough to send him to the door to holler for Rory to hurry up.

"Just a minute," she called back. "I forgot something."

"It better be damned important," he snapped, feeling edgy. They'd been here too long; Chase couldn't hold Talbot forever. He didn't want another confrontation with the man, not with Rory here, liable to get caught up in it. The seconds ticked by, until he was ready to go after her and drag her out.

"It *is* important," Rory said, coming out of an upstairs room and down the stairway, clutching a small overnight bag and something else in her hands. "Very important."

Something about her tone made him wait in the doorway for her, trying not to remember all the times when he'd stood here waiting for his first glimpse of her as she came regally down the wide staircase. She came up to him, a solemn look in her eyes as she held something out to him.

Sean stared at the large, flat inch-and-a-half-thick book she held. A scrapbook. His scrapbook. He recognized the tear at one corner, from when he'd thrown the book across the room in a fit of fury after his accident.

And three years later, after he'd proposed to Rory and she'd accepted, he had tossed the book into the trash, deciding it was time to get on with his life instead of dwelling on past glories that would never come again.

"How...?"

"I saw your face that day, when you found it in that storage box. And when you threw it away. So I went and dug it out of the trash."

He took it from her. The pages of newspaper clippings, of football victories, of long scoring runs, of great catches, and at last of the news that the pros were in town, scouting the San Diego State Aztecs' Sean Holt, meant nothing anymore, he'd told himself that day. He had Rory now, and she would make everything all right. And he'd really believed it—then.

"Why, Rory?" The question broke from him before he could stop it.

"I thought you might want it again someday," she said softly now.

He had, amazingly enough. Years later, when he'd come out of the nosedive her desertion had put him in, he'd regretted throwing away a large piece of his past. But it had been, he'd thought, too late. And now Rory had handed that past back to him.

"And I wanted..." Her voice broke oddly, and he heard her take a deep breath. He looked at her then and saw such a world of pain in her eyes that he was reminded of the moment when he'd thought of her as a victim for the first time. "I wanted our children to see it someday," she finished in a hoarse whisper.

Emotion kicked through him, driving his breath from him as surely as a hit from a three-hundred-pound tackle. It tightened his jaw, made his hands curl into fists, and made his voice as harsh and dry as a Santa Ana wind.

"Then why did you keep it all this time? After you knew damned well there weren't ever going to *be* any children?"

She winced visibly. "I...hid it away. I think I hoped that someday I'd be able to give it back to you."

"The only thing I want back from you is—"

The roar of a car's engine and the squeal of straining tires cut him off. A sleek, expensive European coupe skidded to a stop, blocking their exit from the driveway. Sean didn't need to see the driver; he already knew who it was.

He was going to have that confrontation with Frank Talbot after all.

Chapter 10

Rory had expected Frank to be angry, but the malevolence that twisted his face startled even her. It didn't seem to bother Sean, who turned and casually tossed the bag—and the scrapbook—through the open T-top onto the back seat of his car. But then, Sean had never seen Frank in one of his rages; she doubted he had truly let loose in Chase's office, not at two-against-one odds.

"So you don't know where she is," Talbot said scornfully, glaring at Sean. "I knew you were a liar."

"When in Rome," Sean said, looking pointedly at Talbot.

"I ought to flatten you, now that your big, bad brother-in-law isn't here to save your ass," Talbot spat out.

"You're welcome to try," Sean said mildly, shrugging as if Talbot were no more than a bothersome insect.

Rory's breath caught in her throat. Didn't Sean realize he was baiting a wild beast? Apparently the tiny sound was enough to distract Talbot, because he turned on *her* then.

"And as for you, you silly bitch, you'll get yours. I'll teach you a long overdue lesson—"

"If you lay a hand on her again," Sean said, his voice suddenly deadly cold, "you're a dead man."

Talbot snorted noisily. "And who's going to do it? You, gimp? Don't make me laugh."

"The only laughable thing around here is you. Chase was right, you *are* a clown."

The red evidence of fury rose in Talbot's face. "Sean, don't!" Rory cried out. "He's vicious, he doesn't care who he hurts—"

"Shut up!" Talbot ordered her. Rory didn't even realize until a few seconds later that she had unquestioningly obeyed him. God, was she that weak? Had she become what she'd pretended to be, a docile, submissive woman he would leave alone? Was she trapped in that assumed role now, too weak to break out of it?

"I told you she's not worth it," Talbot said to Sean. "She's a whimpering, spoiled little bitch."

"Then you won't mind if she leaves, will you?" Sean said coolly. "Get in the car, Rory."

"She's not leaving. I own her, Holt. And every second you drag this out is going to make it worse for her later. A black eye is nothing compared to what I'll do to her. And to you, if you don't get your nose out of my business."

"We're leaving now," Sean said, so casually that Rory had to stop herself from shaking her head in wonder. He was treating this as if they were simply guests taking their leave of friends after a chance meeting.

"The hell you are. You're trespassing on my property." Talbot's narrow, pale eyes gleamed with remembered anger. "Two can play that game."

Sean grinned suddenly. "Couldn't bully my brother-in-law, huh?"

The red splotches on Talbot's face deepened, and Rory knew from grim experience that Frank's hold on his always-volatile temper was at its most tenuous. There was nothing that infuriated him more than the idea of someone laughing at him.

And Sean knew that, she realized suddenly as she dared a quick glance at him. He knew it, and he was using it, intentionally acting as if he found Frank merely amusing. But he didn't know, she thought. He didn't know how despicable Frank could be. He wouldn't hesitate to hit Sean, amputee or not.

"Frank, please" she began, trying to draw his attention away from Sean. "Just let me go."

"'Frank, please,'" he mimicked in a whining tone. "She begs so nicely, don't you think? Especially in bed. Oh, but you don't know that, do you? I quite enjoyed discovering—rather painfully for her, I'm afraid—that she was still a virgin. Not even man enough to take her, were you?"

Rory felt Sean tense beside her and wanted to tell him not to let Frank's vile mouth get to him. But she knew she didn't dare say a word, for fear Frank would strike out, as he always did. And this time it might be Sean who was hurt.

"Or was it her? Did she hold you off, maybe with some story about wanting to be pure for her wedding night? Well, she was pure, all right, but it wasn't her wedding night. As if I'd marry a cold fish like her, when I could buy her. Marriage is just a way for a woman to get her hands on a man's money." Talbot laughed, a horrible, malignant sound. "But maybe she was smarter than I gave her credit for, not wanting to go to bed with a cripple."

Rory tensed then, waiting, certain Sean would explode now. But instead, to her astonishment, he relaxed.

"The only cripple I see here is you, Talbot," Sean said. "A cripple and a parasite, a man who can't make it on his own, so he has to suck the life out of those around him, getting fat on others' misery."

"Oh, God," Rory murmured under her breath. Sean was taunting a rattlesnake, daring him to strike.

"You've got a big mouth, Holt. You figure you're safe? That I can't hit a cripple?"

"Why should that stop you?" Sean said, his voice suddenly low and mocking. "You beat up women. Is that all you're man enough for?"

"Sean, no!"

Her cry came too late. Frank launched himself at Sean, swinging from the heels in a roundhouse blow that caught the dodging Sean in the mouth. Sean staggered, lifting the back of one hand to wipe away the blood that was welling up from a split lip. It had been a glancing blow, Rory realized thankfully, or it could have broken Sean's jaw.

Frank whirled back around. He came at Sean again, landing a quick blow against his ribs. Rory heard the dull thud. Her stomach knotted. She looked desperately around for something, anything, to use as a weapon. The car, she thought. Maybe there was a tire iron.

As she tried to get past the sprawling men to the car, Frank drove Sean up against one of the newel posts of the porch. His head snapped back; Rory heard the tinny thump as he hit the rain gutter that ran down the side of the post. There was a clear spot now, at the far side of the steps. She started for it.

Frank backed up a couple of steps. He was breathing hard, but his face was lit with a malevolent pleasure. Sean sagged against the post, as if dazed. Rory's stomach clenched again; she had to do something, had to help Sean somehow. But then Sean moved, and she stopped.

He staggered away from the post, as if thoroughly beaten. Frank took a step toward him, fist raised as if to deliver another blow. Sean took another wobbly step, until Frank was between him and the post. Then, in a movement so smooth and so quick that Rory couldn't quite believe it, he attacked.

He spun on his right heel. His left leg came up, bent at the artificial knee. His left arm came up, his palm open, the heel of his hand forward. He caught Frank below the ear with a driving force and at the same instant he kicked solidly against Frank's tailbone with the rigid, harder-than-flesh prosthesis.

Rory had to dodge out of the way as Frank went slamming back against the post, screaming as he hit one of the brackets that held the rain gutter and it ripped at his face. She stood there watching in shock as Frank slid down to the porch; she'd never seen him bested in anything.

"Get in the car, Rory. Now!"

Rory gaped at Sean. He jerked a thumb over his shoulder.

"Reinforcements are on the way. Get going!"

She spared only a split second to glance at the blond man running toward them from the black sedan now parked crookedly in the street. Frank was howling, clutching at his face, blood welling up between his stubby fingers. Then she was running for the car. Sean was behind her, moving oddly, with a hitch in his gait she had never noticed before. He barely got into the driver's seat before the watchdog came running up the driveway.

The man hesitated, as if torn between the quarry he'd been trailing for so long and the man who had hired him to do it and was now screaming at him to kill Sean. Frank was obviously out of control, and from the studying look the blond man gave him, Rory thought perhaps he was also out of help. For the moment, at least.

"Let's hope he decides to take his boss in for stitches first," Sean muttered as he maneuvered the car over the curb and out into the street past Talbot's silver coupe.

"My God, Sean, where did you learn to fight like that?"

"A friend of mine taught me," he said shortly, concentrating on getting them as far away as he could as fast as possible.

Rory found her gaze glued to the rearview mirror, searching for any sign of the black sedan in pursuit. Her heart was still hammering, her breath coming quickly. When the adrenaline finally ebbed enough for her to look around, she realized she had no idea where they were.

They were out of the neighborhood, on a safely busy and anonymous street, when Sean pulled over to the curb. Without even looking at Rory, he rolled up his left pant leg until it was above the knee of the prosthesis. She understood now why he'd always worn loose jeans; she'd never thought about it before, just enjoyed the fact that they emphasized the snugness of the seat—and the taut curve of his backside.

Wincing slightly, Sean gripped the prosthesis just above the knee and twisted it slightly. It seemed to slip into place, and when he let out a small breath of relief she knew that this was why he'd been walking so oddly after the fight.

She felt a sudden heat and wondered if she was blushing; despite his matter-of-factness, this seemed somehow a very intimate thing to do in front of someone. But the heat faded rapidly as she realized that it probably only meant it didn't matter to him that she was there. That *she* didn't matter to him, not in that way.

He glanced over, catching her watching him intently. She was praying that her thoughts weren't showing on her silly face when one corner of his mouth quirked upward in a wry grin.

"There are some advantages," he said with a shrug. "Even if I do have to put my leg back on straight afterward."

"You were . . . wonderful," she said simply.

Sean stared at her for an instant, then let out a short, compressed chuckle as he shook his head. "I think this is where you're supposed to flutter your eyelashes at me and trill, 'My hero!' isn't it?"

She was blushing then; she could feel the flood of color to her cheeks. "It's just that...I didn't know...no one's ever really fought back against Frank when he gets like that, and..."

"And I was the last person on earth you thought would do it." His mouth twisted. "Or is that *could* do it?"

She opened her mouth, then closed it again. What could she say? She *hadn't* thought he could do it. She never would have guessed that he could move so quickly, strike so swiftly...and so effectively.

"I'm sorry," she said at last. It was all she could think of to say. "I just didn't know."

He looked at her for a silent moment. Then he began to roll the leg of his jeans back down again.

"A friend of mine once drank a toast to honest women. I think I see his point."

He turned back to the wheel and steered out into traffic. For a long time Rory sat still, trying to erase the memory of Frank launching himself savagely at Sean. And savoring the memory of his astonishment as Sean turned on him.

Slowly she began to realize how late it was, and that the sun was rapidly sinking, sending the shadows stretching toward darkness. Then she thought once more about the fact that she had no idea where they were.

"Where are we going?"

"Someplace it'll take Talbot a while to find."

He didn't seem inclined to talk, and she didn't push. But fifteen minutes later, when he pulled off the Coast Highway onto a narrow dirt road that ran along the edge of one of the lagoons that dotted this stretch of the coastline, she looked at him curiously. The only thing in sight was a square warehouse kind of building with a long ramp running almost the length of the front side, angling down from a landing in front of a large, heavy-looking door. A set of steps came straight down from the same landing.

The building was painted a soft tan that blended with the surrounding hills. There were a pair of six-inch wide stripes, one dark red, one dark green, painted near the top of the building, as if its owner had chosen to emphasize rather than disguise the building's square shape.

Parked at the bottom of the ramp was a large blue van, and right in front of the building sat a red four-wheel-drive Jeep wagon. When he saw the second vehicle, Sean muttered what sounded like a swear word under his breath.

"Sean?" she asked. "What is this place?"

"It belongs to that friend I told you about. He lives in it. But he's leaving tonight for L.A."

"The friend who likes Katie, the friend who taught you to fight, or the friend who toasts honest women?"

"Yes."

It took her a second to realize that he meant they were all the same man. She felt a sudden dread of going inside this place. If Sean was as close to this Dar Cordell as it seemed, he'd no doubt told him about her. And she was certain that whatever he'd said wasn't very flattering.

It was getting dark quickly now, so she couldn't see Sean's face very well. But it was clear that whatever had disturbed him about the second car wasn't going to stop him from going inside. At his gesture she followed reluctantly, hanging back, her misgivings growing.

The door at the top of the steps was unlocked. She could understand why; this place was remote enough, and looked so much like only a warehouse, that she imagined it was as safe as any residence behind fences and locked gates.

They stepped into a cool, dim entryway, and Rory could hear a child's shrieks of excitement echoing off the high walls and ceiling beyond the entry wall that blocked their view of the room.

"Faster, Dar! Spin faster!"

It was a little girl. An obviously delighted little girl. And Rory knew even before they stepped around the wall, before she saw the flying dark hair of the child, why Sean had sworn when he'd seen the truck outside. She stayed hidden behind him, ashamedly aware of her cowardice but unprepared for this.

It was a warm tableau, Stevie seated with her feet up on a long, comfortable-looking couch in a green that matched the stripe on the outside of the building, Chase walking around, cradling a tiny, cooing bundle gently in his strong arms. But the centerpiece of the picture was the laughing little girl and the man she was clinging to, who was laughing nearly as much as the child.

It was amazing, Rory thought, how fast he was moving. The bright blue wheelchair he sat in seemed more like an improvement than an impediment. Front wheels off the floor, he was spinning around so quickly, first one way, then the other, that Rory wondered that they both didn't go flying out from the sheer force of it. She'd always thought Sean's shoulders and arms were broad and strong, but this man was like no one she'd ever seen in person before.

But he was clearly the man in the photograph she'd seen in Sean's apartment; the expression on his face was almost identical as he grinned at the little girl in his lap. Except that the photo hadn't done him justice. He wasn't damned near perfect, he *was* perfect, Rory thought.

The photo hadn't done Katie justice, either. She was as adorable as Rory had always known she would be. Her dark hair, as thick and shiny as her father's, whipped around with the movement of the chair. She was clinging to the man in the chair like a limpet, her arms thrown around his strong neck, her knees braced on his muscled thighs. And it was only then that Rory noticed the reason the man was in the chair: his left leg was no longer than Sean's, and his right ended several inches below the knee.

As if her stare had made him aware of their presence, the spinning stopped. The man tossed his tousled hair out of his eyes with a flip of his head as he grinned at Sean. Instinctively Rory drew back out of sight. Katie spotted the new arrival then and shouted her welcome.

"Uncle Sean!" Katie scrambled to the floor and ran toward them. Sean bent and picked up the little girl with an easy motion that belied the fact that he'd just been in a fight.

"Women." Dar's grin widened as he watched Katie hug Sean. "Fickle even at her age."

"What's fickle?" Katie asked.

"Never mind," Sean said. "You'll learn soon enough."

Rory winced inwardly. Had that been meant for her?

Dar wheeled toward them. "Welcome to the party, buddy. Glad you stopped by." He gestured at Chase and his bundle. "I figured if I was going to see the baby before I left for the race tonight, I'd better arrange it myself. You've been on another planet lately, and..."

His voice trailed off, the chair stopped, his dark eyes narrowed, and Rory knew he'd spotted her. She heard Sean sigh. He moved to one side, out from in front of her.

"Dar, Rory. Rory, Dar Cordell."

"I guessed," Dar said shortly.

There was no welcome in his voice, but Rory hadn't expected one. And it wasn't really this man she was afraid of, or even Chase, who had stopped dead in his wanderings with his baby son to stare at her. It was Stevie, who was getting slowly to her feet, also staring. Stevie, who loved her brother so fiercely. And Katie, who was looking at her with her tiny face scrunched up in concentration.

Sean turned then, as if to usher Rory into the huge, airy expanse of the warehouse. The movement brought him into the glow of the room's lights, and Dar whistled, long and low.

"What the hell happened to you?"

Sean's hand shot to his split lip, as if he'd forgotten. His fingertips came away bloody, and he shrugged ruefully.

"I . . . bumped into something."

Rory cringed inwardly as he used her own lame excuse. But Dar wasn't buying it, not for an instant.

"Something with a fist?" he drawled. "And what does the other guy look like now?"

Apparently giving up the pretense, Sean grinned, then winced when the movement pulled on his lip. "He's wearing the imprint of a graphite carbon knee on his backside and is probably in the emergency room getting stitches in his face about now."

Dar laughed. "Good for you."

"I had a good teacher," Sean said.

Dar shrugged. Sean opened his mouth to go on—probably, Rory thought with a wary look at Stevie and Chase, to explain why he had intruded on this warm gathering with the one person they least wanted to see. But before he could speak, a small, green-eyed volcano erupted.

"Go away!" Katie shouted, glaring at Rory. "I know who you are. You're the one who hurt my Uncle Sean! Go away. We don't want you here!"

Chapter 11

"Out of the mouths of babes."

Rory heard the soft words and knew who'd spoken them. She made herself look up to meet Stevie's bright—and accusing—blue eyes. She appeared the same, Rory thought, barely a day older than when Rory had first met her over five years and a second child ago.

Only back then Stevie had never viewed her so coldly; Rory wouldn't have thought it possible for the warmhearted woman to look like that. But Stevie hadn't been staring at the woman who'd deserted her beloved brother then. And Stevie's loyalty to those she loved knew no limits.

Rory's gaze flicked to Chase. His expression was unreadable, and she wondered what he was thinking. She knew he had no more reason to welcome her than Stevie did; he had long since come to regard Sean as his brother in fact, if not in blood. But Chase had learned the hard way to reserve judgment on people who were sometimes driven to desperate actions. At least there was no accusation in those green eyes so like his daughter's, merely a cool, assessing look that made Rory uneasily aware that, when he did make his decision, Chase would be as implacable as the buildings he designed. As implacable as his daughter.

His daughter. Slowly Rory forced her gaze back to the child. Katie's eyes were glittering angrily, and she wasn't listening to whatever Sean was whispering into her ear. There were no shades of gray in Katie's world; she knew how she felt, and she wasn't having any part of being placated.

"No, Uncle Sean. She's a mean lady, and I don't want her to stay."

"Katie..." Sean began again.

"No," Rory said, her eyes brimming at the child's vehement protectiveness of her beloved uncle. Her looks might be her father's, but it was clear that her fiercely loyal heart was Stevie's. "No, she's right, Sean. Don't hush her."

It took all her nerve, but she took a step closer to look into the little girl's face.

"I did hurt your uncle, Katie. Very badly. I was very young and very foolish, and I thought I was doing the right thing."

"You hurt him," Katie insisted, making it clear that, in her young mind, nothing else mattered. "You made him go away for a long time. I was scared he wasn't coming back."

Rory saw Sean's arms tighten around the little girl, but he didn't say anything. Nor did Stevie, or Chase, who seemed content to let their brutally honest daughter say what perhaps they wouldn't. Dar just sat there, watching, an odd expression on his face, making no move except to glance from Katie to Stevie and then back again.

Rory took a deep breath and tried again, wondering why she felt as if this child held the rest of her life in her tiny hands.

"Have you ever done anything you were really, really sorry for, Katie?"

Being asked a question seemed to surprise the girl, and she considered it for a moment. Then, slowly, she nodded.

"I tore one of Daddy's building drawings once. I didn't like it because he worked on it too much and wouldn't play with me, and it was making him cross. I was sorry later, because he had to do it all over."

Rory sensed rather than saw Chase shift as if he were uncomfortable. She didn't look at him, just concentrated on the child.

"But it seemed like a good reason at the time, didn't it?" When the child reluctantly nodded, she said softly, "Well, I had what seemed like a good reason, too, Katie. It wasn't until later that I realized how wrong it was. And how very, very sorry I was."

Katie's delicate brows furrowed. "Really sorry?"

"Really. Sorry for letting down your mommy and daddy after they had accepted me as a friend. Sorry for making you sad and scared..."

Rory swallowed tightly, then made herself go on. "And most of all, sorry for hurting the person I loved more than anyone else...except the person I did it for. If I could take back what I did, I would. But I can't. I can only apologize with all my heart."

She risked a glance at Sean then; he was standing very still as he held Katie. She read in his eyes that he knew exactly whose ears that apology was meant for, what she couldn't read was whether or not he was ready to accept it. He might believe her story now, he might understand why she'd done it, but it was a long high-wire step from understanding to forgiveness.

Sean had finally told Stevie and Chase Rory's story, but he wasn't at all sure it had made much difference. Oh, they'd understood, he thought, and the sight of Rory's bruised face had brought on a bit more tolerance, but their expressions were nearly as mutinous as the now sound-asleep Katie's had been.

He supposed it was to be expected; he'd had a few more days to absorb what had happened than they had. And he'd had the advantage—or disadvantage—of Rory's own emotionally wrenching recounting of her dilemma. Confronted with Stevie, Chase, Dar and the not easily convinced Katie, Rory had remained silent.

Stevie looked up at Sean with concern as they stood in the doorway. Dar had escorted his guests to the door, said good-night, then tactfully left Sean to say his own goodbyes in private.

"Just be careful," Stevie said.

"I will."

Sean reached into the blanket-wrapped bundle Stevie held to brush a finger over his new nephew's cheek. Right now the baby had Chase's dark hair and Stevie's bright blue eyes, and he found himself hoping it would stay that way; he quite liked looking at this child who was a combination of two people he loved so dearly.

"I'm just afraid if you get involved . . . she'll hurt you again."

His gaze shifted to his sister's worried face. "I'm a big boy now, sis." He leaned over to kiss her cheek. "But thanks."

Stevie sighed, nodded and turned to go. Sean glanced at Chase, who was cradling the sleeping Katie in his arms, and saw almost the same expression of worry on his brother-in-law's face.

"Sorry I couldn't hold Talbot any longer," Chase said, eyeing Sean's swollen but no longer bleeding lip.

"It was long enough," Sean said. "Besides, I almost enjoyed it. Thanks. I know you . . . don't approve."

"But I understand," Chase said quietly, his gaze flicking to Rory, who was sitting alone on the sofa with her feet curled under her, looking a little lost and forlorn. "And if you need anything, you know we're always there for you. But Stevie's right. Be careful." He looked pointedly at Sean's lip again. "This could blow up in your face all over again."

"I know. Believe me, I know." He hesitated, then asked, "Can you cover for me at work? Just until we get things settled?"

After a moment Chase nodded. As he turned to head for the truck, Sean saw the glint of the gold chain around his neck, the chain that held the pendant Stevie had given him as a wedding gift, the symbol of all they'd been through. It reminded him of Rory's locket and her father's odd fixation on it at the end of his life. Everything, it seemed, led his thoughts back to Rory.

"Good luck," Chase said over his shoulder, so obviously heartfelt—and doubtful—that Sean wondered if maybe he truly was crazy.

He stepped outside to watch his family drive away, then went down the steps to replace and fasten the T-tops on his car. He needed a couple of minutes to think. And to tell himself that they were right; he'd done as much—hell, he'd done more—than Rory could or should ever have expected. He'd gotten her away from Talbot, the rest was up to her. He should walk away clean and consider himself lucky for having escaped lightly this time.

Then, as he thought of Rory sitting inside, all alone, he knew he couldn't simply walk away. Perhaps it was guilt over what she'd said, how she'd childishly hoped he would come back and fix things, never realizing that he hadn't been able to even fix himself, not then. Or perhaps it was just the knowledge that she hadn't deserted him because she didn't want him.

He should have realized, he thought, when he'd found himself defending her to his family. He should have realized that his subconscious had apparently made the decision he'd been shying away from; he had, in truth, forgiven her. He believed now that, five years ago, she had truly thought she had no choice.

But he still wasn't sure what was left, if anything. He was only sure that if he wasn't careful, he could wind up in bloody pieces again.

To his surprise, when he went back inside, Rory wasn't alone. Dar was actually talking to her. He was relieved at first, but then thought better of it. He needed to find out what was being said first. He headed across the bare floor toward the large rectangle of carpet that marked the living area of the unbroken expanse of the warehouse. It was the same kind of carpet that had finally been delivered to the site; it had been Dar who had first explained the facts of wheelchair traction to him.

"You put him through hell," Dar was saying, his voice sharp with the edge Sean had come to know meant he didn't like what he was feeling, or didn't like that he was feeling at all; Sean had never been sure which it was.

"I know," Rory said quietly. Then, yet again, "I'm sorry."

Dar let out a compressed breath. "If I wasn't sure of that—"

He broke off then, looking up as he heard Sean approaching. He looked defiant, Sean thought, as if trying to convince Sean—or himself—that he didn't care that he'd been caught showing concern over a friend.

"So," Sean said brightly, "you're still leaving tonight for the race?"

Dar nodded.

"All packed?"

"Yes."

"How about the race chairs?"

"Loaded this afternoon."

"Sure you don't want me to go along?"

"Yes."

They'd been through this before, when Sean had wanted to go watch a race but had been bluntly told that Dar would prefer it if he didn't. Win or lose, Dar Cordell raced alone, as he did most things. If nothing else, it made Sean realize how amazing it was that Dar had let down the walls enough for him, and then the Camerons, to get in.

There were times—like now—Sean thought in exasperation, when Dar could be a real pain. Times when he drew back into that protective shell and refused to admit that he gave a damn about anything, refused to let anyone give a damn about him. And Sean was fairly certain it had little or nothing to do with the loss of his legs. Dar's walls were too high not to be the product of a lifetime. And while those moods had become rare around Sean, when they hit, they hit hard.

"Dar's won virtually every road race in the western United States," Sean explained conversationally to Rory. "And he's got orders for his custom race chairs backed up for months."

"That's...nice."

Dar snorted inelegantly.

"Why don't you tell her about your new idea?" Sean suggested.

"No thanks."

Sean went on as if Dar hadn't been utterly rude. "It's an electric chair for children, designed like a toy car, with interchangeable sets of controls that can be adapted to various disabilities. Kids with limited mobility can drive it all by themselves. It's a great idea."

Rory looked at Dar speculatively. "I don't think I dare offer an opinion."

Dar looked startled, then almost embarrassed. But he said nothing. Sean gave up with a shake of his head. Rory got to her feet.

"Don't worry, Sean. I understand. I wouldn't want to talk to the person who betrayed my best friend, either." She smiled wanly. "I respect his loyalty. And I'm glad he's your friend. But I think I've long overstayed my welcome. I'll wait in the car."

She started toward the door but stopped when Dar spoke abruptly. "You really think this Talbot guy will be looking for you, Sean?"

At the edge of his vision Sean saw Rory stiffen, her eyes flicking from Sean to Dar and back again. Was this what really had Dar so on edge?

"Probably," Sean admitted. "Or his hired help will be, at least." He grinned. "I don't think he'll be too mobile himself for a day or so."

A smile flickered across Dar's face then, and Sean silently apologized to his friend for his exasperation. "Stay here, then," Dar said abruptly.

Sean blinked, startled. "What?" He'd only meant this as a breathing space for a few hours, until he had decided what to do. He knew Dar wasn't one to open up his home lightly, and hadn't wanted to ask, knowing how his friend felt about Rory.

Dar's powerful shoulders lifted in a shrug. "I'll be gone nearly a week. You might as well stay. It's far enough out of the way, it might keep him off your back a little longer."

He knew Dar was right, Sean thought later as his friend drove off, but there was something about the isolation of this place that made him wonder if he hadn't made one of the more stupid moves of his life. All alone here, with the one woman he couldn't seem to resist, despite all the painful history between them.

With a sigh he walked back into the warehouse and closed the door. He found Rory standing before Dar's drafting table, looking at the large gold trophy that was holding down a stack of wheelchair designs.

"He's got a closet full of them," Sean said from behind her. "But he only gets one out when he needs a paperweight."

"Why does he hide them away?"

Sean shrugged. "For Dar, it's the winning, not the accolades and awards afterward. If it wasn't for the fact that it brings him business, I think he'd skip the ceremonial stuff altogether."

"He's . . . very much alone, isn't he?"

"He always has been."

"In that picture . . . he was standing . . . ."

"He can. And does. He uses his prostheses enough to keep in practice. He does pretty well, for a bilateral amputee. But he's more mobile, and faster, in a chair. And Dar Cordell never does anything at less than top speed if he can help it."

"He loves Katie," Rory said.

Sean knew she was purposely keeping the conversation on safe ground, but after she'd had to unexpectedly face his family, he thought she deserved a little recovery time.

"Yes," he agreed. "He does. Sometimes I think she's the only human being on earth he does love. I mean, he likes me and Stevie, and Chase . . . but he *loves* Katie. She accepts him unconditionally and has since she first met him when she was about five."

Rory glanced at him then, and looked away so quickly he knew what she had to have been thinking.

"Yes," he said. "She had practice. She grew up knowing about her Uncle Sean's 'funny leg,' as she calls it. The first thing she ever asked Dar was why he didn't just get two legs like mine, so he could walk. I half expected him to close up, like he does sometimes. But he didn't. He just showed her he could walk if he wanted to, and then took her for a wild ride on one of his racing chairs. She came back agreeing that it was much more fun.''

"An honest woman," Rory said quietly.

Sean lifted a brow. He hadn't thought of it like that, but it made sense. Katie hadn't felt sorry for Dar or stared at him, she had just wanted an answer to a simple question. And once she'd gotten it, that was the end of it for her. Dar was her best friend, and that was that.

"She's a beautiful child."

"Yes."

"And the image of Chase."

"Yes."

"I wish . . ."

He didn't prompt her when she stopped. He didn't want to know what she wished, not when it came to children that would never be born.

And that was enough recovery time, he decided. More than enough. The quiet seclusion of this place was starting to close in on him. It would take a loner like Dar to be truly comfortable here.

"What are you going to do, Rory?"

At first she didn't answer. She turned away from the table and walked back toward the living area. She moved slowly, and Sean saw her hand steal up to clasp the locket. He followed her, waiting. The silence drew out.

"I'm not sure," she said at last. Then she turned to face him. "All I know is it makes me ill to think of him in my house or sitting in my father's office."

"So throw him out."

She looked startled, then thoughtful, and Sean wondered how long it had been since she'd felt as if she had the power to do anything of her own volition.

"I could. Out of the house, anyway," she said slowly. "It's mine."

"Then do it." Then the implication of her words hit him. "What do you mean, the *house* is yours? What about the money? The company?"

She sighed. "It's Frank's. All the ready cash and Daddy's stock, anyway. Frank made sure that was in the will. I was the beneficiary on his life insurance, but Frank made me sign that over to him. But Daddy made sure I got the house, and a small trust that couldn't be broken. And this." She touched the locket, but Sean barely noticed.

I wouldn't put it past Frank to try and alter it, or forge a new one to replace it, giving him everything.

Sean gaped as what she'd said came back to him. "Your father disinherited you? For that sleaze?"

"It was part of the deal."

Sean spun on his heel, fighting the sudden churning in his stomach. "I've had about enough of your father and his *deal,*" he snapped. "He was no better than Talbot!"

Rory made a tiny sound, and Sean whirled back to her. Her face was pale, and she was clutching the locket again, her knuckles white with pressure.

"Sean—"

"And if you defend him again, after what he's done, you're a bigger fool than I ever was."

"Sean, don't think I haven't realized he was weak, and far too proud. But he was my father—"

"And he sold you! Sold you to a piece of slime, and then turned your birthright over to him, too!" He strode toward her, hating the way she shrank back before him. "But it's okay, right? I mean, he did leave you *that.*"

He made a swiping gesture at the locket she kept hanging on to as if it were the most precious thing in the world. He froze when Rory flinched, throwing her hands up as if to ward off a blow. Sickness roiled within him at her fear, and he was only vaguely aware of the clatter as the locket, its chain giving under the strain, flew across the floor. His anger drained away, and he let out a long, weary breath.

"I'm sorry. I didn't mean to...scare you."

"I know." It was barely above a whisper, and she was shaking. He couldn't look at her, not like that, not when her trembling cruelly pounded home to him what she'd been through.

He turned and went to look for the locket. He'd seen it skittering out of sight past the end of the sofa, so he headed that way. He found it just behind the front leg, almost out of sight. It had sprung open; he hoped the blessed thing wasn't broken. He bent to pick it up. When he straightened, he looked at Rory curiously. Before he could speak, she started toward him.

"Please, I know it isn't much, and you're probably right about him, but it's their wedding picture, and Daddy was so determined I have it—"

"Why?" he asked, more than curious now.

Rory held out her hand for it. "Because it was my mother's. He left me all her things."

"Then it would have come to you anyway. Why was he so fixated on it at the hospital?"

"I don't know." Rory looked puzzled, whether at the question or his determined interest, Sean didn't know. "I don't even know why he had it with him. The nurse said he just kept talking about it and the jewelry box mother had kept it in. He made her promise to personally hand the locket to me."

She held her hand out again, then seemed to realize the locket was open. She bit her lip. "Would you...close it, please? I can't look at the picture. Not yet."

"Don't worry. You won't have to."

Her brow creased. "What?"

Silently, watching her expression, he held the locket out to her, balanced on his palm, still open and facing her. She took the locket and stared, her brows furrowing even more, and there was no doubting her bewilderment.

"I don't understand."

"Neither do I," Sean said. "Yet."

For a long moment they both stood there, staring down at the locket that held, instead of a photograph, a tiny gold key.

Chapter 12

"It has to be to her jewelry box," Rory said, stopping in her pacing. "It has a lock about this size."

"Probably," Sean agreed. "Since you said he mentioned it, as well as the locket, before he . . . died."

She heard his hesitation over the word. She wondered if he was regretting his outburst against a dead man in front of the daughter who, regardless of whether he deserved it, had loved him. Probably, but everything he'd said was true. It had been a hard thing for her to admit, that her father had been too weak to stand up to Frank and had prized his good name more than his only daughter. But it had been an even harder five years, and her image of her father had been pared down to the imperfect reality.

Rory stared again at the little key, still baffled. She sat down on the couch, a few inches away from Sean, yet close enough to feel his heat. She wished she'd picked somewhere else to sit; she couldn't think when he was so close. She couldn't do much of anything when he was so close, except yearn for things she'd thrown away: his touch, his kiss, his love.

She could have the first two, she supposed. This thing between them seemed to affect him as much as it did her. But did she want them without the third? Without the love? Was that better than not having them at all? Better than never knowing what it would have been like between them? Better than never feeling him caress her again, arousing her to a point she'd never reached with anyone but him, even though they had never actually made love?

She shuddered at the memories. Sean Holt had made her feel more than she'd ever felt before or since, and they'd never gone beyond kisses and touches. She couldn't even begin to imagine what it would be like if they did. . . .

And she was a fool to try. Or to tell herself that she could have anything of this man. It was he who had broken off each time they'd slipped into that maelstrom of sensation. It was he, no doubt fighting the attraction with bitter, painful memories, who had walked away.

She battled the hot, erotic images her silly thoughts had brought on. *Do something constructive,* she ordered herself, *instead of dreaming impossible dreams. Figure out what Daddy meant by leaving you this key.*

"I still don't get it," she said when she could trust her voice. "Why would he take the picture out and put her jewelry box key inside? He even put a drop of glue on it, so it wouldn't fall out when the locket opened."

"Did your mother have a lot of expensive jewelry?"

"Some," she admitted, "but it was mostly kept in the safe in Daddy's den. She only kept sentimental pieces in the jewelry box, like this locket and her old charm bracelet that I loved to play with, that kind of thing."

She frowned as something else occurred to her.

"What?" Sean asked.

"She never locked that box. When I was little she left it open so I could come in and play with what was in it. After she died, Daddy left it unlocked so he could look at her things and . . . remember."

Her voice trailed away brokenly. She couldn't help it. First her mother, then Sean, and now her father. She'd lost everyone she'd ever cared about, made such a mess out of her life. She tried to pull herself together, knowing that if she broke down now, she would never be able to stop.

He reached out and took the locket from her. She shivered as their fingers brushed. His hand hesitated, as if he, too, had felt the little snap of electricity. Then he snapped the locket shut and set it on the large coffee table.

"It's late," he said, "and it's been a hell of a day. We can't do anything more tonight. Get some rest, and we'll figure out what to do tomorrow."

Rory shivered again, wrapping her arms around herself this time. She felt as if she were tottering on the edge of an abyss of despair. Was it true, then, what she had feared would happen when she'd accepted his help? Was she falling in love with Sean all over again? Was she that big a fool?

She looked up at him then, but she could read nothing in his expression. "I'm sorry, Sean. About the fight, about getting you into this in the first place . . . about everything."

"Don't worry about that. But you have to decide what's next, Rory. What you're going to do."

"I know."

"The bathroom's the door on the left, and the bedroom's behind that wall," he said, gesturing.

"No," Rory said. "You . . . slept on the couch last night. I'll take it tonight."

"It's okay. It's comfortable," Sean said. Then, with a slightly weary grin, he added, "It certainly won't be the first time."

Rory shook her head. "Please. Let me take the couch." She gave him a wry smile. "I don't think Dar would appreciate my using his bed. And I wouldn't be comfortable. It's enough that he let me stay here at all."

Sean studied her for a moment. "Feeling pretty sorry for yourself?"

Instinctively she started to deny it, then stopped. Her head came up, and she held his gaze. "Yes, as a matter of fact. Very sorry. You would, too, if you'd made such a mess of everything."

One corner of his mouth lifted. "Maybe you're right. So wallow in it, lady. For now. But tomorrow you've got decisions to make."

"Yes. Tomorrow."

Sean stood up. "There's a blanket and pillow in the drawer of the coffee table."

She nodded. Sean just stood there for a moment, looking at her. Then he ran a hand through his hair. Rory had to stop her fingers from instinctively flexing, as if they could feel the heavy silk of the dark strands.

"Good night, then," he said at last.

When he'd gone, Rory sat trying to sort out her thoughts. But the only thing strong enough to divert her mind from Frank, her father and that silly key was Sean, and thinking of him only made things worse. Much worse.

Then she heard the sound of water running, and her heart caught in her throat as she realized Sean was taking a shower. She closed her eyes, as if she could shut out the images her imagination provided so easily, of his tall, straight and, despite everything, still beautiful body sleek and wet. Of soap bubbles sliding over his skin. Of her own hands, following every path laid down by those lucky bubbles . . .

She smothered a moan as a memory of that last kiss came to her, complete with those spine-chilling yet heat-provoking moments when he had cradled her breasts, caressing her nipples until she had hardly been able to keep from crying out. That memory sparked another, from long ago, of his mouth, his tongue, on that same tender flesh, tasting, suckling, nipping, until she was arching almost double, wanton in her desire for more, thrusting her breasts up to him in innocent need.

Lord, she thought now with a shiver, how had they ever stopped? More importantly, she wondered, *why* had they stopped?

And why should they now? Surely there was no reason. She knew there was no future in it, there was too much water under that particular bridge. But just once... just to know? Surely he was curious, too. He must be, to have kissed her with such heat.

But he had stopped each time, she reminded herself yet again. Except... had he, the last time? Or had the thought of Frank's possible pursuit intruded on a moment that otherwise might have gone on uninterrupted to the conclusion her body had been screaming for? And his, as well, if the state of his arousal was any indication.

At last the sound of running water stopped.

"Just go to sleep, you stupid fool," she ordered herself firmly. Even if you did go to him, he'd turn you away, and rightfully so. Do you want to be humiliated all over again? Just go to sleep.

Sleep turned out to be little help. Sean was there, too, looking down at her with passion-darkened eyes as his hands slid over her, stroking, fondling. And in sleep her mind let loose the restraints she worked so hard to maintain while she was awake. Her imagination had more to work with now, the memory of a broad, naked chest, lightly dusted with hair, a ridged, flat belly, and buttocks tautly curved. And what she had yet to see her mind was more than willing to conjecture about, using the length and thickness of the aroused bulge his briefs had barely covered as a guide to images so heated she moaned in her sleep.

And the part of him that was missing seemed inconsequential. What did a leg matter when the rest was so beautiful? When it was Sean?

Twice she sat up, awakened by her own whimpers of need, and nearly wept because she felt so bereft that it had only been a dream. She wondered if she were tumbling headlong into that abyss.

The third time she awoke, deep in the night, she did cry; she had never, ever felt so utterly alone.

It was just reaction, she told herself. Reaction to the stress of the day, to that awful—wonderful—fight with Frank, and then having to at last face Sean's family.

Then she tried to convince herself that it was that very family that had brought on this feeling. Seeing Sean and his family together. Even the detached Dar was, to some extent, a part of their loving group, making her feel even more isolated.

When that didn't work, she told herself it was the children, fiery little Katie and now the new baby. They had pounded home to her that she would never be part of that group, never be accepted as she once had been. That she would never have a Katie of her own.

She hadn't realized how important that had been to her until it was too late. It had been just her and her father since she'd been twelve, and she'd thought the bonds between Sean, Stevie, Chase and Katie were wondrous when she'd first met them all. And when they'd opened to let her in, for Sean's sake, she'd felt at home as she'd never felt since her mother had died.

But at last she had to admit that, even if all she'd been telling herself was true, her excuses melted to nothing beside the actual reason for this crushing loneliness. And the actual reason was sleeping—peacefully, no doubt—just a few feet away.

She'd wanted Sean Holt with the simple single-mindedness of youth five years ago. She wanted him now for so many different reasons that she couldn't name them all. She just knew that somehow he was the only beacon in the crushing darkness in which her soul was wandering, lost.

And how long would it be before that beacon, that saving light, disappeared? Before he walked out of her life, as she had once walked out of his?

And could she let him go, without ever warming herself with the heat of that light? She shivered at the thought. And turned to look at the wall that separated her from the only man she'd ever loved.

"Rory?" Sean raised himself up on his elbows. "What's wrong?"

She stood there at the foot of the bed, her shape, back-lighted by the dim light from the main room of the warehouse, looking oddly bulky. Then he realized that she had the blanket wrapped around her.

"Are you cold?"

It didn't seem possible. Even here near the coast it barely got down into the sixties at night, and he had long ago kicked off the single blanket on Dar's bed, leaving only the sheet. But she appeared to be almost shivering.

"Do you want another blanket?"

"Yes, I'm cold," Rory said, sounding so odd that Sean pushed himself up to a sitting position. Rory walked around the foot of the bed and came to a halt a couple of feet away. "But I don't want a blanket."

Sean drew back a little. In the faint light he couldn't read her expression, but the way she sounded was making him edgy. There was an undertone to her voice, like the faint hum of a wire stretched tight, ready to snap. He reached over and flipped on the bedside lamp.

"Rory—"

She blinked at the sudden flare of light, but her words didn't waver. "I want you, Sean."

He sucked in his breath, the simple declaration catching him as unaware and much harder than Talbot's surprise attack. The look in her eyes was a second blow. It was that hungry, wanting look again, but more intense, more stirring. Every alarm his common sense could set off was clamoring, but his body was listening only to her, to the pure, raw need in her voice. It responded in a rush that nearly made him gasp. The muscles of his thighs and lower belly tensed in response, as if all their blood supply had been stolen—which it had, he thought, feeling the sudden, slamming hardness.

"Rory," he whispered.

Her blanket slipped, baring one slender shoulder. He stared at that small expanse of skin and knew with stomach-knotting certainty that she was naked beneath the thick blue cloth.

"I want you to warm me. I'm so cold inside, Sean. I have been for so long. Sometimes I thought I was dead. But then I saw you again, and..."

She shrugged helplessly. Sean held his breath as the blanket slipped farther. He didn't know which was more shocking, her words or what the sight of that silken skin was doing to him.

"I just want to feel...real again. I haven't felt real in five years."

He let out a long breath and gave up the effort to control his unruly body; he was losing the battle, anyway. He wasn't sure he hadn't lost it the moment she'd come into the room.

"Do you want me, Sean?" she whispered. "Can you possibly?"

"I think," he grated out, "that would be tough to deny right now."

He glanced downward, but he already knew his arousal had to be obvious to her; the thin cotton of the sheet was tented over his hips. He lifted his gaze back to her face and was totally disconcerted when he saw her expression. She was looking at him as if he were some wondrous sight she'd never expected to see, a miracle when she'd given up believing in them long ago.

"Why, Rory? If it's because you're scared, or confused—"

"I am. I've never felt so alone. But that's not why."

"What, then?" His eyes narrowed as a thought occurred to him, a thought that succeeded in chilling his ardor a little. "You haven't got some crazy idea that because I helped you, you...owe me, do you?"

Her head came up as sharply as if he'd slapped her. Even through the blanket he could see her body tense. "And you think this is the only way I can pay you back?"

He hadn't meant to insult her, not really. He hadn't realized what his words would sound like. And he supposed he had come to truly believe her story and couldn't condemn her as easily as he once had.

"That's not—"

"Never mind," she said, sounding suddenly weary. "I suppose, after what I've done, I deserved that. And I do owe you. A great deal. But..." She lowered her gaze. "I've had quite enough of paying for things that way."

"Then why?"

"Can't I just...want? Want the night we never had?"

Her words made him shudder. He didn't understand himself. Here she was, offering him what he'd been aching for ever since she'd dropped back into his life again. So why the hell was he resisting? Why didn't he just take what she was offering?

"It's not that night, Rory," Sean said, his voice tight. "It will never be that night again."

He thought she shivered then, despite the blanket. "I know. I ruined that for us forever. Maybe I just want the only night we'll ever have." Her eyes met his, and held. "I don't expect any more than that. But things between us are so...unfinished. I can't help feeling that we won't be able to put the past behind us until they are."

Put the past behind us. Such simple words. He'd done it, he thought. He had put her and what she'd done behind him and gone on, although it had taken him a while—and a lot of help—to do it. Yet now here she was, wanting to bring it all back to life again.

"What do you want, Rory, one night together and then we go our separate ways? Again?"

She went very still. "I'm sorry," she said stiffly. "I should never have come in here."

She turned, her shoulders slumped in utter defeat. Stevie had looked that way once, Sean thought, when she had awakened to find Chase had left her, had cast himself back into his own personal hell to keep her safe. Sean had barely been able to stand his sister's pain then. He couldn't bear seeing Rory's now. Even if easing it brought more upon himself.

"Rory, wait."

He reached out and touched her arm. She froze, still with her back to him, as if she were afraid to look at him again. He threw back the sheet and got up to stand behind her, bracing himself with his stump on the bed.

"I can't deny I want you, even though I could give you a hundred reasons why I shouldn't."

"And a hundred reasons why this would only complicate things more?"

"Yes."

She gave a sigh. "I know. But reason doesn't seem to work when I'm around you."

He nearly laughed. It came out as a compressed, ironic chuckle. "I know the feeling. It doesn't seem fair that after five years, you can still do this to me."

"Did you ever wonder... how we stopped? Back then?"

Sean went very still. He lifted his hands to her shoulders and slowly, very slowly, turned her around. He straightened his arms, setting her slightly away from him, so she could see him. He saw her eyes widen when she realized he was naked. Her gaze lowered, and he heard her quick intake of breath. Perhaps she hadn't really looked at him, that morning in his apartment. Not this closely. Or hadn't been thinking about going to bed with him at the time. He tried not to cringe and made himself stop the instinctive movement to reach for the sheet and pull it up to hide the stump of his leg.

"This was why we stopped," he said tightly. "You'd better take a good look before you decide to stay."

Her brows furrowed, and she raised her eyes to his. Her puzzlement was unmistakable. "I don't understand. You're... oh, you mean your leg."

She blushed, and he realized she hadn't been looking at his leg at all. She'd been looking at the jutting flesh thrusting forward from the thicket of dark curls. Heat kicked through him in a fierce burst, hardening him even more. He knew then that he was lost. He could no more say no to her than he could walk away from her right now. It didn't matter that his mind was screaming at him that he was heading for trouble; it didn't matter that the memory of the pain she'd caused was still vivid in his brain... his brain didn't seem to be functioning any longer. He would just have to pray that he could take what he seemed incapable of turning down and still keep his heart intact.

"Be sure, Rory," he said hoarsely. "Be very sure you want this. Want me. Like I am." He had to stop and suck in a deep breath; he couldn't seem to get enough air. "We stopped before. I'm not sure I could now."

Her lips parted as if she were going to speak, but then she stopped. Without saying a word she stepped back. He released her shoulders, half-expecting her to turn and go, her mind changed. Then, still without speaking, her eyes fastened steadily on his, she let the blanket fall.

Sean's belly knotted again, so violently that he couldn't breathe for a moment. She stood there before him, naked, her slender body infinitely more beautiful than in even his most erotic imaginings. Her hair was a silken fall of honey-gold over her shoulders. Her breasts were full and high, and he had a sudden flash of memory, of how she had tasted, how her nipples had hardened against his tongue.

He nearly groaned aloud at the image, and his tongue moved against his teeth as if already anticipating tasting that sweetness again. His gaze slipped down over the indentation of her waist, lingered on the feminine flare of her hips and came to rest on the delta of soft, pale curls below her belly. He felt himself surge in response, and this time he did groan aloud, a throttled sound he was unable to hold back.

And then she was in his arms, and the feel of her skin against his was more than he'd ever, even in the wildest of his dreams, imagined. Suddenly he understood what she'd meant about unfinished business. They needed to resolve this. They needed an end to the unfinished dreams, or they would be haunted by them forever. He pulled her closer.

Sean felt as if he'd lost whatever strength he had left in his leg. He sank down onto the bed, and Rory went with him. He lay back, pulling her on top of him. He was wound so tightly that he thought he was going to lose control, and every time she moved the pressure built.

He felt her breasts against his chest, felt the hard points of her nipples in the center of the soft curves. He wanted more and slid his hands down her back to press her closer. At least, that was what he meant to do; he was so entranced by the silken smoothness of her skin that he spent a few moments just stroking, savoring. Then she moved again, shifting her hips, and the exquisite friction on the aroused male flesh caught between their bodies made him groan under his breath.

Rory heard it and moved again. And again. Sean had a brief impression that she was being very careful not to touch his stump. He felt a qualm, but when he intentionally moved and it brushed against her, she didn't recoil. And by then his mind was so fogged by the feel of her that he couldn't think clearly about anything other than the way she was making him feel.

But he had to think, at least for a few seconds. "Rory . . . wait . . ."

"I don't want to wait, not any longer."

"But . . . are you on something?"

For an instant she didn't answer. Then, "I won't get pregnant."

She sounded sad, Sean thought, not understanding. But then she was touching him again, and he couldn't even care that he didn't understand.

"Damn," he gasped. "You're driving me crazy."

"Good," Rory whispered, leaning close to his ear so that her breathy whisper sent a shiver through him.

"Rory, I mean it. It's been . . . a long time for me. If you don't slow down, I—"

"Good," she repeated, and before he could protest she was kissing him, hotly, fiercely, until he was drowning in the sweet sensation. She avoided the swollen area of his lower lip, but it seemed to make no difference in the amount of pure, boiling sensation that was flooding through him.

He moved his hands to her shoulders, gripping and lifting her away from him. She started to protest, then cried out in surprised pleasure when he lifted his head to nuzzle her breasts. He licked at first one nipple, then the other, bringing them to taut peaks. Then he suckled her, long and deep, until she was arching her back, moaning as she silently begged him for more. He caught one nipple gently between his teeth, flicked it with his tongue until she cried out, then he repeated the caress on her other breast.

She was moaning his name, twisting sinuously against him, and the sweet avidity of her response drove him to the edge. He wanted nothing more than to roll her onto her back and drive into her with every ounce of his strength, but he knew he couldn't. He didn't trust himself not to explode the moment his achingly taut flesh touched hers. And he didn't trust himself to do it with any kind of grace; he hadn't had much practice since the accident. In fact, he'd had damned little, only a few short, usually awkward encounters in the past eight years. So he lay back, partly because he had no choice, and partly because he was being engulfed by Rory's teasing caresses, left breathless by the line of kisses she traced along his jaw and down the cords of his neck.

When she moved downward from there to trail her lips over his chest, he groaned again. When first her lips, then her tongue, found and traced his nipples, he sucked in his breath, then let it out in a gasp.

He reached for her then, pulled her up his body until he could reach her mouth with his once more. He kissed her thoroughly and deeply, his tongue probing, darting, dancing with hers, tiny darts of sensation shooting through him whenever wet flesh met wet flesh.

He slipped one hand down her body, stroking her side, then her hip. He hesitated there, but she moved, as if tacitly giving him permission to go further. He did, parting the soft golden curls, and he groaned against her lips when his fingers found her hot and wet, her feminine flesh slick and ready for him.

He gently stroked her, searching for that sensitive spot, the knot of nerves that would make her as ready as he was. He knew when she gasped and her hips lifted to his hand that he'd found it. He began to rub in a circular motion, slow, then fast, then slow again, until her hips began to move in a similar motion.

He wanted to wait, wanted to be certain she was as hot, as ready, as he was, but he couldn't. He'd never been so aroused, so hard, so ready. He'd already waited for more than five years, and it seemed like a lifetime. He broke the kiss, his breath coming in harsh pants.

"Rory," he gasped, "I . . . can't wait . . . much longer."

"Good," she moaned as she arched against his hand again. "Neither can I."

"You'll have to do it," he managed. "I can't—ahh, damn, that feels good. . . ." His explanation faded into another groan as she moved.

"Yes," she breathed, sounding as if his words had added to an already urgent need. "Oh, yes."

She straddled him then, drawing her knees up on either side of his hips. Sean could feel her heat, his body sensing the closeness of the tempting feminine heart of her, and his arousal surged to a fullness he'd never known before. He lifted his hips up from the bed, seeking. Rory looked at him, her expression suddenly shy.

"I don't know . . . help me, Sean."

He didn't understand her shyness, but he knew that if she didn't take him in the next second, he was going to lose it completely. He put one hand on her hip and reached to guide himself with the other. He urged her gently downward, but at the first contact of his inflamed body with the yielding heat of hers he couldn't stop himself from grasping her hips and arching upward, driving into her with one long stroke.

Rory cried out his name in shocked, wondering pleasure. She nearly fell forward onto his chest, but Sean propped her up, nearly desperate for more of the incredible sensation of being buried to the hilt inside her. He lifted his hips again, feeling the hot clasp of her body around his.

"Oh!"

She made a small sound at his movement. She seemed so surprised by it all, Sean thought vaguely. But then she took a clue from his movement and began to move herself, rocking atop him in a slow, voluptuous motion that squeezed him by exquisite degrees, and suddenly he couldn't think at all.

It had been too long, and he was too close. Her body was driving him to madness, a madness unlike anything he'd ever known or even thought possible. He slid one hand down her body to where they were joined, his thumb searching out the spot that made her gasp and arch. He stroked and caressed as he fought desperately to hold back. He bit his lip until it started to bleed again and forced himself to stay perfectly still. Rory's sweet rocking had already driven him to the edge; any movement he added would send him careening over, and he didn't want to go alone. He switched to the same circular motion as before, only faster this time. Rory moaned, her body bowed, and began to move faster.

He wasn't going to make it, Sean thought. He couldn't stop himself; he could feel it boiling up low and deep inside him. The moment he realized it, Rory cried out, and never had his name sounded so sweet as it did breaking from her throat as her body began to convulse around his.

Sean bucked beneath her, his hands gripping her hips to hold her to him as he thrust upward with all his strength. He heard his own shout, a guttural cry of her name, as all the heat and need and longing of five years ripped through him in a wave of liquid fire that seared him as he gave himself up to the most explosive climax of his life.

Chapter 13

Rory let the water stream over her face, spiking her lashes, washing away the sleep that clung to her eyelids and the droplets from her cheeks. And she told herself it was the water, that she wasn't still crying, she truly wasn't.

She replaced the hand-held shower head—which, along with the sturdy plastic seat built into the shower wall, was obviously designed for Dar's use—in its bracket and reached for the shampoo. That way, she thought wryly, she could always blame her tears on suds in her eyes.

She had thought she'd become an expert at dealing with tangled emotions in the past five years, but nothing had ever prepared her for how she'd felt this morning—this afternoon, actually, she'd realized in shock when she'd gone out to the coffee table to get her watch—waking up in Sean's arms.

Her first sleepy thought had been simply that she felt marvelously rested for the first time in days, not exhausted from a restless night of little sleep, as had been her norm of late. Her second thought had been embarrassment that she had fallen asleep so abruptly, sprawled atop Sean, his body still sheathed in hers. She vaguely remembered giving a sigh of contentment before drifting off.

And that memory, the vivid image of what they had done, how it had felt, had brought her fully awake, her cheeks flaming. Her body ached in several interesting places, adding an immediacy to the scene playing back in her head. She'd been a crazed thing, wanton, wild for him, in a way she would never have thought possible. And she knew, she just knew, she'd screamed when his last touch had sent her flying into a brilliant universe of heat and sensation that mere moments before she would have sworn didn't exist.

She shivered despite the heat of the shower. Even washing had become a sensuous thing as the water slid over her, reminding her of Sean's hands stroking her, his mouth caressing her, and his body at last sliding home, filling her. Nothing in her life had ever prepared her for that, either, for the sheer pleasure of being complete, joined with the man she lo—

"Oh, God," she moaned, cutting off words that were devastatingly close to the truth. She raised her hands to her face to dash away the wetness she could no longer blame on the shower.

Her fourth thought, grim and inescapable, shattered the vision of that wondrous place where Sean had sent her: she didn't deserve this. She didn't deserve such joy, such pleasure. And she especially didn't deserve it from Sean, not after what she'd put him through. Not after what she'd become for the past five years. She had no right to this, and never would have, unless she could pull her life out of this downward spiral. Even then, it would probably be asking too much for Sean to forgive.

Were it not for the fact that she was reasonably certain his pleasure had matched hers—she had the memory of the taut planes of his face and the fierce bucking of his body beneath hers to tell her so—she wouldn't have the nerve to face him at all.

As it was, she'd slipped out of bed quietly, leaving him sleeping, thinking she could face her thoughts much better if the situation were less intimate. And if she had the slightest clue how Sean would react when he woke up.

Would he regret what they'd done? Would he resent her for coming so intimately into his life again, when he'd managed—with a lot more courage and determination than she herself had ever had—to put her and what she'd done behind him? Would he be angry this morning, or simply as confused as she was, glorying in the most incredible act of physical love she'd ever experienced, yet knowing that their lives had become infinitely more complicated because of it?

At last, reluctantly, she turned off the shower. She reached for the towel she'd gotten from a pile on a shelf behind the bathroom door and dried herself off. She dressed quickly in the clothes she'd haphazardly grabbed yesterday, light blue jeans and a paler blue silk blouse. She left her hair damp, only combing out the tangles with what she supposed was Dar's comb; it had been in the medicine cabinet next to a can of talcum powder.

She stared at that can, twin to the one in Sean's bedroom, wondering. He'd said Dar had prostheses, too; did it have something to do with that? It suddenly made sense to her, to powder skin that was going to be rubbing against something all day.... For the first time she really had a sense of the myriad of tiny details like this in the new life Sean had been forced into all those years ago.

She finished with her hair and put down the comb. She barely glanced at the bruise around her eye in the mirror. It was an unbecoming mottled yellow and purple now, and she knew that meant it was healing. It wasn't pleasant to look at, but it served as a constant reminder of what she had to do now. She picked up her watch and saw that she had lingered even longer than she'd thought.

When she got back to the bedroom Sean was awake and sitting on the edge of the bed. He had on his jeans and was pulling on his right sock. Her gaze naturally gravitated to his broad, bare shoulders, to the flex and play of the strong muscles there. She remembered all too clearly what his skin felt like, heavy satin stretched over that taut flesh, and her fingers itched to touch him. She curled them into fists and forced her eyes down to where he was tugging on his shoe. As if he'd felt her steady gaze, he looked up.

"Something wrong?" he asked, and Rory wondered if she were imagining the edge in his voice.

"I . . . no. I was just thinking."

"Don't like my shoes?"

No, she wasn't imagining it. "No. I mean, yes," she said, flustered at his tone and the cool, level look he was giving her after the incredible intimacy of last night. "I . . . they're fine. I was just wondering if you left the other one on all the time."

She flushed, hideously embarrassed at having blurted that out. But, unexpectedly, Sean answered easily.

"Yep. Doesn't make sense not to, unless I'm changing shoes altogether. Plastic foot's a little tough on them, though."

"Oh. I didn't know."

"You never asked," he said pointedly. "Ever."

He was right, she hadn't. Ever. "I . . . was afraid to. Afraid you'd think it . . . made a difference, that I was having second thoughts or something."

"I thought you just didn't want to know, didn't want to face it." He shifted his gaze to the lace he was tying. "Like you didn't want to touch my leg last night."

She paled a little. Is that what had him so edgy? "I didn't know . . . I thought . . . I didn't know if it hurt or not."

His head came up. "Hurt?"

"Does it? Still, I mean?"

He let out a breath. "No. It's...sensitive, at the tip, but it doesn't hurt."

"Oh." She felt a little foolish. But it would be more foolish, she realized, to let misunderstandings grow as they had five years ago. "I was afraid to ask that...before. I didn't want you to think it mattered to me."

He shook his head in wonder. "You were going to marry me. Didn't you think you had a right to know what you'd be dealing with?"

"I did, sort of. I...read a lot. And I asked Stevie."

He blinked, looking startled. "You did?"

She nodded. "She told me how they tried to save your knee, because it would have been so much easier for you later, but it was too badly damaged. And that you had a very hard time at first, but you came around, and pretty soon they were showing you off as their star pupil, and you were giving demonstrations at clinics for people who didn't believe they'd ever walk, let alone run, again."

"Stevie talks too much," he muttered, but he looked almost pleased. Then, after a moment, he said, looking like a man probing a hornet's nest he wasn't certain was empty, "You were up rather early."

"I...yes. But for the first time in ages, I slept so wonderfully...."

Her voice faded away, and she felt herself blush furiously.

Sean smiled then, as if relieved. "So did I."

"Sean, last night was..."

He waited, watching her, saying nothing. He was doing it again, she thought, using silence as a tool. She wondered how often he got more than the other person ever intended to say. With her, at least, it seemed to happen all too often.

She let out a long, audible breath. "It was so many things. I don't think I know them all yet. But there's one thing I do know."

"What's that?"

"It's time for me to take back my life. Past time."

"Yes."

Was it always so easy, so black-and-white, when you weren't in the middle of the forest? Her mouth twisted at the mangled axiom, but she slogged on, more determined than she'd ever been in her life.

"I'm going to start," she said. "Right now. By throwing that man out of *my* house. And my life." She was picking up momentum, the words tumbling out. "Then I'm going to find out why Daddy left me that key. And then I'm going to—"

"Whoa," he said, holding up a hand. "You sound like you're ready to run out the door this instant."

"I am," she said flatly. "I've waited far too long already."

"You'd better think this through, Rory. Talbot doesn't seem the type to give up and quietly go away just because you tell him to. And we already know he's not the most even-tempered of guys. Your eye and my lip attest to that."

"But it's my house. That's the one thing Daddy left only to me. I'll have the police throw him out, if I have to. I mean, it's not like we're . . . married."

She stumbled over the word and lowered her eyes. Color rose in her cheeks, not the blush of embarrassment, but the humiliated flush of shame. God, she hated what she'd done. And sometimes she hated herself, as well. Despite all her youthful arrogance, she'd proved she could be bought after all.

"Don't, Rory."

Her head came up sharply. "What?"

"Hating yourself won't accomplish anything."

Her eyes widened. "How did you...?"

"I recognized the look. I've seen it in the mirror a time or two, remember? I hated what I saw. What I couldn't do anymore. What I couldn't *be* anymore."

"That's different," she said softly. "That wasn't...your fault."

"Believe me, that doesn't make one damned bit of difference when I get out of bed and fall flat on my face because I've forgotten and stepped off on a leg that isn't there anymore. Or when I used to dream that I was looking in a mirror and I was whole, and while I stood there watching, my leg would start to bleed, and then just rot away."

Her stomach knotted up. "Oh, Sean..."

"Feeling sorry for me? Good. Maybe you won't have time to feel so sorry for yourself."

"Sorry for myself?" she said, startled.

"What would you call it?" He shrugged. "You can't change the past any more than I can. You *can* change the future, but not if you don't get on with it."

His gaze shifted, and she realized she had once more reached up to finger her mother's locket.

"Maybe you should figure that out first," he said, indicating the golden heart. "If your father went to all that trouble and was so worried about it even when he had to know he was dying, it must mean something."

She nodded, much more composed today, able to accept his mention of her father's death without any visible sign of emotion.

"I know. It *was* so important to him," she said slowly. "The nurse said he was very insistent, even... at the end."

"Do you know where the box is now?"

"He finally put it away, but it was still unlocked. I found it once, a couple of years after Mother died, in a drawer in his desk."

Sean reached out and lifted the locket, letting the backs of his fingers brush lightly over her silken skin. She shivered, and he drew back, staring at his own hand as if he'd felt the same rush of hot, vivid memories his touch had evoked in her.

"Assuming you're right," he said after a moment, "and also assuming there's no point to hiding a key unless you've locked the lock that it opens...why would he have suddenly locked a jewelry box that had been left open for years?"

"I guess...because there was a reason to now?"

Sean nodded. "It's the only thing that makes sense. He put something there that he didn't want anyone to find. Except you, apparently."

"You think he...hid something there?"

"I don't know." Sean shrugged. "But I think the more knowledge we have, the better off we'll be."

We? She stared at him, fighting down a flurry of emotions: surprise, hope, and, underlying everything else, fear. Fear for him. He didn't know what they were dealing with, not really. He didn't know how far Frank would go.

"No, Sean. You've already gotten hurt because of me. It's my problem—"

"Your friend Talbot," Sean said flatly, "made it my problem when he split my lip yesterday."

"That's what I mean. He's a vicious man, and he doesn't like being beaten. By anyone, but..." She lowered her eyes as her voice trailed off.

"But being beaten by me would be worse? He wouldn't like losing to 'half a man,' is that it?"

She didn't meet his gaze but gave him a nod. It hurt to concede it, but it was true. Frank was rarely bested; having it done by Sean would eat at him like acid.

"That's exactly why I'm going to be right there every step of the way," Sean said, his voice echoing her earlier determination.

She lifted her gaze then, searching his face. "Sean, this isn't because of... last night, is it? I mean, you don't think you... *have* to help me now, do you?"

Sean's jaw tightened, but his voice was even. "I suppose I had that coming, because I insulted you the same way."

She paled. "I didn't mean—"

"Neither did I."

"I'm sorry," she said, her voice frail. "I just didn't want you to think I... expected you to help, because of... because..."

"Because we made love last night?"

She nodded, a small, helpless gesture that belied the angry confidence she'd been brimming with just moments ago. She didn't know where it had gone, but when it came to the thought of Sean being hurt, she couldn't hang on to any of her determination. He'd been hurt too much already.

"I just want this over and done," he said at last.

She winced, at his tone as much as his words. He'd sounded a little raw all of a sudden, as if he were only now facing the ramifications of what they'd done in the full light of morning. As if it had taken him years to swat the last of the stinging hornets she'd turned loose on him before, and now he was wondering if he'd walked right back into the swarm all over again.

She couldn't blame him. If last night had shown her anything, it was just how big a fool she'd been. Just how much she'd thrown away. And it had made clear to her that she didn't deserve to get any of it back. At least, not yet. Not until she'd done everything possible to change what she could. And then? Only Sean could decide. But she couldn't blame him if he wanted it over and done with, as he'd said, so that he could walk away and get on with his life again.

"I understand," Rory said, her voice very low. "And please don't think that I believed...one night would change anything. I'm not that big a fool."

"I'm not sure which one of us is the fool," he muttered.

She cringed inwardly but made herself go on. She might not deserve his love, but perhaps she could regain his respect, at least.

"What you said was right. I have to get on with it. And I have to do it myself, Sean. I got myself into it, I have to get myself out of it."

"You had a little help," he said gruffly.

That sign of empathy, that little bit of understanding, somehow stiffened her resolve.

"You were right about that, too. I can't change the past. Can't change what my father did. Or what I did. All I can do is stop it here. And make sure that Frank is stopped."

Sean studied her for a moment. "Are you going to fight him for the company, too?"

"I can't even think about that, not yet. And I don't know enough about business. I'd have to find someone who does to help."

"I might know someone," Sean said slowly. "I met him a few months ago. His name's Gunnar Royce, and he specializes in helping companies in trouble." He grimaced. "And if Talbot is as bad at business as he is at fighting, Sheridan Manufacturing will be in trouble soon."

"Thank you. Maybe later. But the house has to come first." She gave him a wry, sideways look. "I know it's silly, but it's like the house is...a symbol or something. It's the one thing that's truly mine, that I *feel* is mine, and that I want to fight for. The company...that was Daddy's baby. It never meant much to me."

"Except for providing all that money you grew up with."

He sounded mocking rather than sarcastic, but Rory didn't react to his tone, simply responded to the words. "I know you won't believe this—Daddy never did—but money means very little to me."

He lifted a brow at her. "Oh?"

"It couldn't give me the only two things I ever truly wanted."

The brow came down. "What things?"

"It couldn't save my mother's life. Or give you back your leg."

Sean drew away sharply, staring at her. Rory didn't know if he believed her, and at the moment, she didn't care. For the first time she truly believed what she'd been saying. She couldn't change the past. She wasn't even sure she could make up for it. But she could stop its effect on the future. And stop it she would.

"I'm going back home," she said.

Sean blinked. "What?"

"It *is* my home. And I'm going back to it. I'm going to get my mother's jewelry box and find out why Daddy left me this key. And when Frank comes back, I'm going to throw him out."

"Rory, slow down. You know he's not going to just leave."

"Then I'll call the police and have them throw him out."

"Are you really ready for that? Ready for the questions they'll ask? You'll have to prove it's really your house."

"You're the one who wanted me to call the police in the first place," she pointed out, exasperation creeping into her voice.

"I know. But you said you couldn't, because of what Talbot knew about your father."

The old pain stabbed at her, but it was more distant now, as if she'd taken a step back from it. "Daddy's dead. Frank can't hurt him anymore."

"But he can still smear his name in every newspaper in the state. It wouldn't be any less newsworthy now that he's dead. Are you ready for that to happen, Rory?"

She tried to stifle a shudder. "I . . . don't know."

"Then you'd better think about it. All of it."

She felt suddenly weary, the exhilaration of the night spent in his arms fading before the weight of things that had only been postponed. She made herself get up, made herself move, back and forth across the room, from the weight set to the big television, then back again.

Finally she stopped her restless pacing in front of the cross-country ski machine. She stared at it. The upright post in front had been shortened, and in place of the usual foot straps, the skis had a built-up arrangement that obviously allowed Dar to use it on his one knee and what remained of his left leg. She studied it for a moment while she strove for calm. Then she turned to look at Sean.

"So you think I should just . . . what? Go back to him?"

"You know better than that," he retorted sharply.

"Then what? Just walk away? Let him have it all? Let him win?"

"I didn't say that, either. All I said was slow down. Think about it. It's better to know everything you can before you jump in."

She leaned against the belly pad of the ski machine. "With both feet?" she muttered.

"If you've got 'em."

Her brows furrowed, then lifted in shocked realization. "Sean, I didn't mean anything by it. It was just a figure of speech, really—"

"Rory," he said gently, "it was a joke."

She blinked. "It was?"

"I don't expect them to rewrite the entire English language just because some phrases don't fit me anymore. So feel free to say 'stand on your own two feet,' 'haven't got a leg to stand on,' 'two left feet' and any of the rest of them. My feelings won't be hurt."

Rory stared at him, shaking her head slowly in wonder. Was this really the same Sean who had once gone to such extremes to keep her from ever facing the reality of his loss? She wondered what this Sean would say, had they just met, when the time came to tell her about his leg. She had a feeling it would be quite different from the tense, nervous explanation she'd gotten five years ago.

She took a deep breath to steady herself. "All right," she said. "What do you think I should do first?"

His gaze flicked down to the golden locket, then back to her face. "I've been thinking about your father."

"Join the club," she said, barely even trying to keep the bitterness out of her voice anymore.

"I mean last night, when I couldn't sleep. Before..."

His words trailed off, and Rory saw color tinge his cheeks. Suddenly she felt better; he was as confused as she was over what had happened between them. And perhaps just as affected by the steamy memories.

"What were you thinking?" she prompted.

Sean shook his head, as if to free himself from whatever images gripped him. I know the feeling, she thought, but waited silently, trying, for once, his method of persuasion. He looked at her for a long moment before he finally answered her question with one of his own.

"Did you know your father made a sizable donation to the Laurel Tree building fund?"

Her brows rose in surprise. "Your project?"

Sean nodded.

"No, I didn't."

"He did. Enough to put the fund over the top. We wouldn't have been able to start for another six months if it hadn't been for his money. That's what I came to talk to you about that morning, at the house."

Rory listened in astonishment as Sean went on, explaining what Chase had told him about Jacob Sheridan's insistence on making this donation, and that he had known that Sean would be directly involved.

"I don't understand," she said at last. "Daddy was never much for...charitable donations. He always had his money too tied up in other things."

"I guessed as much. That's why it's been nagging at me ever since I found out."

"But why do you think—"

"I'm not sure. But I've been thinking, wondering really ...what if Talbot was right?"

Rory gaped at him. "Right? About what?"

"Right to be worried about...dramatic deathbed reversals."

She frowned. "What are you saying?"

"I'm saying, what if your father had second thoughts?"

"About what?"

"About what he'd done. Maybe he even felt guilty or something."

Rory's eyes widened. "You mean you think he made the contribution to Laurel Tree to...make up for what he did to you? For what he said that day?"

Sean shrugged. "It's the only thing that makes any sense to me."

Rory's eyes were unfocused as she wrestled with the idea. "It does," she whispered at last. "It does make a weird kind of sense. Daddy always thought money was the way to make everything all right." The memories swirled up, dark and painful. "Even when all his wealth couldn't save Mother, he still wouldn't give up. He would have flown in every specialist in the world if she hadn't finally begged him to stop."

"If we're right," Sean said softly, "then I can't believe that he would feel compelled to make it up to *me* but leave *you*...like he did."

She came back to the present with an almost audible snap. "He wouldn't," she said, knowing he was right. "He wouldn't."

"Then I think the first thing we need to do," he said, reaching out once more to touch the locket, this time carefully avoiding touching her skin, "is find out what's in that jewelry box."

Rory's heart was hammering so loudly that she was amazed Sean couldn't hear it in the confines of the car. They'd taken all the precautions they could think of. Sean, using a made-up name, had called Sheridan Manufacturing and talked to Jacob's secretary; Rory had known Deanna would recognize her voice immediately. The woman had advised him—rather cheerlessly, Sean said—that Mr. Talbot was indeed in Mr. *Sheridan's* office. Sean had simply said he would stop by later and hung up. Talbot was apparently not, he told Rory then, making any new friends at the office.

They had driven in silence back to La Pacifica. After checking for any sign of the black sedan, or anyone else following them, they had pulled around to the street behind Rory's house. They had decided to go in the way she'd come out, through the back, in case her shadow was watching the house to see if she would return.

Rory used the cellular phone Sean had borrowed from Dar's place to call the private number to her father's office, just in case Deanna had been ordered to say Frank was there when he really wasn't, in case Rory called. She knew they were risking tipping him off, but better that than walking in on him if he were lying in wait inside the house.

Frank had answered in the middle of the first ring, his growl of her name sounding almost savage.

"Aurora?"

She shivered, suddenly unable to move.

"I know that's you, you bitch. No one else would call this number. You'd better—"

Sean had silently taken the phone from her then and cut Frank off in mid-tirade. That was when she'd turned to look at him, her heart pounding.

"Let's go," he said, checking his watch. "It may take him a few minutes to decide what to do, but we can't count on it. We have to assume he's already on his way here. We've got maybe six minutes, eight tops."

She nodded and scrambled out of the car. It was her fault Sean was mixed up in this; she couldn't fail him now. She led the way to the side gate and across the Gerards' spacious, elaborately terraced backyard. She heard Pepper barking inside the house, and called to him. He subsided to a muffled whine.

She wondered if Sean would make it over the Gerards' back fence all right, but by literally giving his left leg a hand, he seemed to manage it fine. Those shoulders and arms, she thought, would get him over just about anything. He even landed easily, and started moving toward the house before she did. So far, so good, Rory thought as she ran to the back door.

She realized she'd spoken too soon when her key wouldn't open the lock. She stared at it blankly for a moment before she realized what must have happened.

"Damn him," she swore in frustration. "He's had the locks changed!"

It threw Sean only for a second. "Can you get in the same way you got out before?"

Her expression cleared. "Yes! That window isn't even alarmed, it's so small." She eyed his shoulders. "But you'll never get through it."

"Come down and open the door once you get in. It's going to eat up some time, but I don't want you alone in there."

She wasn't about to argue; she didn't want to be alone in there, either.

They moved quickly to the edge of the concrete, and Sean hoisted her easily atop the patio roof. She ran to the window, hoping that Frank hadn't locked it after her escape. She breathed a sigh of relief when she found it open, and looked in to see the bathroom still strewn with the things she'd piled behind the door to slow him down. She grabbed the windowsill and started to pull herself up.

She was so intent that she didn't realize Sean had pulled himself up after her—those shoulders and arms again—until he came up behind her and lifted her, making what had been proving a tricky scramble easy.

Rory slipped inside and ran swiftly to the alarm panel and shut off the system, breathing a sigh of relief when her code worked. Frank hadn't gotten around to changing that yet, apparently. Sean was back down and at the door by the time she made it there to unlock it.

"Three minutes," was all he said. She nodded, her heart still hammering in her chest as she turned and ran down the long hallway to the big double doors of her father's—it would never be Frank's—den at the front of the house.

They were locked. For a second time she stared at a doorknob blankly. These doors had never been locked in her life.

"I'd forgotten they even could be locked," she whispered as Sean caught up with her.

"We don't have time for subtlety here," he said, backing up and glancing around. One corner of his mouth lifted in a crooked grin. "Stupid," he muttered.

She half expected him to do something dramatic, like try to batter the sturdy doors open, but he merely took out a pocket knife—the same knife, she realized in shock, that she'd given him years ago, after falling in love with the beautifully inlaid turquoise handle—and proceeded to lift the bolts out of the hinges on one of the double doors. They were conveniently on this side of the doors. Or stupidly, she thought, realizing now the reason for his comment. In less than a minute the door was leaning awkwardly to one side and they were in the den.

She had the jewelry box in her hands in seconds. It was heart-wrenchingly familiar; about six inches high and deep by ten inches long; smooth; lacquered ebony with an oriental design painted in red and inlaid with mother-of-pearl on the top. A moment's inspection told her it was indeed locked. She nodded to Sean.

"We're on borrowed time now," he said.

They went quickly back out past the sagging door. They'd known coming in that they wouldn't have time to cover their tracks. Frank would know someone had been here, and it wouldn't take much for him to figure out who. Especially when he realized the alarm had been shut off. She thought about resetting it to make it look like a burglar had just come in the window they'd left open, but she didn't want to take the time, and besides, with nothing else missing, Frank wouldn't be fooled for long.

"Maybe we should have trashed the house," Sean said as they went out the back door, as if he'd been thinking the same thing she had.

"No time," Rory said, breathless from adrenaline as much as exertion. "Besides," she added with grim honesty, "I'm not sure I don't want Frank to know it was me."

"First salvo?"

"Something like that."

Sean grinned at her then, crookedly, and despite her nerves, her anger, her confusion over their future—if they even had one—she found herself grinning back.

They were at the wall when they heard the sound of screeching tires as a car rounded a turn at high speed. Sean glanced swiftly at his watch.

"Frankie's been speeding," he said mildly. "Up and over," he said to Rory, giving her a leg up. He made it so easy, practically tossing her over the wall. He went after her with an ease that belied any handicap at all, and he was on the ground and safely out of sight before they heard Frank's roar of rage echoing from within the house.

They were back in the car and several miles away before Rory's adrenaline ebbed enough for her to even think about opening the box. She snapped apart the locket but couldn't break the bond of the glue that held the key. She made a sound of frustration, and Sean glanced at her.

He pulled into a parking lot behind a building and stopped in the shade of an overhanging tree. He left the motor running, but reached over and pried the key loose. He took a moment to scrape off the excess glue with his thumbnail, then handed it to her.

Rory held her breath as she slid the little golden key into the matching lock. It turned, then clicked. She lifted the lid of the box.

She found the bright red costume jewelry earrings she'd loved to play with as a child. Wrapped in a piece of torn newspaper she found the gold chain bracelet that had so entranced her—she'd known each of the tiny charms by heart, and had loved each one. She smiled sadly when she found the stack of silver bangles—she'd clanged them incessantly on her tiny wrist, until her mother had pleaded for relief and suggested ice cream as a distraction.

When she had the jewelry out, she began to inspect the box itself. Her father must have hidden whatever it was beneath the lining or something, she thought. She pried, poked and probed. She lifted the red satin, felt into every corner.

She opened each tiny drawer and felt under them, and even turned the whole box upside down to check the underside.

It was several desperate moments before she admitted the truth. Except for the cheap jewelry she'd already taken out, the box was empty.

"Dar doesn't open his home often," Sean had replied rather gruffly, concentrating on stirring the eggs, "but when he does, he doesn't put limits on it."

But I wish he did, he'd thought as he watched her pace in the robe that was too big for her. She was covered from her shoulders to past her knees, and she had pulled it firmly around her and belted it securely. There was no casually seductive gap at the neckline, nor any danger that it was going to slip from her shoulders, as she could have arranged easily enough. Instead she wore it like armor, even turning the shawl collar up to provide more coverage. It didn't matter. Sean was all too aware of the slender and probably nude body beneath it.

He was still too aware of it as he watched her continue to pace.

"But I don't understand!" she said yet again. "Why would Daddy go to all that trouble—"

"Rory, stop. You've been chewing at this ever since we got back and not getting anywhere. It's late. Chew on dinner, instead." He grimaced wryly. "And the way I cook eggs, 'chew' is the right word."

He was rewarded for his effort at humor with a fleeting smile and a stop to her nervous traversing of the room. Rory sat down and actually picked up the fork that was on the plate, buried in the pile of eggs, which had, despite Sean's words, come out nicely fluffy. She was still distracted, but she was eating, probably without even realizing it, he thought, but that didn't really matter. She was wound so tight that he was afraid of what was going to happen when she finally let down. When she admitted that their excursion into breaking and entering had been for nothing.

The problem was, he didn't understand any better than she did. He'd fully expected something to be in the box. Nothing else made sense. He tried to quiet his questions with the hard-won knowledge that often things in this world never made sense, but it wasn't working very well.

He ate without much awareness of what he was doing. There was just too much careening around in his head; the mystery of the key; the lingering adrenaline after their narrow escape from Talbot; the ever-present warnings of a mind still lingering on the memory of past pain; beneath it all, the vivid, breath-stealing images of last night, of Rory naked in his arms, crying out his name in a voice husky with passion.

It seemed as if he'd waited a lifetime for that moment, and he wondered with a shiver of trepidation if he was losing the battle to keep his heart intact, if he'd lost the line between what his body wanted and what his emotions were willing to risk. He wondered if, when his body finally decided to listen to the warnings of his mind, it would be too late. If it wasn't already.

It couldn't be, he told himself. He couldn't have forgotten the pain of five years in only five days, could he?

But when he looked up from his plate to catch her staring raptly at his bare chest, he was very much afraid he knew the answer to that question. He wished that she had some other clothes to put on, and that he'd put his own shirt back on, but most of all he wished that they both didn't have this tendency to want to play with fire.

He tried to concentrate on eating. They did a creditable job on the makeshift dinner, and then Rory silently got up and gathered the plates.

"I can do that," Sean said.

"You cooked, I'll clean," she said.

He shrugged and let her go. He wandered over to the coffee table where Rory had set the jewelry box down. He was tempted to pick it up, but she had already examined it half a dozen times, and she would know better than he if there was anything different about it.

He sat down, staring at the box and the small pile of trinkets beside it. He flicked the silver bangles with a finger. They jingled almost merrily, belying his mood. He hooked a finger and lifted the chain bracelet out of the cushioning wad of newsprint it had been in, studying the dozen tiny charms that clanged together.

The bracelet was still dangling from his finger when Rory came back and sat beside him. They had come that far, he supposed; she no longer carefully separated herself from him. He wasn't sure if that made him feel better or scared him to death.

"I used to love to play with that," she said softly, looking at the bracelet. "My mother would make up a story about each charm, where it had come from and why. The angel was the one who brought me to her. The pony was the one I had wished for when I was five."

She reached out to touch the tiny golden cocker spaniel. The charms clanged together again. Her voice was sadly tender when she went on.

"And this was for Charlie, my dog. He died when I was ten. Mother bought this charm afterward. She used to tell me it was because Charlie's love needed a place to go that would always be close to me, so it would always be there when I needed to find it...."

Her voice had become choked, and it was all Sean could do to keep from pulling her into his arms and comforting her.

"Your mother sounds...like a very special woman," he said, a little awkwardly.

"She was. I'm glad she never knew—"

Rory cut herself off abruptly, but Sean knew what she'd been about to say. He wondered how differently things might have gone had her mother been alive five years ago; somehow he couldn't see the woman who had made a simple, inexpensive charm bracelet a magical thing for her child letting that child be sold to save her father's pride and reputation.

Fighting off emotions he was wary of—perhaps he wasn't that much better off than Dar after all—Sean asked hastily, "What about the tennis racket?"

Rory hesitated, then accepted the diversion. She fingered the charm and the bracelet jangled. "She'd wanted to be a tennis player when she was in school. She said the racket was for all the dreams that never came true. You should never give them up completely, she said, because sometimes the dreaming is as important as the doing."

Barbara Sheridan could have taught Maggie Holt a few things about teaching children, Sean thought with a pang. How had such a woman wound up married to a cold-hearted man like Jacob Sheridan? Or had he only become that way after she had died? He could see where the loss of a woman like that would change a man, perhaps forever. Losing Rory had certainly changed him forever.

And up until five days ago, he would no more have put Rory in the category of a woman like that than he would have challenged Dar to a marathon wheelchair race. The thought that he would even think about doing it now made him even more edgy. That, or the noise of the bracelet was really getting on his nerves.

"What about the keys?" he asked, wrenching his attention back to safer ground. "And why the silver one? It looks like just a regular key."

Rory looked at him quizzically. "What silver one? There's only one key on there."

"Only one gold one," Sean corrected, holding up the charm, trying to ignore the inevitable jangling. "But there's this silver one on the other end."

Rory shook her head, looking puzzled as she sat forward. Sean held the bracelet up for her, the silver key looking out of place amid the dangling—and noisy—gold charms. She took it, catching the unmatched piece between two fingers.

"I don't understand," she said slowly. "I was going to take this with me when I left, but I didn't want Frank to find it. If he knew how much it meant to me . . . he'd destroy it. After he taunted me with the threat of doing it long enough, of course."

She sounded thoroughly bitter, and Sean couldn't blame her. If he'd ever wanted revenge, he would have gotten it now, with the knowledge that she'd been living in hell for five years. That it was a hell of her own—and her father's—making didn't seem to matter to him anymore.

The annoying sound of the bracelet didn't matter now, either. What mattered was what Rory obviously hadn't realized yet. But before he could speak, she had steadied herself, as if she were drawing strength from this token of her mother's love.

"So I decided to leave it with Daddy," she said. "But this key wasn't there then. I know it wasn't. I would have noticed. It's so obviously different, just a key, not a charm. And it's fastened on with just a piece of wire."

"I know," Sean said softly, waiting for her to get there. She did suddenly, her gaze shooting to his face, her eyes widening.

"It wasn't there," she whispered. Then, excitedly, "This is it, isn't it? This is what Daddy meant me to find!"

"I think it must be," Sean agreed.

"Oh, God." Rory's voice was still barely above a whisper. "We weren't wrong. We weren't."

"Now all we have to do is figure out what it goes to." Sean leaned back, considering, turning over possibilities in his mind. "It can't be his desk, because that's where the box was."

"He lost those keys years ago, so he never kept anything important in there anyway. And Frank already had office keys, since he's a partner, so it wouldn't be to anything there."

"I presume it isn't a key to that safe you mentioned?"

"No. It's a combination safe." She grimaced. "Frank's already checked it out, anyway. He made me give him the combination so he could see what was in there."

She smiled then, a wintry smile that didn't reach her eyes. "He wasn't happy when all he found were the insurance papers on the house and the pink slip to Daddy's car. Even mother's good jewelry was gone. I think he was hoping to sell it."

Rory was running her finger over the key, as if its shape held the answer. Sean had noticed there was a number stamped on the side, and an odd etched design, but nothing else. No name, no lettering, no clue to whatever the little key unlocked.

"Okay, let's start with the size," Sean said. "It's bigger than the jewelry box key, but too small to be a car or door key. Or a post office box, at least here at the local branch."

"Too small for the lockers at Daddy's club, too," Rory put in.

Sean nodded. "There's no brand name stamped on it, so it's probably not a padlock key."

"It's too big to be a diary key," Rory mused.

"Okay, so what would have a lock this small?" Sean asked. Rory lifted the bracelet, and it jangled again. Sean grimaced. "And how the hell do women stand to wear these, anyway? That constant jangling would drive me crazy."

Rory smiled. "The sound is part of the attraction."

Sean shook his head. "Must be a female thing."

"Sure," Rory agreed easily. "Like jangling spurs are a male thing."

Sean blinked. His eyes narrowed as he stared at her. And deep down, buried in the depths of her eyes, he saw the faintest glint of humor.

"I've never," he intoned with great dignity, "worn spurs in my life."

"Too bad," Rory shot back. "Most women think they're sexy."

That was skating far too close to dangerously thin ice. Talking about "sexy" with Rory was not something he wanted to get into. He was in enough trouble already, and he had little doubt as to where a conversation like that would lead. Especially when Rory was like this, when he was seeing the girl he'd loved in the woman she'd become.

"The key," he reminded her, his voice stern.

She turned her attention back to it, but then gave him a quick sideways look. "Don't feel bad," she teased. "Daddy felt the same way about the noise. That's probably why he wrapped it up like that—" she gestured at the crumpled piece of newspaper "—to keep it from rattling."

Sean wasn't sure he liked the idea that he and Jacob Sheridan had agreed on anything, even something as trivial as the noise of a charm bracelet, but he was too taken aback that Rory had been able to maintain her smile while talking about her father to worry overmuch about it.

"Wise man," he muttered, and reached for the bracelet. Surprised, she released it. He quickly tugged loose the silver key, handed it back to her, then reached for the torn piece of newsprint to wrap up the noisy piece of jewelry again.

"If it's not a door key," Rory said, fiddling with the key, "or a safe, or a desk . . . maybe a file cabinet? But where?" She tapped the key with one slender finger. "And how on earth do we find it? We can't just—"

"It's not a file cabinet." Sean knew he sounded odd; he could hear it himself.

"Oh," Rory said, sounding deflated. Then, as his tone registered with her, she frowned. "How can you be so sure?"

Wordlessly he handed her the piece of paper the bracelet had been wrapped in. She looked puzzled but took it, glancing at both sides, wrinkled but still readable after he'd smoothed it with his hands.

"I don't understand," she said, looking again at what appeared to be a section of the stock market section.

"The other side," Sean said quietly.

She turned it over. She looked, then raised her eyes to his, her expression doubtful. "An ad for a bank?"

"Read it."

With a barely concealed sigh, she did, murmuring parts out loud as if they would make more sense to her that way.

"...six-month CDs...highest interest...full-service bank...free checking, safe-deposit boxes, traveler's checks...home equity credit lines—"

Her breath caught, and Sean knew it had hit her. Her eyes, now wide with a combination of hope and excitement, flew back to his.

"Safe-deposit boxes!"

He nodded. "I don't think it was coincidence that your father chose that particular piece of newspaper to wrap that key in."

She looked at the ad again. "But he never used this bank. It's just a small local one, too small to handle Sheridan Manufacturing."

He leaned back against the sofa cushions. "Maybe that's why he chose it. Because he'd never done business there."

He could almost see her mind racing. "Because there's no way he could be connected with it." Then, her voice rising slightly as she ran with it, "And he knew Frank would check into all of his business dealings at his regular bank."

Sean nodded. Joy flooded Rory's face, and in that moment he was looking at the girl he'd loved, the girl so open and honest he'd often felt he could see right through to her soul. He'd called himself a fool when she'd betrayed him, a fool who couldn't see past a pretty, lying face. He'd spent a long time not trusting anyone, and longer not trusting himself.

"You're right, Sean, I just know you are!" She was staring at him, looking almost transported. "I can feel it.

Daddy did leave something, something that will help. I'm certain of it!''

So now who's the fool? Sean thought wryly as her faith in her father surged back anew. And then, before he had time to linger on the speculation, Rory had thrown her arms around him.

"Thank you," she said, her voice exultant. "God, thank you, Sean. You had no reason to believe me, to help me, but you did.... Maybe deep down I knew you would. Maybe that's why I called you that night."

She was clinging to him, her body twisted so her face could burrow against his chest as she audibly gulped back tears. He felt the warmth of her against him, felt the flutter of her lashes brushing the skin of his chest. Her breath feathered over his left nipple, and he felt it draw up tight. He had a sudden vision of her moving to taste that suddenly aroused flesh, and it was all he could do not to move, not to silently beg her to do just that.

He tried to hold back, more wary now than ever, but at last, cursing himself for his lack of will, he put his arms around her. He reined in his soaring senses. She had given him no indication—except for those hungry looks he'd occasionally caught—that she wanted anything more than help from him tonight. So he tried to turn his thoughts to just that.

"Rory," he said softly, "we'll check it out tomorrow, but don't get your hopes too far up. The higher you fly, the harder you crash."

She tilted her head back to look up at him. Her eyes were suddenly clear of tears, instead wide with an expression of sadness that was so intense he could hardly bear to look at her.

"And you know all about that, don't you?" she asked, her voice sounding like the look she wore. "I'm so sorry, Sean. I—"

He cut her off with a finger pressed to her lips. "I know." He let out a compressed breath. The emotional strain of the past few days had been the worst, he decided. He would take physical exhaustion anytime. "And I believe you mean it."

She sighed. "But it doesn't matter, does it?"

"I don't know how I feel right now, Rory. I understand why you did it, but I just don't know.... But don't apologize anymore."

"I feel like I could never apologize enough. Even if it doesn't make any difference to you."

"What do you want me to say?" Sean asked wearily. "I said I understand. Maybe I've even forgiven. That's all I'm sure of, right now. What else do you want?"

"What I can't have," she whispered.

Then, twisting in his arms, she kissed him. Lightly at first, a mere brush of her lips over his. But then she shifted again, pressing closer, her mouth lingering, as if she were savoring the taste of him.

His body began to heat despite his efforts to control his response. Her hands slid over his chest, warm and stroking. When she began to nibble gently at his lower lip, again carefully avoiding the sore spot, he stiffened, resisting the tiny darts of fire that shot through him.

"Just once more, Sean," Rory whispered, as if she'd sensed his resistance. "I know this doesn't change anything between us, but... let me take this with me. So I'll know forever that it really can be beautiful, not ugly and degrading."

Her words took his breath away. For so long he'd been beyond selective to nearly celibate, rarely daring to risk, because he was the one who'd needed reassurance. Now Rory was coming to him for the same reassurance, and that was such a turnaround that he didn't quite know how to deal with it.

Five days, his mind screamed at him. It's too damned fast. You can't resolve all that's gone between you in five days. *Have sex with her if you have to, but keep your damned heart intact. Don't get yourself tangled up with her again. If you get involved, she'll hurt you again.* All the warnings, all from people who loved him, swirled in his head. And he knew every one of them was right.

But the warnings didn't matter anymore, because Rory was kissing him fiercely, her hands sliding caressingly over his shoulders and upward, until her fingers threaded through his hair. Her touch lit fires in him as only she had ever been able to do, and he knew that, although he might try, he could never resist her. And he wasn't sure any longer that he wanted to.

He felt the wet velvet brush of her tongue over his lips and opened them automatically. She gave a little sigh, but instead of probing forward, she continued to trace his lips with a feathery touch, as if she were a child tasting a sweet, postponing the moment when she would plunge ahead to savor the full treat. The tip of her tongue flicked to the corner of his mouth at the same moment her fingertips found and stroked his nipples, and he was startled at the sudden surge of sensation that made him suck in his breath.

As if that had been the signal she was waiting for, Rory invaded his mouth, stroking, seeking, and Sean felt a shiver ripple down his spine as his body tightened in a rush. His hands went instinctively to her shoulders, and before he realized what he was doing, he'd pulled her onto his lap.

She sagged against him with a sigh of pleasure, never breaking the kiss. The feel of the soft velour against his skin made him tinglingly aware of the body beneath the cloth. He was vaguely aware that one of her thighs was resting atop the upper edge of his prosthesis, but she didn't seem to notice or care, and after a moment he didn't, either. She had begun to nibble her way gently down the cords of his neck to linger in the hollow of his throat, kissing, tasting, until he knew she must be able to feel the pounding of his pulse beneath her lips.

"Rory." It came out as a groan. "Are you sure about this? We may just be making things worse."

She lifted her head. "I'm not sure of anything," she said honestly. "Except that, no matter what happens, I would regret not doing this for the rest of my life."

He groaned again, low and deep in his throat. And then he gave up the battle he wasn't sure he'd ever wanted to win. His hands came up to cup her face, to draw her down to him. It was his kiss this time, deep and hot and thorough. He kissed her until he could barely breathe. He kissed her until she was moaning, soft little sounds escaping from her.

She began to move restlessly, sinuously, as if it were an involuntary reaction to his touch. Her hands moved over his chest, his belly, slowly, as if she were trying to memorize him. He felt the deep muscles of his belly tighten, and, as if those muscles had propelled it, a sudden burst of heat rushed downward to already rapidly hardening flesh.

He let his hands slide over her shoulders and down her arms, then over to cup and lift the soft curves of her breasts. It was a little awkward in their position, and when she moved suddenly he froze, wondering if he'd hurt her somehow. Or if she had changed her mind.

That thought vanished instantly when he realized she had moved only to straddle his thighs as he sat on the couch. She reached for his hands and pulled them back to her breasts, and he let out the breath he hadn't realized he'd been holding.

He began anew, lifting, caressing that feminine softness, until he could see, even through the thick velour, her nipples growing taut. Only then did he move to caress them, rubbing with his thumbs. Rory gasped and pressed herself against his hands, and suddenly that cloth was far too thick.

He reached for the neckline of the robe, then stopped. "Rory?" he asked, his voice already so thick he could barely get it out.

"Yes," she whispered. "Oh, yes."

He tugged at the cloth, and then, when it was loose enough, smoothed it back off her shoulders. It fell from her, pooling around her waist, baring her to his heated gaze. Almost reverently, he reached toward her again. She moaned, arching her back this time, offering her breasts to him. He caught her nipples between his fingers and rolled them gently, until they were tight and hard.

He slipped his hands down to again cup and lift her, his gaze hot as he watched her breasts nestle into his palms. He stared at the rosy crests that had responded so eagerly to his touch, then he glanced upward for an instant and saw the blush that had colored her cheeks. But she never moved, never drew back, never tried to hide herself from his steady gaze.

She was embarrassed, but trying to conceal it, he realized. The woman who had unraveled in his arms last night, the woman who had made love to him so sweetly, so fully, who had asked him to make love to her now, was embarrassed. He couldn't reconcile that with what he had thought she must be, a woman bitterly experienced. But he couldn't deny that she had been utterly, undeniably, amazed by what had happened between them last night and what was happening between them now. It was almost as if she were the Rory he'd once known, open, innocent, untouched. He wondered if somehow, some way, she had managed to hang on to some part of the girl she'd been, some tiny part of her innocence.

It was that girl he felt suddenly compelled to speak to.

"I used to dream of this," he said hoarsely, "when we were together. All I'd ever seen of your body were those gorgeous legs...and your breasts. I used to lie in bed at night and get hard just thinking about that night when you let me touch you there, kiss you...."

A tiny gasp broke from her, a breathy little sound that reminded him anew of that night and of how she'd sounded when he'd first taken her nipples with his mouth.

"Please, Sean . . ."

"What, Rory? What do you want?"

Her color deepened, and she shook her head helplessly.

"Tell me," he urged. "I need to . . . hear it."

Her expression changed then, and the blush abated.

"You," she whispered. "Your mouth on me . . . like you did before."

He'd been waiting only for that. He moved swiftly, taking one nipple in his mouth and suckling her fiercely in the same instant his fingers moved to capture and tug the other. She cried out, a shocked, exclamation of pleasure. He continued until she was moaning his name, then reversed himself and took her other nipple in his mouth and began to tease the first with his fingers. He suckled and teased until she rose up on her knees, drawn bow-tight in his arms.

Sean took advantage of her movement and slid down a little farther on the couch. When at last he freed her breasts she was trembling, her breath coming in quick little pants. Only now she was straddling his hips instead of his thighs, and when she sank back her body came down on his in an intimate caress.

He could feel her heat, even through his jeans, and he smothered a groan. Rory went very still for an instant, as if she only now realized what he'd done and the significance of that ridge of male flesh pressing against the most female part of her.

Sean held his breath, wondering what she would do. Just the sweet pressure of her weight on him, and the image of how she would look now if he tugged the robe away altogether, her naked body straddling him, was driving him out of his mind. And then she moved, slowly, tentatively, her hands coming to rest on his chest, positioned so that she could reach his nipples with her fingertips as she braced herself.

She began to gently rake her nails over the flat brown disks, and at the same time her hips shifted as she rubbed her body against him, stroking herself over his swollen flesh. Her breasts swayed with her movements, her nipples still glistening from his mouth.

It was nearly too much. For the first time since his accident, he wanted to be naked with a woman more than he wanted anything else. He didn't care what she thought of his body. He didn't care if they wound up making love while he was still half-dressed, having to dodge the straps of the prosthesis, he only knew he had to be inside her now or he would shatter into a million pieces.

And if she were repulsed by that idea, he was very much afraid he would shatter anyway. But better to find out now . . .

Better now than what? Than later? Than after he'd done the unthinkable and fallen in love with her all over again? You won't do that, he ordered himself firmly. This is just something you have to get out of your system. Another part of your past that you have to face and put behind you.

That was the last logical thing his fevered mind heard. A harsh, guttural sound ripped from his throat as she pressed down harder over him. His hips moved in response, and he felt himself grow impossibly larger, straining the worn denim until he felt as if he were strangling.

Then Rory moved again, only this time it was to do what he'd wanted to do; she tugged and pulled at the robe until it fell away. Then she went right back to what she'd been doing and Sean could see every little movement, every shift of her body, could see the soft golden triangle of curls against the denim that was barely containing him now.

He almost went over the edge right then. He knew he was frantic, rapidly becoming mindless with need. All he could think of was the incredible feel of Rory's body against his. And how easy it would be for him to simply free himself and be buried deep inside her in a matter of seconds.

You're too close, he thought. Slow down. *Right* . . .

But he tried. He reached out, sliding his fingers between their bodies to find and stroke her, hearing her cry his name as he found the spot that made her open herself for him, asking for more. He circled one finger slowly, then faster as she responded, her hips moving faster. He kept on until she was moaning on every breath, her flesh becoming slick with her own liquid heat.

It was that awareness, that knowledge that her body was ready for him, that broke his already strained control. He reached for the button of his jeans, but his fingers wouldn't seem to work. He realized he was shaking.

"Rory," he choked out, "please...I can't...if you don't..."

He couldn't get the words out. He was dying, and he couldn't even talk. And when Rory moved again, letting her fingers trail caressingly along that rigid column of flesh, he could barely even breathe. His every muscle tightened as he raised himself, pressing against her hand, still feeling the heat of her as she hovered over him.

Another moan broke from her, a hungry sound that made him want to echo it. And then she'd done it, she'd tugged the button of his jeans free and unzipped them, and even as he gasped out his relief at the easing of the pressure, she made him suck his breath back in in a rush as she gently yet eagerly freed him for a lingering caress.

Her fingers curled around his hardness, lifting him back against her lower belly, and the sight of his own erect flesh against the backdrop of her naked body ripped the command from his throat.

"Now, Rory. Right now, or it's going to be too late."

She moved so quickly, took him in so suddenly, enveloping him in her wet heat, that he nearly gave himself up to her immediately. He savaged his lip, tasting blood before he felt he had even an inkling of control back. But Rory wasn't helping. She was rocking on him in an ever-hastening

rhythm, and he couldn't stop himself from echoing her
motions.

"Sean...oh, Sean, I didn't...I never..." Her words came
brokenly, between moans. "Only you," she gasped.

He wasn't sure exactly what she meant, but the look of
agonized pleasure on her face explained all he needed to
know. Urgently his hands went to her hips, then her waist.
With the strength born of the constant usage of his upper
body muscles, he lifted her until her body almost released
him.

Rory made a sound of protest. In answer, he brought her
back down on him and thrust upward at the same time, hard
and fast.

"Oh! Oh, yes," she gasped.

He did it again, and yet again, driving them together. He
heard the sounds, wet, slapping, erotic sounds as they drove
together again and again. He watched her breasts bob with
each thrust, saw her throw back her head and close her eyes,
as if she wanted to concentrate solely on the place where
they were joined. He could feel the growing heat. He
thought it was from her, but then he realized it was boiling
up inside him just as fiercely. He lifted her again and
brought her down with all his strength.

She cried out, and he felt the first rippling convulsion of
her body around his. Her inner muscles tightened around
him, stroking, milking him, and when she called his name
again he knew he couldn't hold back any longer. He gave in
to it, his body going rigid as the dam burst and he poured
himself into her, feeling every pulse of liquid fire as his own
hoarse shout echoed in his ears, melding with Rory's sweet
moans of pleasure.

Chapter 15

Rory leaned back against the porch steps and stared up at the night sky, wondering if her whirling thoughts would ever slow down enough for her to sort them out. She doubted it; they were coming from too many directions and were far too chaotic to be easily subdued.

If only they weren't so overwhelming, she thought. When she caught herself dwelling on what they might find in that safe-deposit box, she became so worried it would be nothing that she began to panic. So she tried to think about Frank, and what pleasure she was going to take in at last booting him out of her life. But then she remembered that he had bested even her father and began to wonder whether or not she could pull it off.

So she would think instead about the only thing powerful enough to take her mind off all the rest: Sean. And the first thing that inevitably came to her mind was what they had done, right there on the couch, Sean still half-dressed. And then again, naked this time, but still unable to wait long enough to leave the couch, they'd taken each other once more, a slower, more languorous loving. And she'd tested Sean's statement that his leg was very sensitive at the amputation site with her hands, her mouth and her body, determined to erase any lingering notion he had that she found him less than beautiful. His frantic response, his groaning shout of her name, the convulsive shudders that swept him, were her proof that she'd succeeded.

She'd never known anything so fierce, so intense, and she couldn't believe it hadn't affected him the same way. They'd driven each other to exhaustion; even now, Sean was still sprawled on the couch, sound asleep in the tangle of his clothes and the blanket she'd spread over him.

But she'd sensed his reluctance, had in fact used the power of the attraction between them to overcome it. She'd wanted him so badly then that she hadn't cared about anything else. And while it had been much more than worth it in those moments when they'd been as close as two people can be, when he'd been sheathed in her to the hilt, when just the taut look of sheer pleasure on his face had been enough to send her flying, now she was feeling a bit guilty. But, she tried to console herself, she was at least wise enough not to make the essentially feminine mistake of thinking that great sex meant a great relationship. No, Sean had far too much to forgive; she didn't think it was possible.

She wondered if her father had thought it kinder to be cruel, five years ago. Perhaps he'd thought it would be easier for Sean if he gave him a reason to hate, rather than hurt. But, she realized now, despite his strength, Sean had been too fragile, still too raw from the maiming of his body to turn the pain from that personal attack into anger. She wished her father were alive now, as she had wished many times before, but for the first time it was so that she could tell him how angry she was, how much she hated what he'd done, both to her and to Sean.

It didn't matter, she told herself, shifting her gaze to look out over the quiet lagoon. She had killed Sean's love, and her father had nailed down the coffin lid. All she'd done now was confuse things even further by resurrecting the undeniable physical attraction between them. He had no doubt been driven by curiosity, nothing more. Certainly not love. He wouldn't be so foolish as make the mistake of falling in love with her again.

And she hadn't made that mistake, either. As she watched the moonlight play over the water, she at last admitted the truth to herself. She hadn't fallen in love with Sean Holt again. She couldn't, because she'd never stopped loving him. Not the day they were supposed to be wed, not in the five years since, and not now. She'd loved him then for what she saw in him, what she'd known he could be; she loved him now for everything he had become.

Except that what he'd become put him far out of the reach of the woman she now was. A cold, bitter manipulator, who'd thought she could sell her body without selling her soul along with it. Far too shoddy a person for the likes of Sean Holt.

And from now on she would keep her hands off him. She would respect his reluctance to complicate things any further, and once she got whatever her father had left her, she would walk away and leave him to get on with his life. It was the least she could do for him, the very least, after the way he'd helped her when he had very little reason to, and every reason not to.

The sky was starting to turn pink with the dawn when at last she got up and went inside. Sean was still asleep, his head cradled in the crook of his arm, his hair tousled and falling over his forehead, his lashes dark, thick semicircles on his cheeks.

She stood looking at him for a long time. The blanket had slipped down to his waist, baring the lean, strong lines of his back and the powerful muscles of his shoulders. She would always regret that he had lost his leg, but he was still the most beautiful man she'd ever known. His loss only made him more so, because it proved to her that his heart, his courage, were just as strong and beautiful as his body.

The body that had taken her to heights she'd never imagined. The body she wanted to know as well as she knew her own. The body that responded so fiercely to her, with such potent maleness, that it stole her breath away. The body she had always wanted to wake up next to for the rest of her life. And it would never, ever happen. She'd had all she would ever have.

She spoke very little all morning and less as they finally left for the bank. There was nothing she could say that wouldn't reveal the depths of her despondency. But if Sean noticed anything unusual, he said nothing. Perhaps, she thought grimly, he was glad she was being silent, keeping him from accusing her of seducing him last night. Ironic, she thought. Frank had always called her the coldest of cold fish, yet with Sean she became a woman she didn't even know.

Or hadn't known for five years. With Sean she felt as if she had held on to some part of the girl she'd once been, before Frank Talbot had taught her more than she'd ever wanted to know about the ugliness possible in the human soul.

But in a way, she supposed, Frank was right. She looked at him and felt cold inside, cold, numbed and empty. To him, she was little less than frigid. Yet Sean could melt her with a look, and turn her into a writhing mass of tingling nerves with a touch.

A sigh escaped her, and Sean gave her a sideways look. "What's wrong?" he finally asked.

"Nothing."

Sean laughed, but it wasn't a humorous sound. "Right. Try again."

"Nothing I can do anything about," she amended.

"Want to talk about it?"

"Not really." Unless you can tell me I'm wrong. Unless you can tell me that when this is over, you won't walk away, thankful you'll never have to see me again.

"We need to talk, Rory."

"About what?" she asked warily.

"Last night, for starters."

Oh, God, she thought. "I'm sorry. I shouldn't have... done that."

"As I recall," Sean retorted, his tone wry, "there were two of us involved."

"But you didn't want to be."

"At first? No. I was already... confused enough."

"I shouldn't have pushed. You said you... didn't know how you felt."

"I still don't."

They stopped at a red light. He gave her another sideways look, but this time she could see in his eyes exactly what he was thinking, what he was remembering.

"But I do know you blow all my circuits, lady. You didn't seduce me, if that's what you're thinking. I was a more than willing participant." That look somehow grew even hotter, and he added huskily, "I thought the top of my head was going to come off."

She felt her cheeks heat. "I...yeah," she finished lamely.

"So what are we going to do about it?"

"I... don't know."

She wanted to beg him then, to tell him that she still loved him, that she'd always loved him, and to please give her another chance. But she couldn't, not now, not until she extricated herself from the snarl her life had become. If she could manage that, if she could somehow ever feel clean again, maybe, just maybe, she might someday feel she deserved his love. If he still had it in him to give.

"I have to deal with this first," she finally said. "I can't think of anything else right now."

He studied her for a long moment. Then the light changed, and as he turned his attention back to the road, she heard him mutter, "Fine." And it was Sean who was silent for the rest of the trip.

They found the bank easily enough and pulled into the lot just before it was due to open.

"What if they won't let me into the box, even if I explain?" she asked, wondering why that hadn't occurred to her before.

Sean shrugged. "Don't explain. Just give them the box number from the key."

"But—"

"Rory," he said patiently, "if your father went to all this trouble, I'm sure he put you on the card to get into the box. Just act like you have every right to it. Because you do."

She felt a little easier then, but the tension inside her started building again as they walked up to the window. Oddly, it didn't ease but tightened another notch when the woman behind the counter looked at the odd etched design on the key and confirmed that it was one of theirs.

"Let me see here," the woman said as she first called up a file on her computer, then cross-checked it with a card file. "Miss Aurora Sheridan, you said?"

Rory nodded.

"Here it is. You are on the card, Miss Sheridan, but the box is in your father's name."

"He's . . . dead."

"Oh, I'm so sorry. I understand, then. Do you have some proof with you, a death certificate or an obituary?"

Rory paled. "I . . . no. I didn't think . . ."

"How about the front page of the local paper?" Sean said dryly. "Jacob Sheridan was big news in this town."

The woman blinked. "I'm afraid I don't live here, so I wouldn't know. But my manager would." She looked over her shoulder. "Patti?"

An attractive, business-suited woman who had been standing a few feet away with her back to them turned and walked toward them. When she came to a halt, she glanced at Sean, smiled with genuine yet detached feminine appreciation, then settled her attention on Rory.

"Yes, I heard," she said when the teller began to explain. "You're Jacob Sheridan's daughter?"

Rory nodded.

"Do you have a picture ID?"

Thank God she'd gotten her purse from the house, Rory thought. She opened it and took out her driver's license. The woman looked at it, checking the photograph.

"What's your father's date of birth?" Rory gave it. "Do you know his mother's maiden name?"

She had to think for a moment, but finally it came to her. When she supplied it, the woman nodded to the teller.

"Let her in," the manager said.

"What shall I put for the proof of box holder's death?" the other woman asked.

Rory winced. She understood the need for security, but her heart was starting to race.

"Write 'personal knowledge,' and I'll initial it." Patti glanced at Sean again.

Rory felt a burst of pique; did she have to look quite so appreciative? And be quite so attractive?

"You were quite right, Mr...?"

"Holt," Sean said.

"Mr. Holt. Jacob Sheridan was big news in this town." She looked at Rory then. "I'm sorry for all the formalities in what must still be a painful time for you, Miss Sheridan. Please come with me, and I'll get the box for you myself."

Feeling a bit petty—she couldn't blame the woman for realizing Sean was a handsome man—Rory followed her into the small vault. Moments later she sat in the private booth, holding the silver key in a hand shaking too badly to fit it into the lock of the long, narrow gray metal box.

She took a deep breath and tried to steady herself. It didn't work. She closed her eyes and thought of Sean, waiting outside. Perhaps flirting with the lovely bank manager...

The key went in neatly. She turned it, took a split second to try to prepare herself for nothing more than an empty box, then lifted the lid.

It wasn't empty. In fact, it was quite full. Her mother's jewelry. Papers, a small notebook, a large manila envelope and—

Rory's breath caught as she saw the folded piece of ivory-colored linen stationery. Her father's stationery; she didn't need to unfold it and see the imperious monogram to know that. When she did unfold it, her eyes blurred for a moment when she saw the familiar bold, heavy strokes of her father's writing.

My dearest child,
If you are reading this, then I must assume it is too late for me to ever make amends. Not that it would be possible; there is nothing I can say or do to make up for what I, your supposedly loving father, have put you through.

I cannot tell you the depths of my shame, Aurora. Had I been less prideful, less arrogant, you would be married now to a very fine young man, and perhaps I would have had a grandchild by now. I am fully aware I have ruined your young life, sold you, in essence, into a kind of slavery. All that is left to me now is to try to give you the key to your freedom.

I think it is all here, Rory. Everything you will need to bring down the man who brought me to this. I am certain of my own fate now, and no hell I may face will be payment enough for what I have done to my beloved Barbara's little girl. I'm only glad she never knew what I've become.

Do whatever you must to regain your life, and someday, if you can, forgive your all-too-human father.

Daddy

Rory smothered a sob at the signature. He *had* loved her, she thought. He had just lost his way after Mother died.

Five minutes later, her eyes red but dry, and her hands rock steady, she came out of the booth. Sean rose from the chair where he'd been waiting and met her at the counter.

"It's all here." She gestured with the papers. "Everything I could have hoped for. And more. All documented and notarized."

Sean let out a long, compressed breath of relief. He started to speak, then stopped as the teller approached.

"Will you be keeping the box, Miss Sheridan?"

"No, I—"

"Yes," Sean interrupted. Rory looked at him quizzically. "Make copies," he said. "Keep the originals locked up."

She immediately saw the wisdom of that. "Yes. Yes, you're right. And I'll leave the jewelry here."

Half an hour later, courtesy of the bank's copy machine and the efficient, kind and too attractive Patti, they were back in the car with an envelope full of copies of everything that had been in the box.

"We'll go back to Dar's," Sean said. "You'll need to read through all that."

She nodded, still staring down at the envelope that held her future. She would do as Sean said, then she would have to make some decisions. It wasn't a pleasant prospect, but nothing could be worse that what she'd lived with for the past five years.

She sat lost in thought until Sean pulled into a fast-food drive-through. They hadn't eaten at all that morning, not so much because there wasn't much food left, but because they were too wound up.

"We could go to a restaurant," he said, "but I didn't think you'd want to be reading those in public."

He gestured at the envelope, and she nodded. "You're right. Thank you."

Rory dug into her fries the moment they were clear of the driveway. Then she stopped, catching Sean watching her with the slightest of smiles curving one corner of his mouth. She'd always gone for the fries before anything else, and he'd often teased her about it, a lifetime ago.

And then, inevitably, she had always started to feed them to him as he drove, which had led to him licking the salt from her fingers, which had led to a kiss, which most of the time had landed them in some secluded place for a series of kisses that had left them both breathless.

If they'd known what they were missing, she thought as her body roused to the memory, they never would have been able to stop. And a glance at Sean's set expression, the tightness of his jaw, made her wonder if his mind had followed the same reminiscent course as hers had.

They had gone several miles before she realized he was checking the rearview mirror about every tenth of a mile. She sat up a little straighter.

"Sean? Is something wrong?"

He shrugged. "That white car's been behind us for a while."

She turned to look. There were two white cars, a small station wagon with a woman and two small children, and a racy coupe with a cellular phone antenna protruding from the top of the back window, occupied by a single man. This was obviously the car that was making Sean edgy.

"It's not that man, the blonde," she said.

"I know. It's probably nothing. I'm just a little paranoid."

Just because you're paranoid doesn't mean they aren't really after you. The old joke rang in Rory's ears as if the words had been spoken aloud. She watched the car for a few more minutes, then, as the man's turn signal came on and he began to slow, she breathed a sigh of relief. She watched as the white coupe pulled into the left-turn lane and stopped, waiting for a break in the oncoming traffic, then turned back to Sean.

"He's turning off."

Sean nodded. Then his mouth quirked wryly. "Paranoid," he confirmed. "Half the world seems to be taking an early weekend today. And they're all on this road."

He was right, Rory thought. The traffic on the coast road, which was no more than average during the week, was much heavier today, as if the lovely weather had convinced everyone that Friday was part of the weekend.

She looked back once more. In the distance, the left-turn pocket was empty, and she breathed a sigh of relief.

The traffic had thinned out a bit by the time they reached the more remote area where Dar's warehouse was. Sean made the turn and drove slowly along the narrow road. Rory looked out at the lagoon that lay serenely undisturbed about ten feet below them. There were some people on the far side, in a small area that was accessible off the main road. Four adults, apparently two couples, all with binoculars. Birdwatchers, Rory guessed, from the way they were pointing at a small flock of water birds paddling around in the center of the lagoon. Thinking of her recent experience at being the watchee, she wondered if the birds minded.

Sean parked the car, and she got out. She was reaching for her purse when she saw Sean's head snap around, back toward the main road.

"What is it?" she asked, looking that way and seeing nothing unusual.

He shook his head ruefully. "I almost thought I caught a glimpse of that car again."

She frowned. "But he turned off."

"I know. Like I said, paranoid." He shrugged. "Even if I did see it, it was probably a different one. There're a million of those coupes on the road." He reached in to pick up the bag of hamburgers, then shut the car door. "Let's go in and eat, and you can tackle that envelope."

It took her nearly an hour, mostly wading through the legalese of the will, before she was through. She sat back in the single chair at the table—if there were others, they'd been moved out of Dar's way—while Sean, who had been doing some tidying up, came over and sat on the edge of the table.

"It's all here," she said, repeating what she'd said in the bank. "The notebook has all the blackmail payments, with dates and times. This—" she held up a sheaf of papers that were stapled together "—is a full confession that Daddy wrote, telling about the money he used and everything that happened afterward."

"Everything?" Sean asked, his voice very quiet.

She looked up at him, knowing what he meant. "He documented my involvement in an addendum. There's a note here saying he did it that way so I could decide what I wanted to do about that part."

"And have you? Decided, I mean?"

"Yes." He lifted a brow questioningly, but she shook her head. "First, I want to tell you about this."

She lifted the papers that had been in the original manila envelope in the box.

"What is it?"

"Daddy's will. A new one, drawn up two months before he died. It clearly states that it supersedes any prior wills. Including the one that gave Frank the controlling interest in Sheridan Manufacturing." She swallowed tightly. "Except for a single bequest, it gives everything to me."

Sean smiled then, a satisfied smile that warmed her beyond all reason. She savored that smile as she finished.

"That one bequest is in the form of a large trust fund. To be used for the furtherance of projects like Laurel Tree. And to be administered by Sean Holt."

Sean had looked puzzled at first, then, as she finished, stunned. He let out a long, compressed breath. "I don't understand," he murmured.

"Maybe this will help."

She handed him her father's note—she'd kept the original of that, somehow needing that piece of genuine proof that her father had, indeed, loved her—and watched his face as he read it. She saw the instant when he reached the part about him, saw his eyes widen in shock. When he'd finished, he lifted his head and stared at her.

"My father was a brusque, proud man, Sean. This is as close to an apology as I have ever seen him give to anyone other than my mother or me."

Still looking a little dazed, he handed back the note. She got up, walked to the coffee table and tucked it into her purse, then looked back at Sean.

"I have something I'd like to tell you," she said.

He studied her for a moment. "Why do I think I should be sitting down for this?"

"It doesn't matter. But I have to say it, Sean. I haven't felt like I had the right, until now. This—" she gestured toward the pile of papers "—is going to help me get my life back. Someday, if I'm lucky, I'll feel clean again." She took a deep, shuddering breath. "I've been thinking about what you said, that before, I was part of your wishing for a normal life."

"Rory—"

"Please, let me finish. I understand how you must have felt. And I know that if that had been all it was, our marriage wouldn't have lasted. It would have crumbled as soon as reality caved in on us."

He didn't—couldn't, she supposed—deny that.

"But I've been thinking of something else, too. Of how you've become everything I ever thought you could be. And so much more. You're an amazing man, Sean Holt. Maybe you really could forgive me, someday."

He straightened up from the table, a hint of color tingeing his cheekbones. He shook his head, whether in denial or simply embarrassment, she couldn't tell. "I...and if I do?"

He was treading very carefully, Rory thought. And she couldn't blame him. "For a long time," she said, "I thought it would be hardest to forgive. But now I think it may be even harder to be forgiven. As if there will always be a thread connecting you somehow to that person."

"And you don't...want that?"

It was she who had to tread carefully now. "I had decided to just thank you as best I could, then walk away when this was over and let you get on with your life. But I..."

Her throat had suddenly tightened, and she couldn't seem to go on. He turned then, his eyes fastened on her intently.

"But what, Rory? Now you're not going to walk away?"

She swallowed heavily. Did he sound anxious, or apprehensive? It didn't matter, she told herself. He had become a strong, centered man, and he wouldn't let himself be forced in a direction he didn't want to go. So what she said would make little difference. Except to her.

"I will, if that's what you want me to do. I certainly don't deserve anything else. But before I go, there's something I want you to know." She sucked in a deep breath and plunged ahead. "I love you, Sean. I never stopped loving you. Ever."

The color faded from his face. "Damn," he muttered, closing his eyes.

Rory watched the flutter of his thick lashes, felt her own eyes begin to sting with brimming tears.

"You were the only thing that got me through every day of the past five years," she said, her voice low and strained. "No matter what I'd done, no matter what my father had done, no matter what Frank did to me...I knew that, once, Sean Holt had loved me." She lowered her eyes. "Sometimes it was the only thing that kept me from doing something...desperate."

His eyes snapped open, and Rory saw a heat there that she didn't dare try to name.

"My God, Rory. Why didn't you tell me—"

He stopped suddenly, his head cocked at an odd angle, just before she heard the unmistakable sound of tires whirring down a dirt road.

Sean's jaw tensed. "I heard the noise, but it didn't register."

They'd been too intent, Rory thought. She ran to the small window—placed low, so that Dar could easily see out—and peered through it. A silver sedan was headed toward them.

"It's Frank," she gasped, backing away with an instinctively protective movement, colliding with Sean, who had come up behind her. She turned her back on the window. "God, Sean, how did he find us?"

"I really must have seen that white car go past here," Sean grated out. "Talbot must have figured we knew the blonde, so he hired somebody else. This guy must have faked that turn, then gotten back in traffic and followed us from there. And he called Talbot when he saw where we went."

The silver sedan came to a halt beside Sean's car. "Damn it," Sean swore, "I didn't even try to lose that guy—"

"Sean, don't! It's not your fault. But what are we going to do? If I tell him about the will, maybe he'll go—"

He went suddenly very still. "Don't bother," he said

Chapter 16

"Oh, God," Rory moaned. "I'll call the police—"

"Forget it, Rory. We're so far out, it would take them ten minutes or more to get here."

She heard a car door open, and panic bubbled up inside her at the thought of Sean hurt, or worse. And it would be her fault, all over again.

"Then I'll go with him. I'll talk to him—"

"You're not going anywhere. Except out the back door." He reached into his pocket and pulled out his keys. "As soon as he's inside, you get around front and into my car. And get the hell out of here."

She backed away from him, staring at the dangling keys as if they were a venomous snake.

"No. I'm not leaving you here."

"Rory—"

"No!"

"Damn it, Rory, go! If he hears the car start, it might distract him enough for me to do something. Then I'll be right behind you."

She hesitated. It made sense. She was the one Frank wanted, and if he thought she was escaping . . . She grabbed the keys and turned to run. But she'd waited too long. She'd only taken half a dozen steps before the front door burst open.

Talbot ran in, wildly waving a lethal-looking chromed automatic pistol. Rory tried to get back to Sean, but Talbot trained the gun on her and ordered her not to move.

"I knew you'd be here together," he snarled. "Thought you were clever, hiding way out here, didn't you? Did you think I wouldn't find you?"

"How *did* you find us?" Sean asked, his voice deceptively mild.

Talbot drew himself up proudly. "I fired that first idiot, after he was clumsy enough to get spotted. Only good thing he did was get me the license number on your car. After that it was easy. Hell, I've had half the PIs in San Diego County beating the bushes for you, after you broke into my house—"

"It's *my* house," Rory said.

He looked as surprised as if one of the tables had spoken. "Merely a formality. You'll be signing it over to me as soon as we get home."

"You'll never set foot in that house again," Rory said. "Or in my father's office. He saw to that."

Talbot froze. "So he *did* do something."

"Oh, yes," Rory said tightly. "He did."

"I knew it, that last time I talked to him, the day he died, the fool. He warned me to let you go, but I told him he wasn't going to last much longer—"

"You bastard," she spat out.

"I told you never to call me that." Talbot's voice was icy, and so threatening that Rory backed up a step. Her movement drew Talbot's eyes to the table, where all the copies were still spread out. "That's it, isn't it?" His tiny eyes danced over the papers. "A new will? And what . . . a confession? How noble!'' He laughed, a vicious, humorless sound. ''Isn't it just too bad that I have them now?''

He started toward the table. Instinctively Rory moved to stop him. Talbot raised the gun again.

''I told you to stay put, bitch. I've worked years for this, put up with you for years. Do you think I'm about to let you ruin all my plans?''

''It's over, Frank. Those are only copies.'' Thank you, Sean, she breathed inwardly. ''Do you think I'd take a chance with the originals?''

''Then you'll get me the originals,'' Talbot said.

''Like hell,'' Rory said flatly. A low, hissing sound of fury escaped Talbot. ''You're through, Frank. Go back to the gutter you came from.''

''Rory,'' Sean cautioned.

''Shut up!'' Talbot whirled to face Sean. His free hand came up to touch the bandage that covered his cheek. ''I owe you a little present, anyway. You sucker-punched me, Holt, and I don't like spending time in hospitals.''

''Especially when you're sent there by a gimp?'' Sean asked, his voice nothing less than taunting.

Talbot leveled the gun on Sean now. ''Maybe I'll just have to get you out of the way first, boyfriend.'' His malignant gaze flicked to Rory. ''I told you five years ago, on your *wedding day*—'' his lip curled in a sneer ''—that I'd kill him if I ever caught you with him again. Now I'll show you I wasn't lying.''

Rory saw Sean go very still, and for a moment he looked straight at her. She saw the knowledge there, the recognition of the last missing piece of the puzzle. He knew now that Frank had not only threatened her father, but Sean himself, if she didn't agree to his terms. She wondered if he also realized that that threat was the real reason why she'd finally caved in to his demands; she'd held on until that day. Frank had as much as told him so, by saying he'd made the threat on what was to be their wedding day, but . . .

Sean's eyes closed for an instant, as if he were in pain. And Rory knew that he had indeed realized exactly what had happened on that day that was to have been their most joyous.

Talbot laughed harshly, and Sean's eyes snapped open. "Tell me, do you enjoy screwing a cold fish, or is that just the best you can get?"

Sean never even blinked. "You know," he said, his voice as casual as his posture as he wandered a few feet to his left, as if mulling over a puzzle, ignoring Talbot's order to stop, "it seems to me I read somewhere that there are no frigid women, only inadequate men." He stopped then, beside Dar's weight rack, grinning as he looked at Talbot from across the room. "How does it feel to be living proof of that, Talbot?"

Talbot swore crudely. "You're a dead man," he said through clenched teeth. The gun came up, Talbot's finger tightening on the trigger. He started toward Sean.

"Frank, stop!" Rory cried. "I'll give you the papers!"

An unholy grin split Talbot's face as he half turned to look at Rory. In that instant Sean moved. He grabbed a dumbbell-shaped weight from the rack, and, in a smooth, powerful motion, hurled it across the room. It caught Talbot on one knee. He went down hard to the floor, screaming. But he never let go of the gun.

"Rory! Run!" Sean yelled.

She hesitated only a split second, long enough to see that Sean was also moving. Then she raced for the door. She yanked it open, glancing back to see that Frank was on his knees, moaning, but clearly still moving. Then Sean was there, urging her outside.

Rory was amazed at his presence of mind when he locked the door before he shut it behind them; getting it open would slow Frank for a few precious seconds. She hurried down the steps two at a time. Sean went over the railing, staggering slightly when he landed, but steadying himself instantly.

Rory watched in horrified anxiety as Sean looked at the silver sedan for a moment, then took a step toward it. The horrendous boom of two rapid shots from the automatic stopped him in his tracks.

"Idiot, he's shooting the door lock," he said. "No time to sabotage his car. Let's go!"

Rory scrambled into Sean's car, ramming the key she still held into the ignition as he got into the driver's seat. He started the motor, and threw the car into gear. Then they took off, careening around a tight turn.

Rory was taking her first full breath in what seemed like hours when she heard the ominous sound of a racing motor behind them. Before she could turn around, she felt the jolt of impact as Frank rammed them. She heard Sean swear as he wrestled with the wheel.

Frank hit them again, harder. Sean fought the slewing of the car. He brought it closer to the high side of the narrow roadway, away from the lagoon. And then Frank was beside them. The silver sedan glinted in the sun. Frank seemed to swerve away for an instant. Then he came back at them. Rory felt her head snap sideways as Frank's car slammed against the driver's side.

Sean grunted harshly. Rory heard the note of pain in his voice and turned in her seat to look at him anxiously. Frank hit them again, even harder. The steering wheel jerked. Sean fought it again, but they were off the packed dirt of the road. Dust flew up around them. It enveloped them in the instant before Rory felt a strange lifting, and she realized they were going up the steep embankment on the right.

Sean never gave up. He hit the accelerator and cranked the wheel to the left at the same time. It worked, Rory thought joyously. They leveled out again.

And then she felt another bone-jarring impact, somewhere to the rear of her. It sent them spinning out of control. Dust flew. Then they were back on the road. Then more dust. And suddenly, terrifyingly, they seemed to be flying. And nothing was ahead but the sparkling water of the lagoon.

The impact as they hit the water was the worst yet, making the entire frame of the car shudder. Rory's head hit the Plexiglas roof of the car, and her vision blurred. She was vaguely aware of something wet on her face and wondered if she'd fainted and Sean was trying to bring her around.

"Rory!" His voice was urgent in her ear. She heard him move, grunt and move again. Then, "Rory, don't pass out. God, you've got to move! We're sinking fast!"

Sinking? She blinked. She touched a hand to her head. The wetness there was blood. But she felt water sloshing around her feet.

Awareness rushed back. She stared in horror at the rising water level outside the car. And the water that was steadily pouring in.

"Rory, listen." She felt him shaking her. She turned to look at him. Blood was streaming over one side of his face.

"Sean, you're hurt!" she exclaimed, never realizing that she must look much the same.

"Damn it, Rory, listen to me! You've only got a few seconds. The electric windows aren't working. You've got to unfasten that T-top, right now. I can't reach the other latch from here. When we go under, you'll never get it open, the water pressure will be too much."

Go under? The water was almost at her knees now. God, were they going to drown?

"Do it!" Sean shook her. "And when it gives, you get out of here and don't look back!"

Her head cleared suddenly. She reached up and fumbled with the latch nearest the door. Already water was lapping near the top of the car, and it was swirling around inside, filling the air with the smell of the lagoon. She was vaguely aware of Sean digging into his pocket and bringing out the knife she'd bought him so long ago. What was he going to do, try to cut through the Plexiglas?

"I can't lift it," she said, fighting down panic. Then Sean moved, stretching up to hammer the Plexiglas top with the ball of his hand. Why didn't he just open his so they could go out that way? she wondered. Then it gave. Water began to slosh over the edge into the car, drenching her. On the outside the water was perilously close to the top of the car; in moments it would flood over the raised window.

"Come on, Sean," she said, realizing that he hadn't moved. You can still get your side open. It's not over the top yet."

"I can't. It's jammed."

So he couldn't get out until she did. She scrambled to her knees, then stood up. Her movement seemed to drive the car down that last inch, and water began to pour into the hole left by the T-top. She hoisted herself up quickly so Sean could get clear. The driver's seat was underwater up to the dash already.

"Hurry, Sean!" she called urgently as she slipped over the top. They weren't too far out, she realized as she treaded water, looking around. And she'd always thought these lagoons were rather shallow. Maybe the car wouldn't sink all the way.

Frank's car lay on its side halfway down the embankment they had apparently flown over after that last impact. He had crawled out and was sitting in the dirt, apparently too stunned to realize what had happened. Not that he would help anyway.

The bird-watchers were running their way, along the edge of the lagoon, but it was heavy going and it would take them—

"Sean!" she screamed, suddenly realizing that he hadn't come out. She heard his voice, muffled and broken by coughing. She thought she must be hallucinating out of fright; she could have sworn he'd said, "I love you."

There was an awful sucking sound as the car settled beneath the surface.

"Sean!" she cried, climbing back up over the window and pulling her way into the car. In the murky water it took her a moment to find him. He was moving, his hand making odd sawing motions over his left leg. Rory went icy cold with fear.

He was trapped.

She could see it now. Sean's left leg was pinned by the buckled metal, caught between the door where Frank had rammed them, the broken seat and the crumpled dash.

She went closer. He moved his head, his hair flowing in the water, saw her, waved her away with a violent motion. She saw then that he had his knife and realized what he was trying to do.

And that he wouldn't have time to do it.

Her lungs were burning, and he'd been under twice as long as she had. Already his movements were slowing. He was going to die. He was going to drown, right there in front of her, and it would be her fault.

You've only got a few seconds. You get out of here, and don't look back!

He'd known. He'd known from the moment the car started to sink that he was trapped. He'd known, and yet he'd fought to get her out.

No!

Her mind screamed the word. She wasn't going to lose him again, not like this.

She pulled her way back out of the car. She popped up to the surface. She looked around in terror; the bird-watchers were coming, shouting and waving, but they were still too far away. The car had stopped sinking, settling into the muck at the bottom of the shallow lagoon, but it was too late now. She took a breath to ease her lungs, then another, the deepest, longest she could manage. Then she dove again, heedless of the pain as she bounced off portions of the car in her haste.

He was still fighting, but barely. She could see that he was starting to fade. She didn't waste a precious second but grabbed his head and forced his mouth to hers. He barely reacted. She could have sworn she heard the gurgle as he gave up what little air he had left and started to take in water. With all the power she could muster she blew into his mouth until her lungs were empty.

This time she didn't climb out of the car, but only stood on the seat until her head was clear to take a deep breath. They were barely three feet under, but for Sean it might as well have been three miles. She made another trip, wondering how long he could keep going on her already breathed air. Long enough, surely? Please, God, long enough.

He was moving now. Using the knife again. It was working, she thought, her heart pounding as she dared to hope. When he saw her, he waited until she was close, then let out the air he'd been holding. Before the bubbles cleared, her mouth was on his again, pushing the air into him.

When she came back the next time he was ripping at his jeans. They gave suddenly, to the side seam. She gave him her breath, and when he started with the knife again, she scrambled to the surface to fill her aching lungs.

When she came back this time, he waved her off. He was hacking at the cloth furiously. His hand jerked. She thought the knife had slipped, but then realized he'd finished the cut. He yanked at the denim. Suddenly she could see the dull gleam of plastic beneath, and a glint of metal. He made two more quick slashes with the knife, and she thought of the straps that secured the prosthesis to his leg.

And then he was moving, jackknifing his lean body up over the steering wheel, kicking, fighting. Rory backed out of his way, forced to go up for her own air. She drew it in, then held it to go back to him.

Sean popped up beside her.

Alive.

Gasping, coughing, choking, but alive. Beautifully, undeniably alive.

She let her breath out on a sob and threw her arms around him, as much to prove to herself that he was truly alive as to support him.

"Sean," she moaned. "Oh, God, Sean."

He was drawing in as much air as he could take between paroxysms of coughing, obviously far beyond being able to talk. But he put his arms around her, and they clung together until he could breathe without choking.

Only then did they become aware of the chorus of shouts punctuated by splashes as the bird-watchers arrived.

"Damn, man, we thought you were dead!"

"You must have been under for three or four minutes!"

"What happened?"

They were clambering all over the car, helping Rory out to sit on the roof, propping up the unsteady Sean, who was still standing on the passenger seat, only his head and shoulders out of the water.

Then one of them glanced at the outside of the driver's side of the car. He swore expressively and looked at Sean almost with awe. "You were pinned in, weren't you?"

He nodded. "Leg," he managed to say before having to cough again.

"How'd you get loose?"

"Didn't," Sean said. Then he looked at Rory, and the grin she saw on his face nearly stopped her heart. "I just took it off."

Sean laughed as the bird-watchers gaped at him, as if they thought he'd suffered brain damage in the crash. But Rory caught his mood, realizing the pure, perfectly balanced irony of it. And suddenly she was laughing with him, giddily, joyously, at the fact that his tragic loss had, in the end, been his salvation.

He braced himself on the car and pulled himself up to sit on the roof. And there, sitting atop the submerged wreck of his car, Sean kissed her. And the kiss was, as they were, different. Their lives had been pared down to essentials in the past few minutes, and the haze of pain and past hurts that had clouded their vision had been washed away.

"Sean. Sean...."

She breathed his name like a litany, a prayer, against his lips. Then she drew back, breaking the kiss. She looked at him, at the deep brown eyes that had so nearly closed forever.

"I thought I...heard you...in the car...." She gulped in a breath that came nearly as hard as the ones she'd held underwater. "Did you really say it?"

He countered with a question of his own. "Why didn't you tell me that Talbot threatened to kill me five years ago?"

She lowered her eyes. She tried deliberately misunderstanding, answering his question, yet not answering it.

"What difference would it have made? You couldn't have stopped him, even if I'd warned you. He would have done it...sneakily, shot you or something." She tried to suppress a shudder. "That's what he always threatened. And I'd already hurt you so badly...emotionally, I couldn't have borne it if you were hurt physically because of me, too."

He was silent for a moment, but Rory didn't dare look at him. Then, softly, the question she'd dodged came again, in a tone that told her he knew exactly what she'd done.

"Why didn't you tell me now, Rory?"

She gave up. "I didn't want you to feel...obligated."

"Like I didn't want you to feel obligated because I was helping you?"

She nodded mutely. Sean reached out and tilted her head back with a gentle finger under her chin. Slowly her lashes came up, and she looked at him. He held her gaze steadily.

"I thought I was going to die," he told her. "And suddenly it all seemed so...useless. All that old baggage... Obligation. Owing. Guilt. Hurt feelings. What the hell does it mean anymore? What does it matter?"

His hand slid up to cup her cheek, and he smoothed his thumb over the water beaded on her skin.

"I love you, Rory. I was going to tell you, back at Dar's, but I didn't get the chance."

A tiny, tortured sound escaped her. "Oh, God, Sean, I never thought...I didn't dare...after what I—"

"Hush," he said softly. "You've been paying for what happened for five years. Isn't that enough?"

"For nearly destroying you?"

"Then how about today? You gave back more than you ever took, Rory. I'd say we're even, but I'm through keeping score. No more of that. Just you and me...and a fresh start. If you want one."

"*If?* Oh, Sean, do you even have to ask?"

He looked at her, a smile curving his lips. "Maybe not. But I do think I need another kiss. The last one was salty."

This time they kissed to a round of applause and whistles from the bird-watchers. And Rory didn't mind the audience at all.

Epilogue

Sean stood just out of sight at the front of the small chapel. It was a measure of how happy he was, he supposed, that he barely thought of the last time he'd been here. It didn't matter anymore. He wasn't that boy any longer, and Rory wasn't that girl. They might never know what would have happened had they gotten married that long-ago day, but he was as certain as he could be what would happen after today.

No, Rory wasn't that girl any longer. She was a woman, and, once freed of the prison her life had become, she was the most amazing woman he'd ever known.

He remembered when he'd first realized just how much she'd changed. She had come home to his—their—apartment, dropped her purse onto the table and gone to sit on the couch, slipping off her high-heeled pumps gratefully.

"Tough day at the office?" he asked, offering her a frosty glass of iced tea.

"Just long. Actually, it was quite nice. Your friend Gunnar—he's quite amazing, isn't he?—convinced the board to accept the new CEO, Jonas Wagner was elected chairman of the board, and I have retired to my humble position as simply a director.'' She took a long sip from the glass. ''It's been a long couple of months.''

She looked much better now, Sean thought. She'd regained some weight, and that haunted look had left her eyes. She looked lovely, poised and polished in a pale blue suit—she'd only worn pink when Talbot had forced her to, she had once told him—that accentuated her slender curves. It made the nights, when she turned into a sensuous, ardent lover in his bed, even more erotic. But nothing was more erotic than the knowledge that Rory had blossomed in these past few weeks, that she had become the woman he'd always known she could be.

''Do you have any idea how proud I am of you?'' he asked softly.

She looked startled. ''Me? Why?''

So many reasons, he thought. Although she would laugh if he told her so, he'd long since seen the nobility in what she'd done five years ago. And she'd been punishing herself for it every day since. But he'd never seen more love and sheer determination than the day she had saved his life by giving him her very breath. Still, he stuck to the safe subject: the courage in what she'd done these past weeks.

''You didn't know the first thing about the business when you went into this, but you went after everything Talbot had touched like a surgeon goes after cancer.''

''I didn't want anything of him to remain in Sheridan Manufacturing.''

''And you handled him like a field marshal. He was thoroughly convinced that unless he dropped off the face of the earth, you were going to make every one of his little scams public.''

''I was. And he knew it. After he read Daddy's confession and the names of the others he'd blackmailed before, and realized I'd make it public if I had to, he knew he'd lost." She gave him a sideways look. "Especially when you threw in that bit about having him arrested for assault with a deadly weapon."

"I'd guess," Sean said, "from the way he panicked over that, that he has a prior offense somewhere. A second conviction on an aggravated felony means some hard time."

Rory sighed. "I know he should be in jail, but..."

"I understand, honey. You didn't want to drag your father's name through the mud if you didn't have to."

She nodded. "Especially when he did save me, in the end."

"You saved yourself," Sean corrected.

"With your help," Rory said.

He shrugged, thinking he'd done very little, really. Then, after taking a sip of his own drink, he sat down beside her. He'd been waiting for this day, but now that it was here, he was a little nervous.

"Now that the easy task is over, are you ready for the tough one?"

She lifted a brow at him. "What tough one?"

"Katie."

Rory blinked. "I...thought we were doing okay. I mean, the other day she even said I wasn't so bad after all."

"I know. But this might be a harder sell."

"What might be?"

He took a breath, then plunged ahead. "Convincing her to be a flower girl again."

Her eyes widened. "I...Sean, I...do you mean it?"

"We've earned some happiness, don't you think?"

Her eyes searched his face, as if she were looking for a catch. "But...your family...I know they've been wonderful about us, but—"

"Don't worry. They're fine."

They were more than fine, Sean thought now. His family was, without a doubt, quite wonderful. His father had quietly spoken of second chances and gently but firmly told his mother to be quiet. Stevie had taken one look at them together and sighed that she'd better go shop for a dress. And Chase, when Rory had shyly asked him, had gruffly said he would be honored to give her away.

Katie had been, as he'd predicted, a harder sell. But Rory had set herself to the job, and the little girl had finally succumbed, saying that if her mommy and daddy and Dar said it was okay, she guessed it was.

Dar. He'd been the hardest sell of all, and Sean hadn't been sure if it was because of his doubts about Rory or his lack of trust in general. But when the chips were down, he'd come through.

"If you want me there, I'll be there."

"I don't just want you there, I want you to be my best man."

Dar had looked utterly stunned. "Me? But...I thought...what about Chase?"

"He's giving Rory away."

Dar had studied him for a moment. "You want me to stand up for you? Literally?"

"I just want you to be there," Sean told him. "*How* is up to you."

And he *was* there. In a tux. And on his feet. They *were* his, he'd told Katie when she'd asked why he was standing up. By right of ownership, if not birth. And when Rory had still seemed more than a little afraid of Dar and of never having the approval of this friend who was so special to Sean, Sean had told her that Dar had been nervously practicing on the sly for the entire two months before the wedding, knowing he was a little rusty at walking. Rory had let out a relieved breath that the superman was human after all and relaxed.

It was all coming together at last, Sean thought. They were setting right so many things that had gone sadly wrong.

This time, when the music started, Katie danced down the aisle, enjoying her moment in the spotlight.

She tossed a handful of petals to her celebrated Aunt Cassie, and Sean smothered a grin when he saw the exquisitely beautiful woman smile at the little girl, then turn her attention back to Dar, her famous green eyes full of lively interest. Dar himself either didn't notice or ignored the attention; if Cassie was serious, she had her work cut out for her, Sean thought. Odd, he thought, that he was related by marriage to a woman many thought the most beautiful in the world, and although he liked her, he had never thought of her as anything other than Chase's little sister.

And then he had eyes for nothing but the woman who appeared at the end of the aisle. Chase stood tall and dark beside her, but Sean barely noticed. He felt as if he'd waited five years for this day. When Rory was at last beside him, he knew he was being given yet another chance, something very few people ever got.

He'd almost thrown his life away when he'd lost his leg. He'd turned his back on it when he'd lost Rory. And he'd very nearly had it taken away not long ago in a California lagoon. But he had finally realized that it was far too precious to waste in regrets or misery or hatred. Life was for hope, for joy, and for savoring every wondrous day. It had been a hard lesson for him to learn.

He took Rory's hand, and prepared to pledge his life to the woman who had made it worth learning.

* * * * *

Dark secrets, dangerous desire...

Lovers
DARK AND
DANGEROUS

Three spine-tingling tales from the dark side
of love.

This October, enter the world of shadowy
romance as Silhouette presents the third in their
annual tradition of thrilling love stories and
chilling story lines. Written by three of
Silhouette's top names:

LINDSAY McKENNA
LEE KARR
RACHEL LEE

Haunting a store near you this October.

And now for something completely different....

SPELLBOUND
ROMANCE

**In October, look for
ANNIE AND THE OUTLAW (IM #597)
by Sharon Sala**

Gabriel Donner rode into Annie O'Brien's life like
an outlaw—and an angel—saving her from the
gang who threatened her safety. Yet the fight of
Annie's life had only just begun, and bad-boy
Gabe would move heaven and earth to save
her again.

**Don't miss ANNIE AND THE OUTLAW,
by Sharon Sala, available this October,
only from**

"HOORAY FOR HOLLYWOOD" SWEEPSTAKES

HERE'S HOW THE SWEEPSTAKES WORKS

OFFICIAL RULES — NO PURCHASE NECESSARY

To enter, complete an Official Entry Form or hand print on a 3" x 5" card the words "HOORAY FOR HOLLYWOOD", your name and address and mail your entry in the pre-addressed envelope (if provided) or to: "Hooray for Hollywood" Sweepstakes, P.O. Box 9076, Buffalo, NY 14269-9076 or "Hooray for Hollywood" Sweepstakes, P.O. Box 637, Fort Erie, Ontario L2A 5X3. Entries must be sent via First Class Mail and be received no later than 12/31/94. No liability is assumed for lost, late or misdirected mail.

Winners will be selected in random drawings to be conducted no later than January 31, 1995 from all eligible entries received.

Grand Prize: A 7-day/6-night trip for 2 to Los Angeles, CA including round trip air transportation from commercial airport nearest winner's residence, accommodations at the Regent Beverly Wilshire Hotel, free rental car, and $1,000 spending money. (Approximate prize value which will vary dependent upon winner's residence: $5,400.00 U.S.); 500 Second Prizes: A pair of "Hollywood Star" sunglasses (prize value: $9.95 U.S. each). Winner selection is under the supervision of D.L. Blair, Inc., an independent judging organization, whose decisions are final. Grand Prize travelers must sign and return a release of liability prior to traveling. Trip must be taken by 2/1/96 and is subject to airline schedules and accommodations availability.

Sweepstakes offer is open to residents of the U.S. (except Puerto Rico) and Canada who are 18 years of age or older, except employees and immediate family members of Harlequin Enterprises, Ltd., its affiliates, subsidiaries, and all agencies, entities or persons connected with the use, marketing or conduct of this sweepstakes. All federal, state, provincial, municipal and local laws apply. Offer void wherever prohibited by law. Taxes and/or duties are the sole responsibility of the winners. Any litigation within the province of Quebec respecting the conduct and awarding of prizes may be submitted to the Regie des loteries et courses du Quebec. All prizes will be awarded; winners will be notified by mail. No substitution of prizes are permitted. Odds of winning are dependent upon the number of eligible entries received.

Potential grand prize winner must sign and return an Affidavit of Eligibility within 30 days of notification. In the event of non-compliance within this time period, prize may be awarded to an alternate winner. Prize notification returned as undeliverable may result in the awarding of prize to an alternate winner. By acceptance of their prize, winners consent to use of their names, photographs, or likenesses for purpose of advertising, trade and promotion on behalf of Harlequin Enterprises, Ltd., without further compensation unless prohibited by law. A Canadian winner must correctly answer an arithmetical skill-testing question in order to be awarded the prize.

For a list of winners (available after 2/28/95), send a separate stamped, self-addressed envelope to: Hooray for Hollywood Sweepstakes 3252 Winners, P.O. Box 4200, Blair, NE 68009.

CBSRLS